TEA ON SUNDAY

TEA ON SUNDAY

LETTICE COOPER

with an introduction by
MARTIN EDWARDS

This edition published 2024 by
The British Library
96 Euston Road
London
NW1 2DB

Tea on Sunday was first published in Britain in
1973 by Victor Gollancz Ltd, London.

Introduction © 2024 Martin Edwards
Volume Copyright © The British Library Board
Tea on Sunday © 1973 The Estate of Lettice Cooper

Cataloguing in Publication Data
A catalogue record for this book is available from the British Library

ISBN 978 0 7123 5566 7
eISBN 978 0 7123 6828 5

Original cover image © NRM / Pictorial Collection /
Science & Society Picture Library

Text design and typesetting by Tetragon, London
Printed in England by CPI Group (UK) Ltd, Croydon, CR0 4YY

CONTENTS

INTRODUCTION

Tea on Sunday is a very readable detective story by an author better known in other literary fields. Lettice Cooper was a well-established mainstream novelist and critic who was in her mid-70s when she wrote this book. Possibly it is for that reason that in some respects the book has the "feel" of a story written rather earlier than its actual publication date, 1973. This is a traditional detective novel of a kind that was perhaps not exactly cutting-edge at the time of publication but which retains the enduring appeal of a well-made, character-driven story.

In a short prologue, we are introduced to Alberta Mansbridge, an elderly lady who has invited eight people to her home in the west end of London for tea on Sunday afternoon. But one of her guests arrives early…

The main narrative is divided into four parts, starting with "The Tea Party". Alberta's guests meet on the doorstep of her home in Porlock Square. They keep on ringing the bell, but there is no answer, so they try to call her from a telephone kiosk. When there is no reply, they ring the police, who force an entry. Alberta is found sitting at her desk, but she has been strangled. There is no sign of any burglary.

The doors and windows of the house were locked and Alberta wouldn't have admitted anyone she didn't know well. None of the guests has an alibi, and it soon becomes clear that a number of them may have had a motive for murdering Alberta. In other words, this isn't a "locked room mystery" involving some kind of apparent impossibility, but it does offer a clearly defined "close circle" of suspects, since one of the eight guests must be the culprit.

Those guests are a diverse bunch. In addition to her doctor, Musgrave, and her man of business, Holdsworth, there are two rather dubious protégés of Alberta's: Barry Slater, an ex-jailbird, and a charmer who calls himself Marcello Bartolozzi. Another guest is Myra Heseltine, who shared Alberta's home until Marcello showed signs of moving in. There is also Alberta's nephew Anthony and his glamorous young wife Lisa, whom Alberta disliked intensely. Finally, there is John Armistead, managing director of the Mansbridge family firm, in which Alberta had a controlling interest.

DCI Corby, the senior investigating officer, isn't a melancholy romantic like Colin Dexter's Morse or a hard-drinking maverick like Ian Rankin's Rebus. He's a likeable, conventional individual whose compassion is evident from the start, as he stands beside Alberta's corpse: "To the end of his time in the force he would feel the same shock as a young policeman called to his first murder, the same sense of outrage that anyone should dare to do this to a warm, breathing fellow-creature." This humanity shapes his approach to his work and also gives him the understanding of people necessary to solve the case. In the closing lines, he reflects that it's strange "how you lived with a group of people for a few days, your mind on the stretch to pick up every crumb of information about them, to understand them, almost to live in their lives. And then it was over like a book you had taken back to the library."

Corby's empathy was, I imagine, a quality that he shared with his creator. Lettice Ulpha Cooper OBE (1897–1994) was born in Eccles, Lancashire; her unusual middle name was inspired, presumably, by the small Lake District village of Ulpha, in the tranquil Duddon Valley. The eldest of three siblings (all of whom became writers) she grew up in Leeds, where her father ran an engineering firm, and

after reading Classics at Lady Margaret Hall, Oxford, she returned
to Yorkshire, spending several years as sales manager in the family
business while writing her first novel, *The Lighted Room*, a novel set
in Lancashire during the Civil War, which was published in 1925. She
wrote more historical novels before turning to contemporary fiction
with *The Ship of Truth* (1930), about an Anglo-Catholic clergyman
working among the mill-workers of the West Riding of Yorkshire:
the book won the Hodder Religious Prize.

Two of her most successful novels, *The New House* and *National
Provincial*, appeared before the Second World War and prior to her
decision to leave Yorkshire for London when Lady Rhondda offered
her the chance to work on *Time and Tide*, where she was an associate
editor. For almost a decade she set her literary career aside, working
during the war as a public relations officer for the Ministry of Food.
She produced ten novels between 1947 and 1986 and also reviewed
fiction for the *Yorkshire Post* for several years.

London became a regular setting for her stories, while her love of
Tuscany is apparent in books such as *Fenny* (1957), which charts the
development of a young English governess against a background of
fascism and the Second World War. She wrote novels and non-fiction
for children, including a book about Robert Louis Stevenson; she
became President of the Robert Louis Stevenson Society in 1958. At
the age of ninety she was awarded the Freedom of the City of Leeds.

For many years she campaigned for authors' rights and was in
the vanguard of the movement to introduce Public Lending Right;
her efforts were marked by the award of an OBE. She never married, but spent many years living in a London flat with her sister
Barbara; Barbara was (like most members of their family) a staunch
Conservative while Lettice was an equally committed socialist, but
when Barbara died, Lettice was bereft. Her nephew, Leo Cooper,
was a publisher who married the novelist Jilly Cooper.

In an excellent obituary for the *Independent*, the distinguished novelist Francis King said: "In the early years of a long friendship with the novelist Lettice Cooper, I used to think of her as a brisk, sensible and sympathetic aunt, indulgent to some of my follies and outspoken about others. Then there was a period when she became a favourite cousin, to whom I could always turn for help and advice. Finally, despite her being 26 years my senior, I came to regard her as a high-spirited niece, whose optimism, zest for life and radical opinions often made me feel intellectually musty and emotionally stiff-jointed. That she had spent a long period undergoing psychoanalysis never ceased to astonish me, since I have rarely met anyone more firmly in control both of herself and her circumstances. Either her analyst was a remarkable man or she herself was possessed of remarkable powers of self-healing."

The novel reflects her abiding interest in the contrast between the two different social worlds with which she was closely familiar, those of Yorkshire and London. Although Alberta is the murder victim, my impression is that, in certain respects, there was a significant element of self-portraiture in the presentation of Alberta, not least in her strong-mindedness and her involvement with the family business in Yorkshire.

Cooper's usual publisher was Victor Gollancz, whose political sympathies she shared, and it may be that Gollancz encouraged her to try her hand at a detective story in the classic vein. She had already veered towards mystery territory with *A Certain Compass* (1960), which concerns a young widow's efforts to discover the truth about her husband's supposed suicide, while her final novel, *Unusual Behaviour* (1986), deals with police surveillance into the IRA.

Tea on Sunday is, in terms of its strength of characterization, arguably comparable with the early books of P. D. James, although it must be admitted that Cooper lacked James's ability to create such a baffling puzzle that the revelation of the culprit's identity comes as a great surprise. Unfortunately, the novel made very little impression at the time of its original appearance and there never seems to have been a paperback edition. Francis King's obituary didn't mention *Tea on Sunday*, perhaps because he felt that her foray into detective fiction weighed lightly in comparison to her other achievements, but perhaps because the book had by then been well and truly forgotten. However, Cooper's account of Corby's investigation is consistently readable and I am optimistic that present day readers will find plenty here to enjoy.

MARTIN EDWARDS
www.martinedwardsbooks.com

A NOTE FROM THE PUBLISHER

The original novels and short stories reprinted in the British Library Crime Classics series were written and published in a period ranging, for the most part, from the 1890s to the 1960s. There are many elements of these stories which continue to entertain modern readers; however, in some cases there are also uses of language, instances of stereotyping and some attitudes expressed by narrators or characters which may not be endorsed by the publishing standards of today. We acknowledge therefore that some elements in the works selected for reprinting may continue to make uncomfortable reading for some of our audience. With this series British Library Publishing aims to offer a new readership a chance to read some of the rare books of the British Library's collections in an affordable paperback format, to enjoy their merits and to look back into the world of the twentieth century as portrayed by its writers. It is not possible to separate these stories from the history of their writing and therefore the following novel is presented as it was originally published with minor edits only, made for consistency of style and sense. We welcome feedback from our readers, which can be sent to the following address:

British Library Publishing
The British Library
96 Euston Road
London, NW1 2DB
United Kingdom

To
Nina Coltart

PROLOGUE

THERE WERE EIGHT CUPS ON THE TRAY. ALBERTA MANSBRIDGE added the ninth, her own, the dark blue and gold Rockingham cup that her father had used till the day of his death. "As I hope to do till mine," Alberta had said to Mrs Bramley on her first morning there. "So I shall always wash it up myself, then it will be no one else's fault if it gets broken."

She carried the tray upstairs to the double sitting-room on the first floor. After putting it down on the table she straightened herself and rubbed her back. She always enjoyed getting these tea parties ready on Sunday when the Bramleys were out, but lately she had begun to find the stairs tiring. She had left a pile of crumpets near the kitchen stove meaning to go down and toast them just before four, but she thought now she wouldn't bother. Let Anthony do it when he arrived. He was, she had to admit, handy and obliging in those ways, much more so than that flibberty-jibbet of a girl he had married. Lisa was a disaster! What sort of mother would she be for the great-grandson of Albert Mansbridge, the boy who should carry on the firm?

The sitting-room was hot, for Alberta could not bear to be without the coalite fire which in this part of London was the nearest thing to a real fire that officialdom allowed her. She had installed central heating five years ago to satisfy Myra who was always shivering—her own fault because she would not wear warm enough clothes nor eat sensible food, though she was as thin as a knitting needle and with her restless energy she was the kind that would stay so. And now she had moved out of the house where so much had been done to please her. Well, no sense in keeping the top floor flat empty and at the same time paying for those dreary lodgings for Marcello in Camden Town. A smile softened Alberta's large, strong-boned face; Marcello would not find this house too warm; he was like a cat for comfort.

She walked across to the window and looked out at the Square. The usually pleasant water-colour prospect was, on this February afternoon, either white or drab. The sky was drab, the pale stucco houses looked drab; the snow that had begun to fall at midday had already melted to a drab-coloured slush on the pavements and in the street, but in the Square garden the lawn was still iced with it; the bushes were rounded white beehives; every branch of a tree delicately supported three times its own thickness in half-frozen snow.

There was no-one about in the Square; already lights were on in several of the houses: on the far side Alberta could see the constant blue flash of a television set. You could tell by the look of every-thing how raw the cold was, and that there was more snow to come. Alberta realized that her guests might not be particularly enthusiastic about starting on their various journeys across London to her house, but it was too late now to put them off, and she was glad. She hated being alone in the house on Sunday afternoon.

She went back to the fireside and settled down in her own chair, the leather saddle-back chair which like the Rockingham cup had been her father's. Albert Mansbridge had been sitting in it on the last afternoon before he finally took to his bed. Alberta remembered kneeling by him, picking up a handful of letters and documents that had slid from his uncertain grasp to the floor. When she put them back on his knee he patted her shoulder; caresses were as rare between them as if she had been the son he had so much wanted.

"Eh lass," he said, "I reckon I'm about finished."

He had dozed off and she, looking out of the window at the moors and the rounded slopes of the Pennine Hills, had forced back behind her eyes the unfamiliar tears. What a relief it sometimes was now to see Marcello laugh and cry as easily as a child! It was as if he was doing it for her, doing what her Yorkshire upbringing and her father's expectations of her had conditioned her not to do. She knew now that it had been a strain for the first forty years of her life making herself over into the son Albert had never had; perhaps that was why she sometimes felt so tired now.

Her head fell back and she shut her eyes. At once with a deeply pleasurable easing of every nerve she sank into a cat-nap, and a snatch of vivid dream.

She was on the moors above Hithamroyd, coming down the path from Snaithwaite Gap, Thor bounding ahead of her, and some undefined promise of happiness in the air, whose sweetness was still with her, when, a minute after, she woke.

It was on that path that she first met Aubrey. She knew as soon as she saw him climbing towards her that the tall, fair-skinned, blond-haired stranger must be Aubrey Seldon, the new Assistant Manager of Firth's Mill in the next valley.

Now, so many years afterwards, she was living again in the scene halfway between memory and dream. The young man climbed towards her with long easy strides. Thor ran to him and stretching himself to his full height put both his paws on the stranger's chest. She called him off saying "He's all right, he's very gentle, really." But the young man, she saw, was used to dogs; he patted Thor and smiled. He said that of course he knew her by sight; he was coming next week to call on her father at his office. A few minutes later they were walking along the shoulder of the hill together while she told him the names of the places they could see from there.

And so began the year of greatest happiness in her life, followed, when Evie came back from her finishing school, by the most acute suffering she had ever known. It was because of that she had decided when her father died to leave Yorkshire; because of that she could not see the blond head of her nephew, Anthony, Evie's son and Aubrey's, without a double pang of love and hate.

One thing I never am, she thought with a flash of intuition, is fair to the boy. But then his shying away from the work he was born to, his silly jobs or no jobs, and his even more silly marriage to that girl, that Lisa, who very likely wouldn't come this afternoon, and if she did would come sulky, and refuse tea, hoping for a drink instead; but she wouldn't get one, not at this hour of the day. Myra used to say I didn't understand the young, but I never was one for pretending. Myra only fancies she understands them. All the same I shall be glad to see *her* again. Silly work we made of it quarrelling like that.

She glanced at the window. It had started to snow again, soft flakes which were coming down so lazily that they looked as if they were drifting upwards. Alberta glanced at the clock. Twenty minutes past three. She heaped more coalite on the fire, regretfully extinguishing the present red glow for the sake of having a better one when her guests arrived.

She wished now that she hadn't asked them. Snow made you sleepy; there was nothing she would like better than to drop off again and to stay in her chair, comfortably drowsing, until the Bramleys came back from Croydon. Well, anyhow there would be time for another nap; nobody would be here for half an hour.

She started awake, confused and irritable, when the buzzer sounded in her ear. She must have slept for half an hour, but it had seemed more like two minutes. Looking at the clock she saw with surprise that that was exactly what it had been. It was barely half past three.

Now which of them had decided to come half an hour before the proper time? That young Barry perhaps; he might have heard that she had been making inquiries about him; well, she had a rod in pickle for him, and if she was going to have half an hour alone with him he might feel it sooner than he had anticipated. Or... her face softened, it might be Marcello wanting a few minutes to themselves, or John Armistead coming to put his case all over again—as if they hadn't spent the whole of yesterday on it.

The buzzer sounded a second time. She jerked herself up in her chair feeling tousled, dry-mouthed and half-awake, but it was no day to keep anybody standing on the doorstep. She picked up the intercom.

"Yes. Who is it?"

The familiar voice speaking from below sounded thin and small.

"Oh, it's you. You're early. Well, come up."

She pressed the button that opened the front door of the house. She got on to her feet, her limbs stiffened by the brief rest. She pulled her woollen stole round her shoulders, glanced at herself in the mirror over the fireplace, and pushed a loose strand of grey hair off her forehead. She went to the door to meet her early guest.

PART I

THE TEA PARTY

CHAPTER I

ANTHONY SELDON HURRIED ROUND THE CORNER INTO PORLOCK Square. He was hurrying not because he was late, which he had not noticed, but because he was cold and wanted to get indoors out of the weather. He was also driven by fury; his mind careered backwards and forwards like a spinning top over the quarrel that he had had with Lisa at midday. When she stood there in the doorway in her long black cloak and her long black wrinkled boots, he could have killed her or seized her then and there and pushed her down on to the bed. These were, he was coming to the conclusion, the only two ways of dealing with her.

"I can see no reason whatever *why* you can't tell me who you are going out to lunch with; on Sunday too," he added with bitter emphasis.

"You wouldn't know them and what difference does Sunday make?"

"It's a day when we are generally at home together."

"And I suppose you want me to cook roast beef and Yorkshire Pudding; and then to wash up while you snooze in front of the fire. And then we toddle off arm in arm to have tea with your aunty? If you wanted that sort of thing you made a mistake to marry me."

"You don't need to tell me that! And you know perfectly well I don't want that sort of thing. It's what I've fought so hard to get away from."

"I'm not so sure. I know you tell yourself that tale, but I think it's your kind of thing really."

"*Where* are you having lunch?"

"Somewhere where you couldn't afford to take me."

"That's all you think of nowadays, isn't it, how much money you can get spent on you."

"Oh shut your bloody trap, Anthony. I'll go wherever I like and when I like and with whoever I like and the sooner you get used to it the better."

"This modelling nonsense has gone to your head."

"One of us has got to make enough to live on."

They paused for a minute like boxers at the end of a round. Then Anthony resumed the attack.

"Are you coming back here after lunch?"

"I don't know. It depends what I feel like."

"If not, will you meet me at Alberta's?"

"I don't know. Probably not. I didn't marry your dreary relations."

"You haven't been there for months. She's been good to us."

"She loathes me. I'm not at all the nice little wife she wanted for you."

"She may have something there."

"She likes patronizing and managing, and I'm somebody she can't patronize or manage. I hate going there. It's different for you. You've got expectations."

"That's just about the most insulting thing you could say."

"True things often are. Now I'm off. Go get yourself a drink at the Duke, and there's some luncheon sausage in the fridge. If you want Yorkshire Pudding you can bloody well make it. Bye."

Through the window of their basement flat he saw her boots tramping up the steps and the skirts of her dark cloth coat swinging round them.

It's no use, he thought as he turned into Porlock Square, we can't go on like this. I'm sick of it. I can't get any creative work done.

He had at the moment a job in a men's boutique in Kensington. In his spare time he was writing a play, or had been until he married Lisa last April, since when he had been living in a whirlpool which hardly allowed him to breathe, let alone write. It was a dead failure, their marriage, a mistake; it couldn't possibly last and he would be glad to be out of it—only the rest of life would be so horribly dull without her.

He walked round to the other side of the Square. It was snowing again now; he felt the soft explosions of cold on his face and hair; the sky was gravid with swelling snow.

As he turned the corner he saw a group of people between the pillars of No. 31 getting what shelter they could from the portico. He walked faster so as to be there to go in with them when the door opened.

The door seemed to be a long time in opening. The people on the step, five men and a woman, shifted and stamped about. He saw now who they were; all people he knew but none of them people he particularly wanted to see this afternoon; not that he disliked his aunt's doctor, Ewan Musgrave, nor her man of business, Russell Holdsworth; on the whole he liked John Armistead, managing director of Albert Mansbridge at Hithamroyd, whom he had known all his life, and who was a decent old chap. Good God! There was Myra Heseltine, huddled in trendy furs to the tip of her sharp nose. He was surprised to see her. She had been Alberta's chief buddy for years, but they had quarrelled and Myra had left or had been turned out of the top flat at No. 31; he had had no idea that she and Alberta were still on speaking terms. For Barry Slater, the unfortunate legacy of Alberta's spell of prison visiting, and Marcello Bartolozzi, her latest genius, he had nothing but distaste. What really sickened him about all these totally irrelevant people was that *they* were here, but no Lisa. What on earth were they all waiting for? He said,

"Have you rung?"

"Five times," Holdsworth answered precisely.

"Shall I try again?"

"If you think you can do it better than we can," Myra Heseltine snapped at him.

He pressed the bell without answering. He kept his finger on it but no voice came from the aperture.

"The thing must be out of order."

"Of course, of course," Marcello agreed fretfully. He turned up the collar of his waisted periwinkle coat and buried his chin in his velvet cravat.

"Better knock."

"We have."

"Try again."

John Armistead grasped the old-fashioned brass knocker, and banged it vigorously against the iron plate behind it.

In the next house but one a woman threw up a window on the first floor and looked out to see who was making such a din. Meeting the inrush of snow on her face and hair she slammed the window down again.

"She must have heard that if she's in."

"She must be in. We can't all have come on the wrong day... seven of us."

"I suppose she might have forgotten, or thought it was next Sunday she asked us for, and gone out."

"It would be very unlike her," Myra said. "She never forgets appointments. She never goes out on Sunday afternoon. The Bramleys always go to their married daughter at Croydon, and Alberta has a thing about the house being left for long; she stays on guard. Besides, for Heaven's sake, where would she go to on an afternoon like this? It's much more in her line to make us all come out to see her."

Barry Slater, shivering inside his thonged leather jacket, said,

"That's right. But we can't stop here all night, not in this cold. Why don't we try the back door?"

"The Bramleys always leave it fastened and go out by the front door. There are Grantham locks on every window and door in this house. It's a fortress."

"Still, we may as well have a look at the back."

Dr Musgrave disappeared round the side of the house. He returned a minute or two later.

"Locked up and dark. I banged on the door but there's evidently nobody there."

"If she's in, you'd think there'd be a light on by now in the sitting-room."

"If she is in at all, she must be very sound asleep."

"Try throwing something at the window."

Anthony stooped, moulded a handful of snow into a ball and threw. He covered the long window with splodges of snow, but there was no answer.

"She can't be in," Myra exclaimed. "I wonder if she suddenly heard some bad news from her family in Yorkshire and rushed off to catch a train."

"I should have heard any news like that," Anthony said. "They're my people too."

Russell Holdsworth turned to the doctor.

"Do you think she can have had some kind of seizure, a heart attack?"

"She might have had a fall. She could have broken her leg or her hip and perhaps be lying somewhere unable to answer us. I think we must find out."

"I suggest," Holdsworth said, "that we find a call box and ring her up. She has an extension of the telephone on the small table by her chair."

Myra nodded. "And another one in her bedroom."

"I'll go and ring her," Anthony offered. "There's a box in Cheriton Street."

"I'll come with you." Myra Heseltine followed him down the steps.

"No, for God's sake don't. What's the sense of two of us getting soaked?"

"I'd rather walk anywhere than go on standing on this step; my feet are getting frostbite."

"I do not see that it is at all necessary that we should all stay here and catch a *pulmonite*," Marcello complained.

"You go home, then." John Armistead set his broad back against the door. "I'm stopping here until we see if there's anything wrong."

The Italian muttered something and moved irresolutely down the steps, but then shrugged and came back again.

Anthony and Myra, shoulders bent and heads down, turned out of the Square into Cheriton Street, and pushed into driving snow.

"Let's hope," Anthony shouted, "that the telephone box hasn't been vandalized."

"Have you seen Alberta lately?"

"Not since Christmas."

"I haven't seen her since last August, when she threw me out of the house. You knew about that, I suppose?"

"I heard you'd left."

"And you know that the Italian adventurer is moving into the top flat? And into Alberta's bed too, I shouldn't wonder. But Signor Marcello Bartolozzi as he calls himself isn't going to prey on a fool of an old woman much longer. I've found out things."

Recoiling from the intensity of feeling behind her tone, he said vaguely,

"I suppose he's not such a bad fellow really. Oh, blast!"

The telephone box was not vandalized but occupied. A bearded young man was speaking, his arm round a girl who was wearing the same kind of high-necked sweater and dufflecoat as he was.

Myra and Anthony stood outside the box looking as impatient and menacing as they knew how. After a minute or two Myra rapped smartly on the glass. At this the two inside came out looking indignant.

"You go in, Myra," Anthony said; "you'll get a bit of shelter while you're ringing."

"I don't want to. I haven't spoken to her for six months. I'd rather you'd do it."

He pulled the folding door to and took off the receiver. He heard the bell ringing steadily and waited long enough to allow anybody to get to the telephone from any part of the house. He came out of the box.

"It was ringing all right, but no answer."

"Then the others can't have got in. We'd better go back."

They trudged along Cheriton Street not attempting to talk. Anthony was thinking about Lisa; why on earth couldn't she just *say* who she was lunching with? Since she had begun to make a success of modelling she had picked up so many new friends. He knew some of them but not all, he was only on the fringe of that glamorous expensive world, and he thought she preferred him to stay there.

But up till now they had always spent Sunday together; he looked forward to it all the week. And now that seemed to be going. If he could only finish his play, get it put on, win £25,000 with his ten premium bonds, do anything to make himself more interesting… and less hard up. It flicked across his mind that if Alberta had had a fatal accident inside that silent house he most probably would be less hard up. He buried the thought, not liking it.

They turned out of Cheriton Street into the Square. The group under the portico of No. 31 was still there, but Anthony saw with an uprush of joy that Lisa had joined them. She was standing at the foot of the steps, indifferent to the weather except that she occasionally shook the snow off her hair: she had tied it behind her neck and tucked most of it into the high collar of her cloak. Anthony thought romantically that she looked like a gallant young lieutenant in Napoleon's Army contemplating the retreat from Moscow.

"We found a telephone and I heard the bell ringing, but no answer. Now what do we do?"

"Barry?" Lisa suggested. "Can't you climb up to that window? You must have been good at that sort of thing."

At this reference to the career that had landed him in prison Barry looked furious.

"No, I can't. It's too high."

Russell Holdsworth suggested, "I think one of us should go back to the telephone box and ring the police."

The doctor agreed. "I'll go."

"We don't want to bring the police into it for nothing," Barry protested. "Miss Mansbridge wouldn't like it at all."

"We shall have to risk her not liking it. Don't you agree, Anthony?"

"I should think so, yes."

"Where's the call box?"

"I'll come and show you."

As he walked off beside the doctor he felt an arm slipped through his.

"I might as well join the party," Lisa said.

Oh, with her caprices, her sweet surrenders, she was a thousand times more worthwhile than any dull, placid wife! Anthony pressed her arm against his side; he was no longer cold or dejected as they walked along Cheriton Street towards the call box.

CHAPTER II

CHIEF DETECTIVE INSPECTOR CORBY WAS ONE OF THE MANY people in London glad not to have to go out on that raw Sunday afternoon. The case on which he and the rest of the C.I.D. staff at Blent Street had been closely engaged for a fortnight had concluded with two arrests at four o'clock that morning. The Inspector had come home to seven hours sleep, a leisurely bath, and an excellent lunch cooked by his wife, who was now sitting opposite him working with concentration on the detailed finish of a dress that she was making for their elder daughter.

The room was warm and quiet. The house was in a cul-de-sac and the noise of traffic from the main road was muted by a row of intervening houses. The hardly less strident noise of pop records was diminished because his three children were playing them at the back of the house. The Inspector had a Sunday paper spread across his knees, and a book, a life of Palmerston, at his elbow. Biography and good novels were his favourite reading, a discovery of his own as he grew up since he came from a family who only read if they were ill in bed. But for him such books helped to satisfy the acute curiosity about what people did and why they did it that made him a notable detective.

At the moment he was lazily skimming the Sunday paper. Once or twice he looked up, glanced across at his wife and smiled. When Lucy was intent on something she was sewing she put out the tip of her tongue at critical moments; every now and then she pushed back the soft flop of hair that swung across her cheek. Once, looking up from her row of delicate stitches, she laughed.

"I suppose I'm wasting my time. It would be all the same to Jessica if I cobbled it together anyhow."

"But you can't?"

"No, it would be no fun for me."

"I can understand that."

His own job depended on precision, and when anything didn't come off, it was generally for want of it.

"Now you will probably be able to come to Tilly's birthday party. It's on Friday, do you remember. It starts at six. She'll be tremendously pleased if you can make it."

"I'm sure I can if nothing new turns up. There are only small things on the books. I've got quite a lot of paperwork to catch up on. I shall be glad of a quiet week."

He always spoke favourably of quiet weeks when he hadn't had one for some time, she reflected, and he was always bored by the end of them. He liked quiet weeks and paperwork just about as much as she, who was an inspired and adventurous cook, enjoyed cooking regular meals for very young children.

"What I should like still better at the moment," he said, "is a week off. Only it's not much good in this weather. But as soon as the Spring breaks I'll get one. You and I will go down to the West Country and pick primroses."

"I'll hold you to that."

She looked at him lying comfortably back in the deep armchair, square dark head and square shoulders against the pile of red cushions; one arm dangling, one leg crossed over the other; one felt slipper off, one hanging from a toe; the picture of a man at ease on Sunday afternoon. But even when relaxed he seemed to her more compact of energy than most people when they were in action.

The telephone bell rang. Lucy plucked the instrument off the top of the bookcase that ran all round the room. She rested it on her knee while she took the receiver off.

"God, I hope that's only one of your talkative friends, Lucy."

"Yes he's here," she said. "It's Blent Street, Frank." She made a rueful face as she passed the telephone over to him.

He listened for a full minute.

"31, Porlock Square. Send a car for me here at once, please. Get Dr Singleton, of course, and the D.F.I. and photographer. Bennet was going away for the weekend. Get Marsden. Newstead is on his way there, I suppose? If he hasn't got there yet, speak to Rothery and remind him that of course nothing must be touched until Dabs has been over her and everything in the room. Tell him to keep the guests all out of the room; he must shut them up somewhere together and Bates must stay with them until some more of our men get there. And of course no one to enter or leave the house."

He replaced the receiver and groaned.

"Bad luck!" Lucy said.

"Yes. I don't know what time I shall be back. I'll ring you as soon as I get a chance."

He ran upstairs to change. Lucy heard him run down again as the Station car stopped outside the house. She sighed, but she was accustomed to these sudden calls. It meant for her a lot of small disappointments, but it enhanced their enjoyment of holidays and uninterrupted evenings together.

In Porlock Square two police cars, their roofs already white, were parked outside No. 31. Two small boys, diverted from a half-finished snowman in the Square garden, were watching with their faces pressed against the railings. A man in the uniform of the Metropolitan Water Board, evidently answering some emergency call about a leaking tap or a burst pipe, stopped on the pavement to see the third car arrive.

Otherwise the Square was empty and silent; soft dry snow was falling. It was nearly dark and lights were on behind the curtained windows.

The front door was ajar and a uniformed constable was standing in front of it.

"We can't shut it, sir: it's a Grantham lock and so far we haven't found any keys. Sergeant Newstead is here and Dr Singleton has arrived."

"Good."

"The body's upstairs on the first floor."

"And the people who were coming to tea?"

"They're in the dining-room and P.C. Bates is with them. The dining-room's on the ground floor."

"Right. I'll go upstairs first. Thank you."

Corby stepped into the hall and experienced what was almost more the first smell than the first sight of the place where something had happened. Fierce central heating, welcome when you came in out of the raw air, but would be too much for him, anyhow, to live with. A big, old-fashioned, prosperous house; the furniture of the hall solid, late Victorian, very well kept for nowadays; wood glossy with polish; carpet that your feet sank into, and except for the track made by wet boots from the door to the stairs, speckless; silver, some of it looking like presentation cups and bowls, shining behind shining glass doors.

Above the table hung a large oil painting of an elderly man. He was ruddy, bearded, with deep-set eyes, untrimmed eyebrows and an impressive forehead. He was standing by a bureau, one hand resting on a pile of ledgers. Through the window behind him there was a spread of purple moors; very, very purple. The creator of this masterpiece was no landscape painter, but he had managed to endow his central figure with authority. Yes, he was a presence.

Corby had a feeling that he might still be the ruling spirit of the household.

The Inspector saw Sergeant Newstead coming down the staircase. Before he had crossed the hall to meet him he had time for a flash of regret because it was Newstead and not Bob Randall, who had worked with him for five years and had only just gone off to be head of the C.I.D. in a North London Station. To start on a case with Bob had been like slipping into gear. Newstead, Corby had already found out, was an efficient detective; thorough, accurate in his observation and painstaking. But costive; he seemed to have swallowed the book of words whole and got a permanent stiff neck from it; so far no fun in him. Oh well, it was early days yet.

The two men met at the foot of the stairs.

"An elderly lady, sir, name of Alberta Mansbridge, Miss. Strangled while sitting at her desk. Probably with a scarf or a stocking, but there's no sign of anything that could have been used The forensic people may be able to give us some help there. Dr Singleton thinks that it was some time between three and four, probably about half past three."

"Any signs of breaking in?"

"Not possible. The whole house was fastened with Grantham locks. P.C. Bates had to break the kitchen window and squeeze through."

"So she let her murderer in herself…"

"It looks as if she must have done. She's got one of those intercom tubes so that you answer if anybody calls up from the front door, and then press the spring that opens it.

"There were eight people coming to tea with her. They met on the doorstep. When they kept on ringing the bell and didn't get any answer, one of them went to ring her up from a call box and when there was no reply to that they rang the police."

"She was alone in the house, of course?"

"Yes. There's a couple who live down below in the basement flat, but they're out for the afternoon.

"I've put the people who were coming to tea in the dinning-room and Bates is with them. There's only seven of them now. It seems one got tired of waiting out there in the cold and went off home."

"I'm not surprised on a day like this, but he'll have to come back."

"One of the guests was Miss Mansbridge's own doctor, Dr Musgrave. Rothery let him have a look at her just to make sure she was dead, though he said he didn't have any doubts. He didn't let the doctor move her.

"There's three older men in the party, and two young men and two women. One of the young men is Miss Mansbridge's nephew. He told us about the couple living downstairs.

"There doesn't seem to be anything turned over as if a burglar had been at it. We've had a look round, of course, and left everything until the D.F.I. could go over it for prints. There's a locked flat upstairs, but we haven't any keys. I daresay they are in her bag, it's on the floor by her, but that'll have to be printed before we touch it. The D.F.I. should be here in a minute, and the photographer is on his way. They've had a job to get hold of one on a Sunday afternoon."

They had reached the top of the stairs. On the landing another uniformed policeman stood on guard by a half-open door. He moved aside to let Corby and Newstead go into the room.

It was the shape of hundreds of other first-floor rooms in the West End of London; once the front drawing-room had no doubt been divided from the back drawing-room by folded doors; now these were replaced by an archway. A dying fire still made a red glow in the hearth. The big chair beside it was of worn padded leather, not upholstered in champagne-coloured velvet as the other chairs in the room were. The walls were covered with a cream and gold striped paper, an unexpected contrast to the sombre colouring and dark wood of the hall and staircase, as if up here another hand had been at it. A gate-legged table bore a silver tray loaded with cups and preparations for a substantial tea. On the work table by the big armchair was a piece of knitting carelessly bundled so that one needle had slipped out of half a row of stitches.

The Inspector looked along the room through the archway. In front of the handsome old bureau the woman's figure in a dark red dress was stooping forward, one arm resting on the open flap of the desk, the other dangling. By her side Dr Singleton was shutting the fastener of his bag.

Corby walked across and stood beside the dead woman, looking down at her. He stooped without touching her to look at her face. To the end of his time in the force he would feel the same shock as a young policeman called to his first murder, the same sense of outrage that anyone should dare to do this to a warm, breathing fellow-creature.

The hand stretched out over the desk flap was a large old hand, with clusters of brown freckles on the skin; the knuckles looked swollen; she probably had difficulty in pulling on and off the two fine old-fashioned rings. Her hair was grey, thick with a good deal of brown still left in it. She wore one diamond earring. Looking down he saw the blue shine of the other one on the carpet.

"How long ago do you think, Singleton?"

"Difficult to tell with the room at this temperature, but I should say not much more than an hour and a half. Probably some time between half past three and four."

"She struggled but not as much as you would expect; she looks a strong woman."

"She must have been taken by surprise from behind."

Corby leaned forward to look at the flap of the desk where
an open cheque book was half hidden by the dead woman's arm.
What he could see was not written on; her sleeve covered the
signature end.

Her handbag, a solid affair in good leather, was on the floor a
yard away from her foot as if she had kicked it in her struggle and
it had come open.

"I want that left on the floor where it is, until it's been photographed and Dabs has been over it for prints."

The policeman at the doorway said, "The D.F.I. is here now, sir,
and Mr Marsden is bringing his camera upstairs."

"You stay here with them, Newstead. I'll go and see the people
in the dining-room."

The people in the dining-room, five men and two women, were sitting round the long mahogany table in various attitudes of tension.
Corby's eye was first caught by the older woman; she was shivering,
huddled in her fur coat in spite of the warmth of the room.

"I am very sorry I have been obliged to ask you all to stay here,"
Corby said. "But I am sure you will understand that I have to ask
you to help me. I will let you go as soon as possible. I believe one of
you is the nephew of Miss Mansbridge?"

The tall young man with the very fair head said, "Yes, I am."

"Then will you give me the name and address of any other near
relations who should be informed of her death?"

"Oh God! My mother… her half-sister. My father has been very
ill lately. It will be a ghastly shock for them."

"Perhaps you would like to telephone them yourself?"

"No, I… yes, I suppose I ought."

"Bates, will you call another constable to take… Mr Mansbridge,
is it?"

"No, Seldon, Anthony Seldon."

"… to take Mr Seldon to the telephone. You can speak from the one in the hall. Before you go may I have your parents' address?"

"Oh yes, it's Mr and Mrs Aubrey Seldon, The White Cottage, Kirby Waterlow, Yorkshire."

"Right. Well, you go and speak to them."

Corby saw the young man throw an anguished, appealing glance at the dark girl on the other side of the table, but she was engaged in lighting a cigarette, and seemed determined not to catch his eye. He went out with the policeman.

The Chief Inspector looked round the table.

"Wasn't there another guest?"

"Yes, Barry Slater. He got tired of waiting outside in the cold and went off home."

The handsome dark young man at the far end of the table said,

"Why do we not say at once that he went after he heard that we were going to telephone the police?"

"Does anyone know his address?"

The grey-haired man with the bi-focals took out a pocket diary and turned the pages. His movements were precise and unruffled.

"I have it. I had certain arrangements to make with Slater on behalf of the late Miss Mansbridge. It is 16, Lawnswood Road, N.1."

"Thank you." Corby looked round the table. "I shall be able to see you all in a few minutes. In the meantime I hope you will not object as a matter of routine to having your fingerprints taken."

The young foreigner began an indignant protest, but the broad-shouldered, elderly man next to him put a hand on his arm.

"Now then, lad, we've got to do what's necessary."

The young man subsided, muttering.

On the stairs Corby met Marsden, the photographer, carrying his camera and appurtenances.

"Sorry to have had to disturb you on Sunday, Marsden. Will you let me have the plates at Blent Street as soon as you can."

He went into the long drawing-room where Forbes, the Divisional Fingerprint Inspector, was packing his bag. Newstead was covering the still figure at the bureau with a sheet.

"There seem to be any number of prints about the room, Chief Inspector; so far as I can tell they're nearly all the same person's. I should think the cleaning woman's because they're all over the furniture and the window sills and the cupboards. It's a woman who lives in, I understand."

"Yes, she's out for the afternoon."

"I shall want her dabs as soon as she comes home. There are some more which I should think are the dead woman's, they're on her bag and on the desk, and on some of the things on that tea tray. We didn't get much from the body but of course the murderer wore gloves; it's a backward criminal who doesn't know that nowadays. Well those won't help them much longer when we have our new process going."

"Will you get the dabs of all the people in the dining-room as you go out. I've explained to them. And of course the whole lot from the house as soon as you can possibly manage it. After I leave here I shall be at Blent Street for the rest of the evening."

CHAPTER III

"THEY WANT TO KNOW IF YOU WILL SEE THE OLDER LADY, Miss Heseltine, first, sir. She's feeling ill. Bates says she nearly passed out after you left them."

"Right, Newstead. Bring her in."

The slip of a room in which Corby was sitting at one side of a beautiful old walnut wood table gave the impression of being less lived-in than the rest of the house. Books in glass cases lined two walls. On the other long wall hung an old framed map of seventeenth-century Yorkshire, and a photograph of the shed of an engineering works, with the same elderly, bearded man of the hall portrait standing in the entrance. Alberta Mansbridge had clearly cherished her family past, and it might be necessary to understand it to find out why she had been murdered in the present.

This phase of an investigation, the first encounter with each character separately, getting to know the feel of them, picking up the threads of their lives, was like beginning to read a new book. Corby had known for some time how deeply he enjoyed having all his senses stretched to apprehend what was behind the obvious or underneath it.

Newstead brought in Miss Heseltine and ushered her to a seat opposite the Inspector. He himself sat down on a chair near the door and took out his notebook.

"I am sorry to have to bother you, Miss Heseltine. You have had a most fearful shock, and I am sure you want to go home and rest, but you will understand that to discover who killed Miss Mansbridge

I have to find out anything I can from the people who knew her. As soon as possible I will send you home."

"Thank you. May I smoke?"

"Of course."

He saw how deliberately she steadied the trembling of her hands as she took her cigarette case out of her bag and chose a cigarette. He leaned forward and held his lighter to it.

"May I have your full name?"

"Myra Joan Heseltine."

"And your address?"

"Flat No. 48, Lyveden Court, W.2."

"Oh yes, I know, that tall block on the Bayswater Road overlooking the Park."

She volunteered, "I am a buyer of women's dresses and woollen suits for Gamlins."

"That must be very interesting work."

She had no feeling that he was staring at her with any particular curiosity, but he could by now have given a detailed description of her... handsome, gaunt, emaciated, with greenish grey eyes that must have been very fine before the wrinkles puckered the skin round them and the lids drooped over them; grey hair beautifully dressed; make-up heavy but skilful, now exposed by the greyish pallor of shock. She was wearing a well-cut black and brown jersey dress, under the fur coat which she huddled round her again as soon as her cigarette was alight. People being interrogated by the police are generally tense, but in Myra Heseltine he had an impression of a permanent tension augmented by her situation.

"You were a great friend of Miss Mansbridge?"

"I was until last August. I lived in this house for twelve years, in the flat at the top."

"Did you leave it for any particular reason?"

"Yes. We had a violent quarrel. Alberta told me I had better go and I replied that I didn't want to spend another night under her roof. I walked out and later sent for my things. I had not seen her since then until I saw her dead body half an hour ago."

A bold woman, he thought, and too sensible to try to conceal or diminish the quarrel which must be known to other people.

"Have you any idea at all as to who might have killed Miss Mansbridge?"

"No, I haven't." She added with forced calmness, "I realize that at this stage in your inquiries it's probably a waste of time to say that I didn't do it, but it happens to be true."

"You don't know of anyone who had a grudge against her or who could hope to profit in any way by her death?"

"No. Alberta wasn't exactly easy to get on with. She was very strong-willed; she wanted her own way. She was inclined to interfere with people, but she was essentially kind and generous, and as upright as the day. I can't believe that she ever provoked anybody to the point of murder. It must have been some thief who broke in."

"But how? The whole place was secured by Grantham locks. Isn't it clear that it must have been somebody whom Miss Mansbridge admitted herself? Probably somebody she knew, or else somebody who gave a very good reason for seeing her."

A long cone of ash trembled on the end of her cigarette. Newstead came forward quietly and put an ashtray in front of her. Myra saw his uniformed sleeve and then glanced round.

"Is he taking notes?"

"It's the usual practice."

"When the police are interrogating suspects. Yes, I see. Any of us could have slipped in early and done it; is that what you think? Any one of us who had the nerve to come back half an hour afterwards and stand on the doorstep knocking and ringing with the others. What a horrible… but it must have been somebody else really, somebody she wasn't expecting. It *must* have been."

"What I am trying to do at the moment, Miss Heseltine, is to get a picture of Miss Mansbridge, of her life and character and the kind of people she knew. Have you known her a long time?"

"Nearly fifteen years. But John Armistead has known her for over sixty years I should say. He's the managing director of the firm in Yorkshire that was her father's. I've only known her since she came to live in London."

"How did you come across her?"

"She came into Gamlins to buy herself an outfit. I was having lunch in the restaurant, at the small table I always have kept for me. The place was full, there wasn't a seat to be had. I saw Alberta come in and look round. I noticed her because of her rather old-fashioned clothes, and because, although she was a strong, finely-built woman with a good deal of dignity, she also looked like a lost child. She saw the empty seat at my table and came across and asked if it was vacant. I should normally have said I was keeping it for a friend, I like to plan my work and look over my notes while I have lunch, but something about her made me let her join me.

"Alberta began to talk. She told me that her father had owned an engineering business in the West Riding of Yorkshire, and that he had died lately. She had been fully occupied during the last few years nursing her father and I gathered doing half his business for him while he was failing. She was going to buy a house in London but first of all she wanted some new clothes. She hadn't had time to think about them and she had suddenly realized that she was shabby and out of date.

"I don't need to be," she said. "I'm not poor. It's just that I've had so many other things on my mind."

"I liked her at once. There was something candid and fresh about her. I took her after lunch to buy an outfit. She never hesitated over the price of a garment if she thought it was worth it; she was willing to pay well for good clothes but she wanted value for money. She wouldn't have one very becoming suit because she thought the cloth wasn't good enough for the price, and she was right, although if I had been as well off as I was beginning to realize that she was, I should probably have bought it because it suited me.

"She asked me to dine with her at her hotel that evening. She wanted to buy a house, I set about finding one for her.

"She liked this one at once. The rooms were spacious and would take her solid furniture. She thought the house was worth the price. There was this top flat to let in it, so after we had made friends she said to me, 'Why don't you move in?' And I did."

"Would you mind telling me, Miss Heseltine, why you moved out last August? What was the quarrel about?"

"I see you'd have to ask that but I'd rather not tell you. It involves another person."

"I must all the same ask you to tell me."

"We quarrelled about Marcello Bartolozzi, as he calls himself."

"Is that the young foreigner in the blue coat who is here today?"

"Yes."

"Why do you say 'as he calls himself'? Isn't that his real name?"

She spat out, "No, it's not." Corby saw her pause for an instant to get control of herself.

"I've been making inquiries about him through a channel that I suppose you wouldn't approve of: a private eye if you want to know."

"I don't know why you should think that we disapprove of people getting help of that kind if they need it. But you must have felt very strongly to have taken what is obviously to you a drastic step. What was the upshot of your inquiries?"

"That Marcello is, as I always told Alberta he was, a complete fake, a charlatan. I don't like telling you this…"

That, Corby thought, is untrue, but she doesn't know it. She seemed to him a woman who was prepared to go a long way in love or hatred.

"… but there can't be any real harm in my telling you because if anybody did wish Alberta dead, it wouldn't be this… this…" she was stammering with hate but stopped herself, "this adventurer. Berto Fospo is his real name. He would be the last person who could have any motive for murdering her. It was to his interest to keep her alive. He was sucking her. He was making himself out to be a sort of Messiah of industrial design. He was going to revolutionize the modern world by bringing beauty into industry. He said he had a degree in architecture from Rome University and had had two exhibitions of his work in Rome and Venice. There wasn't a word of truth in any of that. There was nothing new in his design, he'd never been to any University, nor had any exhibitions in Italy. But Alberta set him up in an office and was planning an exhibition for him, and he was going to move in here. She seemed to have lost all her usual sense, to be quite out of touch with reality about him. And she wouldn't forgive me for trying to open her eyes."

No, Corby thought, that's a thing that people don't forgive easily.

"Did Miss Mansbridge often give these tea parties on Sundays?"

"Quite often. She liked having company when the Bramleys were out. She was a very nervous woman, really, though she didn't appear to be."

"Were there a lot of other people whom she sometimes invited to tea on Sunday?"

"Not a lot. She didn't make friends easily. There were a few people connected with her Church—that's St Stephen's, Cheriton Road—the vicar and his wife, and the curate and the deaconess who worked in the parish; then there was the matron of the nursing home where she once went for an operation, and a few people she had known in Yorkshire who had moved to London, and oh, I don't know, one or two others I think. She was too masterful for most people; I soon gave up trying to mix her with my friends."

"The couple downstairs, the Bramleys, they were here with you?"

"Oh yes, for three years."

"Were they on good terms with Miss Mansbridge?"

"Certainly. Mrs Bramley is a very good worker and a thoroughly nice woman."

"There are just two more questions that I should like to ask you. How were you invited to this tea party?"

"By a typewritten note. Alberta hardly ever wrote a letter by hand."

"Were you surprised to receive the invitation after the breach?"

"At first I was, yes, but Alberta had a good heart. It didn't surprise me when I thought about it that she should be the one to take the first step. I couldn't have done it, but she was more generous than I am."

"I don't suppose you kept the note?"

"Yes, I have it here in my bag. You can see it if you like."

Corby took the sheet of solid notepaper with its plain dark-blue heading.

"I should like to keep this if I may. You shall have it back later. Sergeant Newstead will give you a receipt for it. Now one more question, Miss Heseltine, a routine question. Can you tell me where you were this afternoon between three and four?"

"Of course. At three I was in my own flat getting ready to come here."

"What time did you leave your flat?"

He saw or thought he saw wariness creep into her eyes.

"About a quarter past three."

"Did anybody see you leave the building?"

"I don't know. The porter may have. I didn't notice whether he was at the desk or not."

"How did you come?"

"In my car."

"You started early, Miss Heseltine. It would only take you a few minutes to drive from Lyveden Court to Porlock Square."

"Yes, I left early on purpose, because of the bad weather. I was afraid my car might not start."

"Did you have any difficulty?"

"No."

"Then you must have arrived here soon after half past three?"

"No, I didn't."

There was a pause. Corby waited for more, saw her struggling with her disinclination to give it. Then she said reluctantly,

"I stopped the car in St Stephen's Square at the other end of Cheriton Road and sat there in it until five minutes to four. I wanted to arrive exactly on time. I was nervous about this meeting. I didn't know whether any other people had been asked to tea. I hoped there would be some more, and I wanted to give them time to arrive so that I shouldn't have the first few minutes with Alberta alone. On the other hand I didn't want to be late because she couldn't stand that; if she asked you to tea at four she expected you to arrive at four and not at five minutes past. So I timed my arrival very carefully and when I got to this house it was exactly four, and John Armistead and the doctor were already on the doorstep."

"Thank you. We'll get that typed out now at once and perhaps you will sign it before you leave."

She said abruptly, "Alberta was killed a short time before we got in, was she?"

"Probably between half past three and a quarter to four."

"Would it be a painful death?"

"It would only last three or four minutes."

"But those would be… dreadful, suffocating, terrifying?"

"I am afraid so, yes. But it is all over now."

"Yes but why *should* it be? She was very much alive, she liked living. It's a mistake to think that only young and beautiful and successful people like living. It's nonsense. Old ones, even unhappy ones—and I don't think Alberta was—we all like it."

"I agree with you," Corby said. "And I shall do my very best to find out who deprived your friend of it. Meanwhile if anything occurs to you that might be relevant I hope you will tell me. Just ring Blent Street Police Station and ask for me. And I have to ask you not to go out of London at present without letting me know."

"I have to go to Paris for my work the week after next."

"I hope that by that time we may not have to restrain you at all, but please get in touch with us before you go. Do you feel equal to driving yourself home now, or shall we send you in one of our cars? Yours can be driven back for you."

"I am perfectly capable of driving myself, thank you."

When she had gone out, Newstead observed,

"She's got it in for the Italian all right."

"He seems to have imposed on Miss Mansbridge very easily. But unless this one's told us a cock-and-bull story he stands to lose by Alberta's death, probably more than any of them. What did you make of Miss Heseltine?"

"She seemed to be very upset; very jumpy, and trying not to show it."

"More jumpy, do you think, than that kind of woman would be after the sudden shock of losing her great friend?"

"She'd quarrelled with her."

"I don't think that would make losing her any easier. Rather otherwise, perhaps."

"She's got no alibi. Do you believe that story about her sitting in the car in St Stephen's Square? Seems thin to me."

"I think I do believe it. She strikes me as being both tough and sensitive. I can imagine that she was shaking all over at the prospect of her first meeting with Alberta after the quarrel, and hoping there would be other people there. We'll have the nephew in next."

CHAPTER IV

"MAY I HAVE YOUR FULL NAME PLEASE?"
"Anthony Albert Mansbridge Seldon."
"And your address?"
"Flat 1A, 45 Brittany Street, S.W.10."
"Did you get through to your parents all right, Mr Seldon?"
"Yes thanks. I spoke to my mother. She's terribly upset, of course. Not that she and Aunt Alberta were absolute buddies, but still, half-sisters you know. They were brought up together. My mamma was always a bit afraid of Alberta. But of course… she said she supposed she ought to come up, but it's difficult for her to leave my father unless she can get one of my sisters to come, and they've both got young children…"

Anthony's voice trailed off. "But you don't want to hear all that…"

"I want to hear anything that you can tell me that might throw light on your aunt's murder."

"I don't know anything. I simply don't understand it. I feel as though it couldn't really have happened."

"You don't know if she had any enemies?"

"I shouldn't think so, not that kind of enemy. She annoyed people sometimes, but after all people don't…" He stopped. "Well, of course somebody has… but I can't think who… It must have been somebody who broke in to rob the house. It couldn't be anybody she knew… it wouldn't be, it just doesn't seem probable."

A nice-looking young man, Anthony Albert Mansbridge Seldon, if a touch on the girlish side with that white skin and the blond hair curling into his neck. But he had good shoulders and long legs and a straight back. He wore a thick, dark blue sweater with a high roll collar and a pair of dirty pink corduroy trousers, which his aunt almost certainly would not have considered suitable for her tea party. He gave an impression of candour, but looked harassed and nervous.

"She did get across some people," he murmured.

Corby nodded. "But people don't as a rule murder anybody who just happens to irritate them."

"That's it exactly." Anthony relaxed.

"Have you seen much of Miss Mansbridge lately?"

"No, not as much as I ought to have. Because she's always been good to me in spite of my being such a disappointment."

"How did you disappoint her?"

"By not being like my grandfather, Albert Mansbridge. That's him." Anthony waved a hand towards the photograph of the engineering shed.

"A formidable fellow I should think."

"You're telling me! He wanted a son to carry on the business, but he only had Alberta by his first wife, who died when she was a baby. Then when he married again of course he was mad keen to have a son and that time he only got my mother. So Alberta had to be a sort of son to him, helping him to run the business when he got old. Of course when my mother married the old man hoped for grandsons, and was furiously disappointed when my two sisters were born. Then after a gap of seven years I came along, and Albert and Alberta thought they were home, the future of the firm and all that. But they were unlucky, it wasn't my thing."

"What do you do, Mr Seldon?"

"At the moment I'm working in a boutique in Kensington... men's clothes."

He said this without much conviction. He seemed, Corby thought, to feel a creeping discomfort about his occupation, as if he was still feeling the tug of family expectations.

"I don't make much money, you see, and everything seems to need so much money nowadays. I'm married, too."

"Does your wife work as well?"

"Yes. She's been on a women's fashion paper for two years. Lately she's gone in for modelling. She's begun to do very well at it. She's a success."

"I see." Corby did see, and felt sorry for this ingenuous young man.

"Will you tell me please how your aunt invited you to this tea party?"

"She rang up."

"When?"

"Tuesday evening, I should think it was. No, we were out Tuesday. It must have been Wednesday."

"Did she sound quite normal?"

"Oh yes, quite. I mean she said we were always out and it was a long time since she had seen us, but it was rather dull for young people to come and visit an old woman, and so on."

"But you did come. How did you come, Mr Seldon?"

"How? Oh, I took the bus to Earls Court Station, and then the tube to South Ken. and then I walked the last bit."

"You say 'I'. Your wife came with you, didn't she?"

"No, she—" Corby saw the startled movement of his eyelids, "I mean, yes, of course she did. She's here in the next room."

"I know that. But I don't think she did come with you, did she? These are routine questions, Mr Seldon, which I shall have to put to everybody. The sooner you all answer truthfully, the sooner this will be over."

"Yes. I see. As it happened Lisa didn't come with me, because she had been out to lunch with some friends and she came straight from them."

"From whom?"

"I don't know," Anthony said desperately. "That's true. She didn't tell me where she was going. She doesn't always."

"Well, let's get back to you. At what time did you leave your flat?"

"I should think it must have been about a quarter past three or perhaps half past—or a bit later."

"Didn't you look at the clock or at your watch before starting?"

"No, my watch wants mending and we haven't got a clock. I just thought it would be about time to start."

"Did anybody see you leave your home?"

"Not that I know of." He added more hopefully, "The people in the flat above might possibly have heard me bang the door when I went out. They have been complaining to us that we never go out without banging it. I've been trying to be careful but I might have forgotten—they may not have been in, though."

"Will you give me their name and the number of their flat?"

Anthony unhappily gave them.

"I suppose if they didn't hear me I haven't got an alibi." He brightened. "Oh yes I have. All the other people were on the doorstep already when I arrived, all except Lisa."

"As I said, these are routine questions, Mr Seldon."

"Yes of course, I understand. Will you be asking everybody?"

"For the moment let's stick to what I have to ask you. Do you know anything about your aunt's affairs?"

"No. Mr Holdsworth, the man in the dark grey suit who wears bi-focals, is the one to ask about that. He took care of a lot of them for her."

"From the look of this house she appears to have been comfortably off."

"She was rich, I do know that."

"Do you know who inherits from her? Have you ever been told the terms of her will?"

"No."

Corby saw his face redden.

"Your mother, I suppose, is her next of kin. Is it possible that to avoid death duties she has left her estate direct to your sisters and yourself?"

"I don't know. It's not a thing Alberta would ever have told me."

"So you don't know whether you stand to inherit a share of your aunt's property after her death?"

"No," he added with a visible effort, "but I expect I do. Of course I've heard talk about it, at home, and so on."

"Naturally," Corby said. Anthony again relaxed.

"Will you think very carefully about your aunt's life and the people she knew, and tell me if anything comes into your mind that could explain her death? Anything unusual that you know of that has happened lately?"

"Yes. I can't think of anything at the moment but I will try."

"And don't go out of London without letting me know at the Blent Street Police Station."

"I don't suppose I shall want to go out of London. Oh, I don't know about Alberta's funeral, where it will be. I suppose she may have wanted to be buried in Yorkshire, and I might have to go. I'll let you know."

"Thank you. I'll see your wife now, and then if you like you can both go home. We shall take charge here for the present. Your aunt's body will be taken to a mortuary."

"Can I stay in here while you see Lisa?"

"No. Newstead, will you bring Mrs Seldon in here and then take Mr Seldon back to the dining-room."

So Anthony had no chance of a word with Lisa in the passage. He saw her swing in, the skirts of her long purple dress trailing round her. She gave him a quick look of inquiry. Then Newstead pulled back the chair opposite the Inspector for her, and said to Anthony,

"This way please, Mr Seldon."

CHAPTER V

YOUNG MRS SELDON, THE INSPECTOR OBSERVED, DID NOT SO much sit down on the chair as drape herself over it, one arm in its narrow purple sleeve hanging gracefully, the other crooked behind her head. It was a very pretty head, with the dark hair drawn back from a rounded forehead, with dark eyes carefully set off though the mascara on the eyelashes was now a little rubbed; with creamy cheeks and a lightly-painted bow mouth, the whole presented with a deliberate air of nonchalance: young Mrs Seldon gave or intended to give the impression of a girl whom nothing could shock, not even murder.

"May I have your name, please?"

"Lisa Seldon."

"Where did you have lunch today, Mrs Seldon?"

"You're as bad as Anthony. He asked me that and I told him to mind his own business."

"But you can't say that to the police, can you? Where did you have lunch?"

"At the Savoy."

"Who with?"

"I could have been lunching there alone, couldn't I?"

"You could, but it seems more likely that you weren't. May I have the answer to my question, please?"

"I was lunching with Mr and Mrs Joseph Cresset Hirsch of New York. She's the American editor of *Young Mode*. There were two other people there: Jeremy Destrick, the photographer, and his friend Leslie Crew."

"Did you come straight from the lunch party to this house?"

"Not exactly."

"What do you mean by 'not exactly'?"

"I suppose you're trying to find out whether I got here early and murdered Alberta."

"I'm making routine inquiries."

"And the next thing is I shall be described as helping the police with them. But I didn't do it, although I don't altogether blame whoever did."

"Don't you?" Corby shot at her with such sharp emphasis that her head jerked and she moved her arm from the back of the chair.

"Well—murder is an out-thing, I suppose, even now when so many people are getting killed all over the place that you feel one more doesn't make much difference. But in many ways Alberta was asking to be murdered. She would interfere with everyone so much and try to improve them. Like that wretched little Barry Slater. It would have been far better for him if he'd never got mixed up with her in that prison."

"Are you telling me that Miss Mansbridge had been in prison?"

"No, of course not, nothing so human. She was a prison visitor for a bit, that's how she met Barry."

"Shall we come back to you? You haven't told me yet where you went after the lunch party and before you came here."

"I didn't go anywhere. I mean I left the party as soon as we had had coffee because I was bored. It was in the Hirsch's private suite and I like lunching in the Restaurant. And Jeremy and Leslie are really too awful when they are plastered. Jeremy started trying to sit with his arm round my neck which shows just how drunk he was. I took his arm off my neck and put it round Leslie's. Then old Hirsch began to make up to me which wouldn't have done me any good with *Young Mode*. So I left and sat in the lounge downstairs while I had another drink on my own."

"What time did you leave the Savoy?"

"A quarter to four. I know exactly because I hadn't meant to go to this groovy tea party at all, and then I thought perhaps I would. I looked at my watch and saw that there was still plenty of time, so I took a taxi and came here. And there they all were shivering on the doorstep, except Anthony and Myra who had gone to telephone"

"Did you see any of your lunch party again before leaving the Savoy?"

"I saw Jeremy and Leslie trying to get through the swing door arm in arm."

"Did they see you?"

"No, they did not. I took care of that. I hid behind a pillar. Not that they were in a condition to see anybody."

"We shall have to find your taxi."

Lisa opened her eyes wide, with striking effect. "Do you seriously suspect me of murder as much as all that?"

"Murder is serious. I have to take steps to clear everyone who could have had motive or opportunity to kill Miss Mansbridge."

"You'll be busy! It might be anybody in the whole of England."

"No. It was somebody to whom Miss Mansbridge herself was willing to open the door. Probably somebody who knew that her couple downstairs went out for the whole of Sunday afternoon. Now this is possibly where you can help me."

He asked her about Alberta's friends, but she shook her head decisively.

"No, I hardly ever met any of her friends; she didn't give parties. I should have thought they would be old battle-axes like herself. Why don't you ask Myra? She lived here for years, she was the chief buddy."

"If anything unusual occurs to you about any of Miss Mansbridge's acquaintances will you get in touch with me at Blent Street Police Station?"

"I will, but it won't occur to me. I've never thought about them."

"It's surprising what comes back into anybody's mind in a case like this. Now, please let me have the addresses of the people you were lunching with."

"Mrs Hirsch is flying back to New York this afternoon and it wouldn't be a good thing for the editor of *Young Mode* to think I was mixed up with the police."

"We may not need to get in touch with Mrs Hirsch if you give me the addresses of the two men."

"It's one address." She gave it. "Can I go now?"

"Yes."

She stood up with one hand on the back of the chair, in a model's pose, but she said in a voice that to Corby sounded less indifferent than she meant it to sound,

"What about Anthony?"

"He is in the dining-room with the others. Sergeant Newstead will tell him that we have finished with you, and there is no reason so far as we are concerned why you shouldn't both go home now. But as I said to your husband, you must not go out of London without letting us know at Blent Street Police Station."

"I never do want to go out of London in the winter. I don't often want to at any time unless it's to somewhere with real sun. I grew up in the provinces. I've had them. But I want to know about Anthony. Has he got an alibi?"

"He has as good an alibi as you have, Mrs Seldon."

"And that's not one at all unless you find my taxi."

"I don't think that will prove to be beyond us."

"Well I shan't worry because if you're good at your job, and I'm sure you are, you'll find out that somebody else killed Alberta, not Anthony or me. Good-bye."

CHAPTER VI

"WHAT DID YOU THINK OF HER, NEWSTEAD?"

"She seems a very up-to-date girl, sir, and what I should call showing off all the time."

"So should I. She's a baggage and very anxious that we should think her still more of one than she is. I wonder if she's longing for Seldon to beat her."

"He doesn't look that sort."

"No, he doesn't, but she may drive him to it."

Newstead, abandoning these idle speculations, asked,

"Would she have had the strength to strangle the old lady?"

"I don't know; I was looking at her hands. She's thin, but she's a well-built girl for all her droopy ways. I doubt if she did it all the same—or her husband."

"They've neither of them got alibis."

"We know well enough that honest people seldom have good alibis. They've no reason to think about covering their tracks. Seldon seems candid, but I think we shall find that he will be better off for his aunt's death. And his wife's making more than he is and I should think she's hard to hold. But if he had killed Alberta, I can't see him having the nerve to join the rest of the tea party on the doorstep. Well, we'd better have one of the others in."

Newstead came in a minute or two later, ushering before him a squarely-built grey-haired man with a ruddy complexion. His shoulders were a little too broad for his length of limb, but he carried himself with dignity.

"Mr Armistead, sir."

"Please sit down, Mr Armistead. May I have your full name and address?"

"John William Armistead, The Red Beeches, Witches Hill, Hithamroyd, Yorkshire." He added in his comfortable, broad voice, "You'll maybe want my address at the works too, in case you want to get in touch with me in the daytime. It's c/o Albert Mansbridge Ltd, Hithamroyd, Yorkshire. That's all you'll need."

"Have you worked for a long time in the firm of Albert Mansbridge, Mr Armistead?"

"Forty-nine years. I came there as a lad of fourteen to be office boy. I'm now managing director."

"If I may say so, a record to be proud of. So of course you knew Miss Mansbridge very well?"

"I've known her ever since I can remember. My father was a crane driver at Mansbridge's and our cottage was just down the road from the Old Hall where Albert Mansbridge lived. When I was playing around the doorstep I used to see Miss Alberta go past with her governess.

"Later on when I was working in the drawing office she used to come down to the Works at the end of the day to fetch her father home. Then when things were getting too much for him near the end of his life she generally spent part of every day with him in the office helping him.

"She had a good business head had Miss Alberta. If she hadn't been there the old man would have had to let go sooner. Some thought it would have been better for him and for the business, but most of us admired Miss Alberta for the way she kept the old man in the saddle. She made mistakes sometimes. She lost us a customer or two by speaking out when she had better have kept quiet. But we all knew she meant well by the firm and by us and had a right good heart."

"Her death here today must have been the most terrible shock for you."

Beads of sweat appeared on John Armistead's forehead. He wiped them and blew his nose loudly.

"It has that. I saw her there dead with my own eyes but I can't believe it, that anyone could have murdered her like that. It must have been a burglar who broke into the house expecting it to be empty; then I suppose he found her there and killed her out of fright."

"Nobody could have got in unless she let him in. Every door and window in the house was locked except the front door which Miss Mansbridge controlled from upstairs. No, one thing's certain, whoever killed her was either somebody she knew or somebody who could give her on the intercom a good enough reason to open the door when she was expecting a tea party.

"Here's where I hope you may be able to help me. Perhaps you don't know her friends and acquaintances down here so well as some of the others will, but she probably had connections in Yorkshire who came up to see her. Do you know of anybody there who had a grudge against her?"

"No, I don't. There's no one that I know of that would even wish her dead, let alone kill her."

"Do you know of anybody who might expect to profit by her death?"

There was a pause. John Armistead put a hand squarely on each knee, and looked across the table at Corby.

"It's likely," he said slowly, "that I shall benefit."

"Miss Mansbridge, I suppose, is probably still a shareholder in the firm. Do you know if you stand to inherit part of her interest?"

"Nay, I doubt if she will have left me any of her shares. She's got her own nieces and nephew to think of. I didn't mean it that way. It's like this. Miss Alberta holds, did hold, sixty per cent of the shares in

Albert Mansbridge Ltd. I've got ten per cent that I've bought over the years. Mrs Seldon, Miss Alberta's sister, holds the best part of the rest."

"So Miss Mansbridge still had the controlling voice?"

"Yes she had and that's why I came up to see her this week. You see, Inspector, times have changed. Albert Mansbridge has been a sound firm making a good profit right up into the sixties. But for the last few years the profits have been falling.

"Our sheds and our machines are old-fashioned. We've put in a new one here and there, as we could, but the time has come when the whole place needs modernizing; we get priced off the field by people with up-to-date equipment. But to bring the whole place in line would cost more than we could afford.

"Mind you, Inspector, we're still a going concern. We've a lot of good-will, not only in the neighbourhood, and we're still getting a lot of work, and turning it out well, but we're not making enough on it. We're solvent, and we should be for a few years yet, but without alterations that would break us we shouldn't be solvent halfway through the seventies. So the best we can do for our staff in the office and for the men in the works and for our shareholders in my opinion is to sell the business now to a large firm that can afford to do what's necessary and that wants a branch in the West Riding."

"Would you be able to find such a buyer if your profits are falling?"

"Aye, we've got an offer now, from Morchard Williamson. You'll have heard of them perhaps?"

"Yes, of course."

"That was what I came up to see Miss Mansbridge about. I dined with her on Friday evening, and I spent the whole of yesterday afternoon and evening going through the figures with her and arguing with her. But she wouldn't hear of selling. 'The name of Albert Mansbridge,' she said, 'must never be allowed to die in the West

Riding.' I tried all I knew to persuade her. I reminded her that the name would be kept alive in other ways. There's the orphanage, the Albert Mansbridge Home for Orphan Boys he founded and endowed in his will. But she said the firm must go on under his name too, choose how."

"Which in these days is an impracticable resolution?"

"It is that. But she said, 'Nobody shall take over Albert Mansbridge Ltd in my lifetime.'"

There was a pause in which the whispering noise of Newstead's pencil was the only sound in the room.

"Since she felt so strongly about the firm," Corby said, "isn't it rather surprising that Miss Mansbridge didn't go on living at Hithamroyd to keep an eye on it?"

"She kept an eye on it all right. She came up for board meetings; she's been a director of course. I came to see her every time I was down here and she always went over the half year's and the year's accounts with me, as sharp as an accountant she was. But I think there were personal reasons why she didn't want to go on living in Yorkshire after old Albert died. But you don't want me to take up your time with old history, Inspector."

"Yes, I do. I want a full picture of Miss Mansbridge and of all those who were closely connected with her."

"It was this lad Anthony's father, you see, Aubrey Seldon. He came up to the West Riding from the South to be Assistant Manager of Firth's steel works in the next valley to ours. Alberta was young then—well, thirty about she would be—she and he were around together dancing and that at Harrogate and Leeds, and playing tennis and golf and walking on the moors.

"We were all pleased for her. She hadn't had much of a girl's life, she wasn't the kind of girl most men take to easily; she was masterful you see. She was good looking in her way, but my wife always said she didn't know how to make the most of herself. I don't know about that but I know you could no more have flirted with her than with a riveting machine. But Aubrey Seldon seemed to like her very much. I don't know if he had any idea of marrying her. He couldn't have helped knowing that it would be a fine thing for him to look forward to being Albert's successor, though mind you I don't know that he had that in mind. But then Evie, Alberta's half sister, came home from finishing school in Switzerland as pretty as a primrose, and full of little airs and graces. In six months she and Anthony Seldon were engaged to be married.

"I don't know what Albert thought about it. He never let on. We all knew that Evie didn't count with him compared to Alberta. Alberta didn't let on either, but she seemed to change in a few months from a young woman to a middle-aged one. They gave Evie a slap-up wedding, and Albert bought a house for her—about three miles away from the Old Hall it was. And I think all that threw Alberta more back on to her father and the firm, but when he died she may have been glad to get away from the place and start a new life."

"Do you know anything about Miss Mansbridge's will?"

"I've never seen her will. Albert Mansbridge was a warm man, he made a lot of money and invested it well. Alberta was a rich woman. I don't know what she had decided to do with the rest of her estate, but I know she told me once she was leaving the shares in the firm to be divided in three equal parts between the young Seldons, that's the lad Anthony you've just seen and his two sisters, both older than him and both married with children."

"Did Anthony know this?"

"He wasn't supposed to. She was very close with her private affairs was Alberta. And I always had an idea she might change her will. She was disappointed with Anthony for coming down here and what she called 'fiddling about with silly little jobs' and for marrying a girl she didn't like before he was in what she considered a position to support a wife. Silly work, she called it."

"So it looks as though Anthony will benefit from his aunt's death and might have been worse off if she had lived longer?"

"He probably will be better off if the Morchard deal goes through. But the lad's not a murderer, Inspector, and neither am I. I shall be able to accept the take-over bid now. Evie Seldon's children won't have the same romantic feeling about the name of Albert Mansbridge. But I would no more have killed Alberta to get my own way than Anthony would to get his share of her estate. Nobody could say he's made up to her for what he could get, he's been a bit too much the other way by all accounts. As for me, I've always liked and admired her and I shall miss her. I hadn't given up hope of getting her round to my way of thinking about the take-over. After I'd spent all yesterday afternoon and evening arguing with her, we said good-bye at bedtime, and I was going out to see my son at Rochester today, but when Alberta rang me up this morning and asked me to tea, I put that off because I thought her wanting to see me again meant that she was in two minds after all."

"You will understand I am sure, Mr Armistead, that I have to ask you a few routine questions. Where did you come here from this afternoon?"

"From my hotel, the York and Lancaster in Barnaby Street. It's a bit old-fashioned now, but it's quiet and central. I've stayed there for years."

"So the staff know you well, I expect. Probably somebody, the hall porter for instance, saw you leave the hotel and will remember what time you left?"

"There's been plenty of staff changes lately. The old people would know me all right, but there's a new fellow in the porter's desk on Sunday."

"Was he on duty when you left the hotel this afternoon?"

"He was, but I don't know that he took any notice of me. He was busy talking to one of the waiters. I just pushed my key across the desk towards him."

"What time did you leave the hotel?"

"At three o'clock."

"It would hardly take you an hour to get from Barnaby Street to Porlock Square, would it?"

"I had to change trains at Baker Street and you never know how long you'll have to wait, Sundays." He added, "I meant to get here a few minutes before the time in case there was anything more Alberta wanted to say to me. I was on the doorstep before any of the others."

"Who came next?"

"Miss Heseltine drove up in her car as young Slater came round the corner. Mr Holdsworth was just after him, and the doctor and the Italian a minute later. We all knew our hostess liked punctuality. Only Anthony was late. He came when we'd all been ringing and knocking for about ten minutes."

"When did you intend to go back to Yorkshire, Mr Armistead?"

"I've a sleeper booked on the eleven-thirty tonight."

"You can go back to Yorkshire tonight if you want to. I'll let you know if we want you again. But I must ask you not to leave the country without letting us know."

"I've no intention of leaving the country at present."

"There's just one other thing. Were you wearing a scarf this afternoon?"

"A scarf? Yes, a woollen muffler."

"Will you let Sergeant Newstead have it? He will give you a receipt for it and of course it will be returned to you."

The blood rushed up Armistead's face, and sweat broke out again on his forehead. He said, "Good God!" and glared furiously at Corby, then checked himself. "You've your job to do," he said abruptly. "The Sergeant can have it. It's hanging up with my coat in the hall. I won't waste time telling you I didn't strangle her. I've no doubt you'll find out who did and I hope it will be soon."

"If anything occurs to you that might have a bearing on her death will you let us know?"

"I will that. There's nobody wants justice on poor Alberta's murderer more than I do. Good day to you, Inspector."

He got up from the chair with the movement of a man still vigorous and active, nodded to Corby and followed Newstead out of the room.

CHAPTER VII

NEWSTEAD, HAVING SEEN JOHN ARMISTEAD OFF, CAME BACK and found his chief sitting with one hand propping his forehead, the other doodling on a blank page of his notebook.

"If that one's a murderer, Newstead, I'll give up and take to market gardening. What would you have done if you hadn't been a copper?"

Newstead blinked. "I joined the police as a cadet when I was sixteen." He seemed to feel that some further answer was required, and added, "When I was a kid I sometimes thought of going to sea." With a relieved air of getting back to business he observed, "They don't seem a likely lot so far."

"No, they don't."

"I don't think much of his alibi."

"Oh, I don't think he has one. I don't suppose for a minute that the hall porter who was talking to the waiter noticed what time any keys were left on the desk. I shall be surprised if there's a real alibi among these people."

"Armistead says he got here first."

"That, if he's speaking the truth—and why should he make it up?—could be a fairly damaging admission. But how much first? The murderer would only need about a quarter of an hour. Ring the bell, walk up, either find Miss Mansbridge at her desk or ask her to sit down and write a cheque for somebody, strangle her and walk out of the house again. If he got here about half past three he could have been away well before Armistead appeared. If Armistead did it he could have walked round the corner, pushed the stocking or scarf or whatever he used down a grating, and walked back and stayed on the doorstep until someone else came. He had a fairly strong motive, though it's not the sort that generally leads to murder.

"One thing we must do is to organize a house-to-house inquiry. Did anybody in the Square see anybody approaching this house or coming out of it or standing on the doorstep between 3.15 and four? Or anybody in the Mews behaving in an odd way, lurking or putting anything down a drain, and the same in Cheriton Street? The weather's against us. There wouldn't be many people about. But somebody may have been looking out of a window or letting the cat in. Well, let's see another of them."

Newstead came back alone a minute later.

"Mr Holdsworth, sir, wants to know if he may telephone to his wife. He says she was expecting him home at six, and she always worries if he's late."

"Take him to the telephone in the hall, and stay with him of course. We'll see him next and then he can get off home."

Alone in the room Corby leaned back in the chair and shut his eyes. One full night's sleep had not entirely removed the fatigue of a week of short and broken nights. He could easily have dropped off. Instead he deliberately directed his attention to his mental photograph of the room upstairs. Was there something he had missed, anything that could give him a clue? He heard the door open and sat up.

"Mr Holdsworth, sir."

Mr Holdsworth was a man of medium height and medium build, probably about fifty; dark hair beginning to turn grey and receding from the temples, a decisive chin, small grey eyes behind bi-focals; a well cut charcoal grey suit and a sober tie. He was less visibly agitated than any of those who had occupied the chair before him. He sat down carefully pulling up the knees of his trousers, and looked expectantly at Corby.

"May I have your full name?"

"Russell Holdsworth."

"And your address?"

"The Twin Gables, Acacia South Park Road, Putney, SW12 7YC."

"I hope you got through to your wife, Mr Holdsworth?"

"Yes, thank you. If I or the children are late coming back from anywhere she immediately imagines we have been run over." He smiled faintly. "My boy and girl, teenagers, have not much patience with this, but I try to relieve her anxiety whenever I can."

"Did you drive here?"

"No, I came by tube. I did not feel inclined to take my car out with the roads in this state."

"I am sure you will understand, Mr Holdsworth, that I have to ask all of you certain routine questions. What time did you leave home?"

"At about 2.30. Tubes are sometimes few and far between on Sunday, and I was anxious to be punctual, because Miss Mansbridge was very particular about punctuality. On my way here I had an interminably long cold wait at Earls Court Station," he added calmly, "I cannot prove that of course. You are naturally looking for alibis and I suppose I haven't one. My wife was resting upstairs when I left and my daughter was out. The boy is away at school. I stopped at the tobacco shop at the end of Acacia South Park Road to buy some tobacco, but on Sundays the shop is staffed by casual labour, mostly from the Far East. All I can tell you is that when I arrived here Mr Armistead and Miss Heseltine were already on the doorstep, and had begun the futile bell-ringing and knocking on which we spent about a quarter of an hour before taking further action."

"Are you an old friend of Miss Mansbridge?"

"I have known her for over twenty years, though it is only since she came to London that I have seen much of her. For the last ten years I have looked after her affairs to some extent. I am an accountant; I have my own firm, under my own name, Russell Holdsworth Ltd. My office is in Freemantle Street off the Strand."

"You say you looked after Miss Mansbridge's affairs to some extent. What does that mean? Did you, for instance, draw up her will?"

"No, and although I am one of her executors I am not even fully aware of its contents. Miss Mansbridge's solicitors are in Yorkshire: the firm of Herbert Clough & Sons in Medford.

"The position is rather peculiar. Old Herbert Clough, who is now dead, was Albert Mansbridge's lawyer, and his great friend. When he died his son, another Herbert Clough, became head of the firm, but Miss Mansbridge had a strong prejudice against him." Again Holdsworth smiled faintly. "She once told me that she never felt able to trust the younger Herbert Clough because he cut two dances with her at her first ball. 'Deliberately,' she said. She met him in a doorway and saw by the look on his face that he had not just forgotten. Whether she was right or not I don't know, but she never forgave him."

"So that lost him a client years afterwards?"

"No, not entirely. Miss Mansbridge's loyalties were as strong as her prejudices. She would not take all her affairs out of the hands of the firm which had been her father's lawyers, but by degrees she put more and more into my hands. I first met her because my wife had cousins living near Hithamroyd and when we went up to stay with them we used to be invited to the Old Hall where Albert Mansbridge lived.

"When Miss Mansbridge came to live in London after her father's death she remembered us and asked us to her house. She began to consult me about her affairs and by degrees I did more and more for her."

"Do you know anything at all about the cheque?"

"What cheque?"

"The cheque that Miss Mansbridge was writing when she was killed. She had only written the date."

"No, I did not realize that she had been writing one."

"It was on her desk under her arm when we found her."

"She helped a good many charities and she had various protégés from time to time. Two of them were here today. One went home before we got into the house."

"That was Barry Slater. Can you tell me anything about him?"

"I should prefer to leave you to find out, which should not be too difficult for you."

"What do you mean?"

"Young Slater has a record. Miss Mansbridge came across him when she was doing a spell of prison visiting at Wormwood Scrubs."

"What was he in for?"

"Breaking and entering."

"I gather that you think he has been an unworthy object of Miss Mansbridge's kindness?"

"In my opinion young Slater saw his opportunity when Miss Mansbridge first began to visit him in prison. He played up to her and persuaded her that under her influence he was going to turn over a new leaf. When he came out she found him a job, and established him in a decent lodging. She made him a small allowance, which I paid to him for her. It was conditional on his keeping straight. She arranged for him to go to evening classes and got the vicar of the nearest church to call on him and enrol him in the youth club, and so on. She even paid for him to have a holiday, though at that time he was earning a good wage.

"I did once venture a protest. I thought she was spoiling the young man, and that he was taking all he could get but felt little affection or respect for her. She said to me, 'You leave that to me, Russell. Barry knows that so long as he keeps straight he's got a good friend in me. If he goes back to his old ways, even once, I've told him he'll get no more help from me and what's more I would tell the police straight away. I'm not soft,' she said. 'No one plays tricks with me and gets away with it.'"

"Was that true?"

"Yes, I should say it was in the long run."

"You said two of her protégés were here today. Do you mean her nephew was the other one?"

"No. Miss Mansbridge was deeply disappointed in Anthony because he wouldn't go into the family business and she didn't like the girl he married. But she had strong family feelings, and liked to keep an eye on him; she would have helped him at a pinch. In fact she did once. But I shouldn't have called him a protégé, it was a much more ordinary relationship. I sometimes thought he must feel it, the fuss she made of young Slater and of the Italian, but I think it will be found in her will that she thought more about Anthony, really, than about them."

"What about the Italian—Bartolozzi, isn't it? You spoke of two protégés. Is he the other one?"

Russell Holdsworth folded his lips.

"Yes; in my opinion Miss Mansbridge has been very injudicious about him, and he is simply an adventurer who has been taking advantage of her. I have not seen very much of him and I cannot claim to be an authority on industrial design, but I did once ask Miss Mansbridge if she had consulted anyone who did know something about it as to the quality of Bartolozzi's work. She only said, 'So far I am following my instinct. Marcello says that I have a natural eye, and that if I had had the training I should have made a very good industrial designer myself.' So..." he shrugged his shoulders, "an older woman's fancy for a personable young man is not always an easy thing to counter. I left it to wear itself out in time. It was very much her pattern to be taken in by somebody at first, but to see through him in the end."

"Did Miss Mansbridge give Bartolozzi a lot of money?"

"Not through me, anyhow. She was averse to giving money to her protégés; she preferred to pay expenses for them. She paid Bartolozzi's lodgings through me, and the rent of the room he is using for an office. She was planning to finance an exhibition for him."

"Perhaps she didn't really trust them as much as she thought she did."

"I think that is quite possible."

"Do you know of anyone who might have any grudge against Miss Mansbridge? Or could have any motive for killing her?"

"I cannot imagine anybody who could possibly want to kill her for any reason. I am inclined to think that somebody who wanted to rob the house must have called up on the buzzer with a hard-luck story begging to be allowed in, and must then have panicked and killed her, and escaped without taking anything when he saw that preparations were made for guests."

"One more question, Mr Holdsworth. Were you wearing a scarf today?"

"No, I hardly ever wear one."

"Not even in weather like this?"

"No, I am not inclined to feel the cold. In fact I prefer being too cold to being too hot." He passed a hand over his forehead. "The central heating in this house has often seemed too much to me."

"Thank you for answering my questions so fully and patiently. I needn't keep you any longer. You will want to attend the inquest. We will let you know when the time is fixed. And I must ask you not to leave the country without first getting in touch with us."

"Certainly. I have no plans at all for leaving the country at the moment."

"And if anything occurs to you that could have any bearing on Miss Mansbridge's death, please let us know at Blent Street."

CHAPTER VIII

"WELL," CORBY GROANED, "THERE WE ARE. ANOTHER responsible citizen. He could be right about a discarded protégé; perhaps a hopeless case whom she sent packing when she found out he was hopeless."

"If she gets her friends out of the nick," Newstead said with disgust, "she might pick up anyone."

"Not, I think, without Myra Heseltine knowing something about it. She clearly kept an eye on Alberta's dependants, felt she needed protecting from them. Or thought they might push her out, as indeed one seems to have done. I have an idea that when Mrs Bramley gets back we shall learn more about the people who came to the house. Let's have the Italian."

Marcello Bartolozzi was apparently unwilling to come. Corby heard an indignant voice raised outside the door, and Newstead's firm "Now then, sir, the Inspector wants to have a word with everybody who was coming to tea. This way, please."

Bartolozzi sat down on a chair with a movement that in a woman would have been called a flounce.

"Before you accuse me of anything," he flung out, "I demand the presence of my solicitor."

"At the moment, Mr Bartolozzi, I am not accusing you of anything. I want your help. You may be able to throw some light on the murder of Miss Alberta Mansbridge."

"I? Why should you think that I more than any of the others…"

"I don't. I am asking all of you in the hope that one of you may have heard or seen something that could give a clue to the murderer's identity."

"How could we? We were outside on the doorstep in the snow, unable to enter the house. There we were, shivering, in danger of a *pulmonite*. Until the police broke in we knew nothing at all of this terrible tragedy."

"If you really want your solicitor here during this interview, of course you can have him. That is, if you can get hold of him on a Sunday evening. If not you will have to come with him to Blent Street Police Station tomorrow morning."

"The *avvocato* of my family lives in Rome. He is a very important *avvocato*. He does a great deal of work for our government and for world organizations."

"You mean you have no solicitor in this country?"

"I have had no need for one. All the practical difficulties in my path have been smoothed out for me by Miss Mansbridge. She was anxious only that I should be able to go on with my creative work with a quiet mind. Mamma Mia! I have lost one who was a second mother to me."

Genuine if perhaps easy tears came into the young man's large brown eyes. Indeed, Corby thought, apart from any real affection that might he there, this member of Alberta's circle certainly had something to cry about. He probably would not easily find such another backer.

"I think, Mr Bartolozzi, you must want to help me to track down the murderer of someone who was so good to you."

"Naturally I want it. If I could find the murderer I would strangle him with my bare hands."

Bartolozzi paused, evidently realizing that this was not the most suitable ambition to admit to at the present moment. He substituted "I mean I would hand him over to justice."

He wiped his eyes with unselfconscious ease, and then smiled brilliantly on the Inspector.

"*Of course* I do not need a lawyer to be here. I was distracted with grief. I did not know what I was saying. I place myself in your hands. I am a very great admirer of the English police. All Europe admires them. Grosvenor Square! Show me how I can help you."

"First of all may I have your full name?"

"Marcello Perotti-Bartolozzi. Perotti-Bartolozzi is a hyphened name."

"Is it your own name or your professional name?"

"My own name. The Perotti-Bartolozzi are a very old family. They have lived for over four hundred years on their estate near Viterbo."

"Have you got your passport on you?"

The descendant of the Perotti-Bartolozzi looked affronted.

"No, I do not carry it."

"Then will you bring it to Blent Street Police Station tomorrow morning."

The Italian hesitated, shrugged and said sullenly,

"That is my professional name, the name I am always known by among the artists of Rome."

"And your real name?"

"Berto Fospo."

"May I have your address, please?"

"41, Garforth Street, Camden Town, N.1."

"How long have you been in this country?"

"About sixteen months."

"How long have you known Miss Mansbridge?"

"For nearly a year."

"How did you first meet her?"

"I was introduced to her at a drinks party." With obviously rising spirits he added, "The party was at your Savoy Hotel. A friend of

mine who gave the party, an artist, very contemporary, very well
known, presented me to Miss Mansbridge." He added quickly, "Alas,
my friend has since died."

She had picked him up somewhere, Corby thought, an elderly
woman, clearly prosperous, probably sitting alone in a café or restaurant; a young foreigner on the prowl, perhaps diffidently asking
for some information, and then feeling his way in. The young man
was exceptionally handsome.

"I believe," Corby said, "you were coming to live here in the flat
upstairs?"

He was surprised at the vehemence of the reaction.

"Who has told you that? It is that Heseltine bitch, that *putana*
who has always tried to make trouble for me."

"Why are you so much upset about it? There's nothing wrong in
taking a flat in a friend's house, is there?"

"Of course not, nothing wrong at all. It would have been a very
good thing for Miss Mansbridge; I would have been a son to her. I
would have looked after her much better than her own family. But
Miss Heseltine has always been jealous of me! She has been my
enemy! She tried to make Miss Mansbridge think badly of me. She
could not stay any longer here in this house because her temper was
so bad that it was not possible for anyone to live with her. It was a
good thing for Miss Mansbridge when the Heseltine left. Her temper
was so uncontrolled that I have always been afraid that something
dreadful would happen. Of course I do not accuse her of anything…"

"Are you sure? It sounds to me as if you are trying to imply that
you think Miss Heseltine may have killed Miss Mansbridge."

"I imply nothing. I accuse nobody. I am only telling you the facts."

"Let's have some of them, then. Do you know of anybody in
Miss Mansbridge's circle who had a grudge against her or had any
reason for wanting her out of the way?"

"I can think of no-one who could want to kill her. Why should they? She was a great lady."

"If anything at all occurs to you that might be connected with her murder will you let me know when you bring your passport to Blent Street?"

"Certainly."

The Italian was beginning to look more cheerful, as if he felt that the interview had passed off harmlessly.

"Now I have to ask you a few routine questions. Did you come straight here from Garforth Street this afternoon?"

"Why do you ask?"

"Because I want to check the movements over a certain period of time of all the people who were coming here to tea."

"But we are all her friends. Why should any of us need an alibi?"

"I told you that these are routine inquiries. Will you tell me where you were between three and four o'clock this afternoon?"

"I was in bed until almost half past three. Last night I was out with friends; we went to an Italian Club, we enjoyed ourselves and drank much wine. This morning I had an overhang, so I took some aspirin and stayed in bed to sleep it off. When I woke it was late, there was only time to eat a slice of bread and salami and dress myself and catch the bus."

"Did anyone see you leaving the house?"

"No. My room—it is a poor one, Miss Mansbridge thought it not fit for me—it is over a pastrycook's shop kept by a Greek. He and his family live behind the shop but they always go on Sunday to the grandmother in Soho. There was nobody in when I left the house. But why should I be suspected? Can you not see what a loss Miss Mansbridge is to me?"

"Yes I can. Did you by chance happen to see anyone you know on the bus?"

"No, I do not know the people in that neighbourhood."

"Well, that's all I need trouble you about at present, Mr Bartolozzi. Remember to bring your passport to Blent Street tomorrow."

The Italian raised his eyebrows as if he thought that the English police might have been all right in Grosvenor Square, but were very fussy and interfering at close quarters.

"If you wish it. I can go now?"

"Yes, certainly. Good night."

"Good night." With the air of a *grand seigneur* in grand opera he stalked out of the room.

CHAPTER IX

"So far as one can see at present, Newstead, it would have been worth more than he's got to that young master-piece to keep her alive."

"He's the only one that's made a fuss about coming in here. Arguing with me all the way along the passage he was."

"Well, he is travelling under a false name and I should think a pretty good case could be made out against him for obtaining money under false pretences."

"Seems he didn't obtain much money, by what the accountant said."

"He got the equivalent, and was likely to get more. Let's see, who have we got left?"

"The doctor, and Slater. They're taking their time about bringing Slater in."

"If they don't come back with him soon we'd better put out an alert to all stations. Will you ask the doctor to come."

"Please sit down, Dr Musgrave," Corby said. "I am sorry we have had to keep you here so long, but we shall be able to let you go when you have answered a few routine questions, and given us any information you can."

"Of course I understand. I am entirely at your service."

"Then first your name and address, please."

"My name is Ewan Musgrave. My home address is 27, Chestnut Tree Avenue, St John's Wood, N.W.8. My consulting room is at 354, Harley Street."

"What is your particular line in medicine?"

"I am a general physician and I also specialize in diseases of the nervous system. I am consultant to the Barchester Hospital on those."

"You have been Miss Mansbridge's personal doctor?"

"Yes, for the last seven years since I returned from Australia."

"But you are not as a rule a general practitioner?"

"Not now. I started as one. My first practice was at Hithamroyd in the West Riding of Yorkshire. I was first assistant and then partner to Dr Lawson, who was the Mansbridges' family doctor and close friend. Both Miss Mansbridge and her father were very kind to me and to my first wife; Miss Mansbridge was an extremely faithful friend. During my time in Australia she always kept in touch with me. As soon as I came back here I came to see her and she asked me to look after her."

As I, Corby thought, should have liked to do in her place. The doctor struck him as a man to inspire confidence. It was an attractive face, intelligent, the face of a sensitive man who had his sensibilities well under control and used them to apprehend other people's. He looked at the moment as though he were suffering from shock but had that again well under control.

"I believe you were the first to go into the room after P.C. Bates?"

"Yes. I came up the stairs ahead of the others. When I looked across the room and grasped that something was very wrong, I asked the others to wait a minute and went in after the constable."

"Will you tell me what you saw?"

"Miss Mansbridge was sitting at her desk with her back to us. Her head was slumped forward. A vase had been knocked over and was lying on the floor. Her bag was open on the floor near her foot. The constable stepped up to her and stooped down to look at her face. He said, 'I think she's dead, sir. Will you have a look?'

"I didn't, in that first moment, think of murder. I thought she must have had a sudden heart attack. I was surprised because I had examined her a few days ago and her heart was perfectly sound. When I stooped over her I saw that she had been strangled. The Constable said 'Don't move anything, sir,' but I had already realized that necessity.

"The others had followed me into the room, and I heard a scream behind me and turned round to see that Miss Heseltine had fainted. I helped to carry her out of the room and lay her down on the settle on the landing. I attended to her until she came round.

"The Constable told us all to stay where we were while he telephoned to the Station, and the other policeman stayed with us."

"You are a very accurate observer, Dr Musgrave. Can you tell me anything about the immediate reactions of the other guests?"

"Anthony Seldon, her nephew, had been into the room with the policeman. He came out looking very green. He went to his wife and tried to put an arm round her, but she shook him off. She's a capricious little monkey at any time. I don't think I noticed much about the others except that I heard Bartolozzi ejaculating 'Dio Mio' over and over again, and that Holdsworth went into the bathroom and brought some water for Miss Heseltine."

"Did you happen to notice on Miss Mansbridge's desk an open cheque book in which she had begun to write a cheque?"

"I saw the cheque book but I didn't notice that she had written anything in it."

"How in your opinion was she killed?"

"By someone who came up behind her and strangled her, I should think with a scarf, a stocking or a piece of rope. I don't know if you've found anything. She obviously struggled, but the attack must have been so sudden that she was probably losing her strength before she reacted."

"Can you make a suggestion at all as to who might have done it?"

"Clearly not anyone breaking in. She herself must have pressed the spring that opened the front door. So the inference is that it was somebody she knew or somebody she thought she knew. The fact that she was sitting at her desk beginning to write a cheque suggests to me that it was somebody making an appeal to her. But why anybody who hoped for help from her should want to kill her, I can't understand."

He threw out his hands in a gesture of perplexity. They were, Corby noticed, strong and flexible; and of course of all the tea party he was the one who would have known best how to do it. He was a likeable fellow but to what extremities are likeable people sometimes pushed!

"You don't know of anybody who had a grudge against her or who might hope to profit by her death?"

"I can't think of anyone who would have a serious grudge against her. As for profiting by her death, I don't know the terms of her will; I suppose her nephew Anthony might reasonably expect to be better off for her death, but really one can't see Anthony as a murderer. In fact I thought when I saw everyone on the doorstep that the tea party was designed to bring all her closest friends together. My wife could not come because the baby had a slightly upset stomach."

"Was your wife a close friend of Miss Mansbridge?"

"Yes. I don't think she was very much in her confidence: she is of course a good deal younger. This is my second marriage. My first wife died in Australia. I have only been married to Elaine for two years. My first marriage was not happy and Alberta was very pleased when I married Elaine; she took a great interest in the whole thing and offered to be godmother to our son, who is now six months old. But I don't think Alberta talked much to my wife about her own affairs."

"But she talked to you, probably? Women, especially those living alone, do talk to their doctors. Did she tell you of any difficulty in any of her other relationships?"

"She used to grumble a bit about Anthony, she couldn't forgive him for opting out of the family business, but it was the sort of grumbling that didn't mean much. I think she was really fond of him."

"I am sure you will understand, Dr Musgrave, that I have to ask everybody a few routine questions. How did you come here today?"

"In my car."

"Did you come straight from home?"

"No, I went to Harley Street on the way and called at my consulting rooms. I wanted to look up some notes about a case before I went to the hospital tomorrow morning."

"What time did you leave home?"

"About half past two."

"There is a housekeeper, I suppose, in the Harley Street house?"

"Yes, but I didn't see her. She always has Sunday off. I had my key and let myself in."

"How long did you stay there?"

"About three-quarters of an hour. I could not at first find my notes. I have a new secretary-cum-receptionist who has her own peculiar interpretation of my filing system. When I found the right file I sat down to read it through."

"So you left for the tea party… when?"

"I can tell you that exactly. I looked at the clock. It was twenty minutes to four."

The doctor looked steadily at the detective. "Nobody saw me go into the Harley Street house, nor come out of it. I have no alibi for the time at which Miss Mansbridge must have been killed. It is probably pointless to say to you that I didn't do it, and could have no possible reason for wanting to do it. I have every confidence in the police and I am sure you will find the murderer. It is not likely that you will find him among the people who were coming to tea here this afternoon."

"What about the one who isn't here now, and who is said to have bolted as soon as he heard that there was any question of calling the police?"

"Barry Slater? I don't think he would have had the nerve."

"But you think he might have had the wish?"

"No. I don't mean that. I didn't think he was likely to justify the kindness that Miss Mansbridge lavished on him. But I thought that she was bound to discover that in time. Her kind heart sometimes deluded her, but she was shrewd too. Meanwhile it was not to Slater's advantage to have her out of the way."

"How were you invited to this tea party?"

"By a telephone message last Wednesday. Miss Mansbridge spoke to my wife."

"Did she seem quite her usual self?"

"My wife said nothing about anything unusual when she gave me the message."

"One more routine question, Dr Musgrave. Were you wearing a scarf today?"

The doctor looked grim but replied calmly,

"Yes, a silk square. It's with my coat in the hall."

He agreed with a hint of disdain to let Newstead have it.

"I don't think we need keep you longer. We'll let you know about the inquest."

Corby paused. The doctor waited quietly for his final dismissal.

In that pause Corby had the feeling that there was something he had missed, something more that the doctor could have told him. With him this was a fairly usual coda to an interrogation, especially when he was tired.

"You cannot think of anything, Dr Musgrave, that could account for what has happened? Tell me anything that comes into your mind, however trivial."

A quiver of some kind of agitation passed over the keen face before him.

"Well? Does anything occur to you?"

"Nothing at all. It still seems to me incredible that anyone could have murdered Miss Mansbridge."

"Then I think that's all for the moment. You won't leave the country, please, without letting us know."

"I have no plans for going abroad until I go to a medical conference in Zürich in May."

Newstead, coming back into the room after seeing the doctor out, grumbled, "Another one without an alibi."

"Damned inconvenient they all are, aren't they? Why couldn't he come straight here from his home instead of fiddling about for an hour in an empty house in Harley Street. But I can't see any motive… not as much as young Seldon might possibly have, or as Armistead owned up to."

"Unless Miss Mansbridge had left a legacy to him or his wife."

"If she had, and if he knew that she had, I should think that he could afford to wait for it. Although of course you never know; we shall probably have to look into some of their banking accounts."

"The doctor is the one who would know exactly how to do it, of course."

"Yes, there is that."

"Only you would think that there would be an easier way for him to do it. He could prescribe some pills, and slip a bit of poison in, gradually deteriorate her health, and then increase the dose. It has been done."

"Yes it has—and found out too often. No, if I were a doctor and wanted to murder a patient I should choose some way that wouldn't depend on medical knowledge, some way that anybody could use. Not that I think he did. I should guess he's a person of good quality of mind and heart… only…"

"Only what, sir?"

"I wonder what he's so frightened of."

CHAPTER X

THE QUIET OF THE HOUSE WAS SUDDENLY DISTURBED BY THE sound of voices and footsteps, different voices and footsteps from those of the police.

"Better see what that is, Newstead."

It was a few minutes before Newstead came back.

"It's the Bramleys home from Croydon. I've put them in the dining-room; Bates is still there. Will you see them now?"

"Yes. Mrs Bramley first. She probably knows more about her late employer than all the rest of them put together. Have you broken the news to her?"

"Yes. She's upset of course, but she seems a sensible woman. Her husband went as white as a sheet and began to shake all over."

Mrs Bramley came in looking as though every muscle of what must generally be a round and pleasant face was frozen by shock. She was still wearing her coat, a green and black checked affair of stout cloth, buttoned up to her throat. Long black boots covered her legs to the knees. From the scarf of an almost matching green which protected her hair, snow melted by the heat of the house was running down into her eyes. She put up a hand vaguely to brush it away.

"Please sit down, Mrs Bramley. I am very sorry indeed that you have had to hear this terrible news."

"I can't believe it! It can't be true!"

"I am afraid it is."

"But why... how can it be? How did it happen?"

"Somebody came into the house and strangled Miss Mansbridge at about half past three this afternoon. The people who were coming to tea with her arrived at four, and when they couldn't get in and couldn't get any answer on the telephone they rang us at Blent Street Police Station."

"But how could anybody get in? We left all the doors and windows locked. I looked round last thing; I always do before we go out."

"We think that it must have been done by somebody for whom Miss Mansbridge herself opened the front door."

"She wouldn't open it to anybody she didn't know, that's for sure. But why should anyone *want* to do it? That's what I can't understand."

"Perhaps you can help us to find out. If it was somebody Miss Mansbridge knew it may have been somebody you knew too."

"I know all the people that come to the house, but there isn't one of them that would think of doing such a thing! Why should they? It must have been somebody that wanted to rob her, or one of these young men that are set on violence, Hell's Angels or muggers or whatever they call them, must have got in somehow. But then Miss Mansbridge would never have opened the door to anyone like that without he told her a tale: said there been an accident in the street outside or something, and they wanted to use the telephone. But then she'd have gone down to the front door herself most likely and showed them the telephone in the hall."

Mrs Bramley asked suddenly, "Where is she? Is she in her bedroom?"

"No, we have had her taken to the mortuary."

As if the full impact had reached her, Mrs Bramley began to cry.

Corby left her alone for a minute while she sobbed and wiped her eyes. Then he said gently,

"I know it must seem hard to you that I should bother you with questions now, but I am sure you will want to give us all the help you can to discover the murderer. I have to ask you a few routine questions. What time did you go out this afternoon?"

"It was just before two. Miss Mansbridge always has her lunch early on Sunday, as soon as she comes in from church, so that we can catch the 2.36 to Croydon."

"Do you think anybody could have come in before you left and hidden in one of the rooms until after you had gone?"

"Nobody could have come in at all this morning without Mr Bramley or me seeing them. Mr Bramley was in the kitchen all the morning, except when he carried the rubbish out to the bins, and then he locked the back door after him when he came in, I saw him do it. The front door was locked and I was about between the rooms and the kitchen, when Miss Mansbridge went to church. I met her when she came back. She said to me that it was a raw cold day with snow coming and I should be sure and wrap up warmly to go to Croydon. She thought about other people, Miss Mansbridge did."

"When you got to Croydon where did you go? Did someone meet you?"

Mrs Bramley sniffed and gave Corby a sharp glance of understanding.

"Oh yes, if it's an alibi for us you're wanting there's no difficulty about that. My daughter's husband met us at the station with his car, and the little girl was in it. We went straight to my daughter's house. Her husband's mother was there and her other son, the one that's in the Army, and his girlfriend... you can ask the lot of them if you like, if you're thinking Mr Bramley or I are murderers."

"I have to ask these questions, Mrs Bramley. I have had to ask all the people who were coming to tea here."

"Oh." Corby saw that for the first time the possibility that one of the guests might have killed her employer had crossed her mind.

She said, "But that's just ridiculous. Why should any of them want to kill the poor old lady?"

"Did Mr Bramley or you have one of the keys of the house with you?"

"We had our own key, we've had it since soon after we first came here. It was in my bag."

"And you had your bag with you all the time?"

"Of course I did. No, whoever got into this house it was nothing whatever to do with us. And now I've told you this I hope you won't have to ask Mr Bramley. He's troubled with his nerves sometimes, and anything like that would prey on him and keep him from sleeping. There's nothing more he can tell you than what I can, and if you don't want me any more I'll be glad to go and see that he changes his socks—he's not wearing boots like I am, and this soft snow gets into everything."

"I won't keep you for more than a few minutes. You must have known all these people who were coming to tea with Miss Mansbridge. Do you know if any of them had a grudge against her, or any reason for wanting her out of the way?"

"There isn't one of them that would be likely to murder her. Miss Heseltine, who used to live in the flat upstairs, had a great quarrel with Miss Mansbridge last summer and moved out. In August it was, just before we were going on holiday. I know I was afraid it might be difficult for us to get away and leave the house. Miss Mansbridge would never sleep here alone. But she got the young Italian, Bartolotsky or whatever they call him, to sleep in the spare room so we could get off. That suited them both so well that he's moving into the flat upstairs next week. I daresay Anthony, that's her own nephew, will be sorry now that they didn't move in here while we were away. His aunty asked him first, but I think his wife wouldn't."

"Do you know what the quarrel with Miss Heseltine was about?"

"About Bartolotsky. Miss Heseltine couldn't stand him. She was always saying that his drawings were nonsense and that he was a fraud and trying to get all he could out of Miss Mansbridge."

"What do you think of him?"

"I think he's out to get what he can, but at the same time he did give Miss Mansbridge a lot of pleasure. When you're getting older and you've no children of your own you like to have somebody young about and whether it was to get things out of her or not he was nice in his ways with her. Mr Bramley and I have often said that if Anthony, her own nephew, had been about the place more it would have been more natural like, but his wife isn't one to put herself out for anybody old."

Mrs Bramley paused to draw breath and to wipe away a few of the tears that were coming into her eyes all the time.

"But don't go thinking that Miss Heseltine could have murdered Miss Mansbridge. She'd never do a thing like that. She's very nervous and irritable, but she's an educated woman that knows how to behave. Was that Barry Slater here? I know he was expected."

"Yes, he came; he was on the doorstep with the others, but he went off before they got into the house."

"Smelled trouble most likely, and didn't want to get mixed up in it. It wouldn't be the first lot he's been in. Miss Mansbridge has been worried about him lately."

"Do you know why?"

"She'd heard one or two things about him."

"She came across him first when she was a prison visitor, didn't she?"

"That's right. She took a great fancy to him and she was sure he was going to turn over a new leaf. She used to say to me that what he'd done wasn't really his fault, it was his bad home background and the company he'd been keeping. When he came out he was going to live a different kind of life and she was going to look after him and help him to go straight.

"She went to meet him at the prison gates with a car. She'd a new warm overcoat for him over her arm, and a parcel of things she'd made up for him the night before—a pullover that she'd knitted herself, and a pair of pyjamas, and some tins of food and cigarettes and chocolate and a new wallet with some money in. 'You see, Mrs Bramley,' she said to me, 'his mother never took any trouble over him; she went off and left him when he was four years old. I'm trying to give him some of what he missed.' So, like I said, she met him in a hired car and took him straight off to the room she'd found for him; she got him a job, and she made him join the youth club at a church and she was always on at him to go to evening classes and improve himself."

"Did you think he was keeping straight?"

"I thought he was at first. Mind you I never liked him, nor Mr Bramley either. He's a very good judge of character is Mr Bramley. He said to me, 'Once a wrong 'un always a wrong 'un.' I said, 'Well, Barry's young, and there's *some* that make good after being in prison. You've got to give everyone a chance.' But lately I know Miss Mansbridge has been worried about Barry. She found out he'd never been to the youth club but once or twice at the start, though she'd been giving him money to pay his subscription. It wasn't more than a pound or so, I don't know exactly, but one thing Miss Mansbridge couldn't stand was anybody trying to deceive her. She said to me last week about young Slater, 'Mrs Bramley, I'm not at all easy about Barry. I'm afraid he's deceiving me. I'm going to have a word with his employer, and see the social worker in his district that I asked to keep an eye on him.'"

Corby smiled. "I begin to feel some sympathy for Slater."

"Well, I know what you mean. You've got to let people lead their own lives. Mr Bramley said to me, 'You can't make a silk purse out of a sow's ear with youth clubs and evening classes.' Mind you," Mrs Bramley added equitably, "you've got to keep on trying I suppose, and I daresay there's some that do respond…"

"Can you tell me anything about this tea party? Did Miss Mansbridge often have them on Sunday afternoons?"

"Yes, she did. She always liked to have somebody here when we were at Croydon. She didn't like being alone in the house. I was sorry for her when Miss Heseltine moved out, and I thought it wouldn't be a bad thing after all when Bartolotsky moved in, though I thought it would have been better if it had been Miss Heseltine moving back again. It was more suitable."

"Did Miss Mansbridge say anything to you about inviting Miss Heseltine here again?"

"No, she only said that she'd got people coming to tea, and she'd like me to make a fruit cake, because Mr Armistead was coming up, and he liked my plain fruit cakes particularly. When I took her coffee into the drawing-room last night after dinner she told me who was coming. Mrs Musgrave had just telephoned to say she wouldn't be bringing the baby as he was a bit upset. 'So there'll be eight of them,' Miss Mansbridge said to me, and she told me who they were. I was surprised that she had asked Miss Heseltine again."

"Were you surprised about any of the others?"

"No, they often come here. Miss Mansbridge reckoned a lot to Mr Holdsworth, he helped her with all her business things; and she was very fond of Dr Musgrave. As for having Barry Slater and Bartolotsky together I thought that was just asking for trouble. But I thought, well, they won't play up much with Mr Armistead and Mr Holdsworth and the doctor there. So I made the cake and minced some ham for sandwiches. Miss Mansbridge was very fond of minced ham sandwiches."

The tears came into her eyes again, and spilled over on to her cheeks.

"I shan't make any more for her now. I wish we hadn't 've gone to Croydon this afternoon."

"I understand how you feel, but you can't blame yourself for taking your usual Sunday afternoon out."

"Oh no we're not to blame, I know that, but I wish we'd been here. We did once think of not going with the weather so bad, but then we wanted specially to go this Sunday with my son-in-law's mother and brother and his girl coming over. But I wish we'd been here all the same. There'd have been no murder done in this house with Mr Bramley in it, I can tell you that."

CHAPTER XI

T HE FORMIDABLE MR BRAMLEY WAS SQUARE, SHY, BRAWNY, grizzled and half paralysed with shock. He came into the room as if he was walking in his sleep and sat heavily down in the chair opposite the Inspector, with his knees apart and his hands firmly planted on them. When asked for his name he said Ernest George Bramley in a voice so husky from nervousness that Corby had to ask him to repeat it. Corby himself had to repeat his first two or three questions before they began to register.

Mr Bramley's statement about their afternoon confirmed his wife's in every particular. He had much less to say about the various members of the tea party, except for a more emphatic statement that Barry Slater was a wrong 'un. He could not think of any reason in the world why anybody should want to murder Miss Mansbridge. He opined in a sudden flight of imagination that it must be one of the I.R.A. When Corby pointed out that Miss Mansbridge herself must have pressed the spring that opened the door to the murderer he said positively, "She wouldn't have done that. Not to a stranger." A look of bewilderment crossed his face and he said, "But she must have done." He could not contribute anything else and, to his visible relief, Corby let him go.

"Well, Newstead?"

"We don't seem to get much further on do we, sir?"

"No, we don't. They're as unlikely a lot as you could meet."

"Except for this Slater, and it's my belief he must be the one. Say he came early, to ask for some money, or else she'd told him to come early so that she could have a word with him about his goings on. Perhaps he begged for money and she told him what she would give him and sat down to write a cheque. Perhaps it wasn't as much as he had expected or he was afraid of her finding out other things about him and lost his top and killed her. We shall have to look up his record, but if he was in for breaking and entering he was probably prepared for violence if he didn't actually do any."

"And where is this charmer now, I wonder? Why haven't they picked him up by this time?"

"It looks as though he's done a bunk."

"Which would seem to support your theory."

"If it isn't him it seems as though it must be somebody who didn't come to tea."

"Lord, yes, perhaps, and that throws it wide open. Alberta appears to have been a woman who collected dubious protégés. There may be one or two that these people don't know about. Perhaps somebody she had found out and sent packing. I have a hunch myself that it is one of the tea party, though I can't give any reason for it and we mustn't take it into account."

Newstead's face showed very clearly that he would never take anybody's hunches into account. And quite right too, of course.

"I suppose we get our people in Croydon to check the Bramleys' alibi?"

"Yes, and we must find the girl's taxi from the Savoy, and ask the people who live overhead if they heard Seldon go out and have any idea what time it was, but my guess is that they've heard that door bang so often that they won't be able to put a time to it. As for the others, we shall have to ask the porter at Armistead's hotel what time he left his keys and the porter in Miss Heseltine's block of flats if he noticed when she went out, and the tobacconist at the end of Holdsworth's road if anybody knew him and noticed what time he came in… and much good may all that do us! London's not the place to be in C.I.D., Newstead. You want a small country town where everybody knows everybody by sight, and notices what they do. In this over-crowded cosmopolitan jungle everybody is incognito. Still we must do the routine follow-ups of course. But we must get on with the house-to-house call round this Square and the streets behind. Borrow extra men if necessary."

"Daly's come in now, sir, and Hunter."

"We must get the Square done tonight while there's a chance that somebody may remember something. I expect half a dozen imaginations will get to work, and their owners will be convinced that they saw sinister-looking characters behaving in suspicious ways outside this house, but we can't help that. We might just have a bit of luck. The weather is against us: people would draw their curtains early and huddle round the telly. Still we've got to try it. Will you get that started at once?"

"I'll see to it." Newstead snapped the elastic round his notebook, and stowed it away in his pocket.

"We may get something from the fingerprints. Dabs should let us have them by the time we get back to the Station, but I doubt if we shall get anything. This is a very clever murder, so simple and so well timed. Have they all gone now, except the Bramleys, of course?"

"I'll see."

Newstead went out. Corby leaned back in his chair and shut his eyes. Slowly one at a time he recalled the people who had been sitting opposite him. He had found that so often by running the first interviews through again as if they were a section of a film being replayed he picked up some clue that he had missed the first time. It was surprising what your subconscious could regurgitate for you given quiet and time for concentration.

Corby played the reel back slowly, but nothing that he had not already made a note of emerged; yet he had a feeling that there had been something, a movement of the eyes or hands, a change in the tone of voice, which he ought to have got and had missed.

If they had given him nothing significant about themselves they had given him a fairly full picture of Alberta Mansbridge. She was, they all agreed, a woman who could be irritating sometimes, but whom nobody would want to murder. But somebody had wanted to murder her—from fear of something she knew? For something they hoped to inherit? It would be necessary to find out about her will and their circumstances. Or was the reason further back in the past, in that early life in Yorkshire that had been dominated by Albert Mansbridge?

Newstead came in again.

"They've got Barry Slater, sir."

"They have, have they? Where did they find him?"

"He was in the youth club of St Philip and St James' Church near where he lives. He was singing hymns."

CHAPTER XII

"WHAT'S THIS? YOU'VE GOT NOTHING ON ME!" BARRY Slater protested before his bottom touched the seat. "What are you bringing me in for? I bin going straight, 'aven't I? You can't prove anything against me. What's going on here?"

"I am hoping you can help me to find out."

"I'm not helping the police with no inquiries. Why should I? I've done nothing. You can't charge me. You'll 'ave to let me go."

"Take it easy. I'm not charging you with anything."

Barry Slater was small, but tough, muscular and wiry. His manner was at the moment a mixture of fear and aggression. He had eyes that should have been a girl's, dark blue with long lashes; probably a touch of Irish blood. Perhaps it was his eyes that had fetched Miss Mansbridge. His hair was dark and curly, cut unusually close to his head for these days. A narrow chin and a thin-lipped mouth, a bit of a rat face. He was wearing a real leather coat beautifully cut, obviously new. A present from Miss Mansbridge? Wouldn't she have been more likely to give it to the Italian? Slater looked guilty and furtive, but probably no more so than any man with a prison record when picked up again suddenly by the police.

He glanced round the room and saw Newstead by the door with his notebook open on his knee and his pencil poised.

"What's he taking notes for? I tell you I 'aven't done anything. I was asked to tea here this afternoon by the old lady. I come here and seen a lot of other people on the doorstep pushing the bell as if they wanted to push it out at the back of the house. When we couldn't get in an' we was all standing round in the perishing cold I reckoned she'd forgotten and gone out, so I cut and went off 'ome."

"You didn't go home because you heard that someone was going to telephone for the police?"

"Nah. I didn't 'ear nothing about the police. I went home because I bin sick with tonsillitis last week, and I didn't want to get a chill, see."

"And after that you went out again in the cold to the youth club. Do you often go there on Sunday evening?"

"Not to say often. But I'm a member, aren't I? I've a right to go there if I want, 'aven't I?"

"I should think so, certainly, if you've paid your subscription."

"It 'as bin paid regular. Miss Mansbridge paid it for me," Barry said with the open manner of one who would never conceal anything from the police.

"I just wondered if you went there this Sunday evening because you had any particular reason for wanting to establish your character as a respectable citizen?"

"I went because it's nice and warm in the parish hall. I like a bit o' classy music for a change, hymns and that."

He glanced sharply sideways at Newstead and his notebook.

"But for Chrissake what am I supposed to have done? Been a robbery 'ere or something? It's nothing to do with me if there has, I've not been inside this house for weeks. What's going on? Where's Miss Mansbridge? She'll speak for me."

"Miss Mansbridge is dead."

"What? No!" His hand went up to his mouth, his eyes dilated, his nose twitched like a rabbit's. Corby thought the shock reaction was genuine.

"What she die of—heart or something?"

"No. She was murdered. She was strangled by somebody to whom she must have opened the door about half an hour before you all arrived here."

"Jesus!" Slater muttered hoarsely. "Then when we was all on the doorstep ringing the bell, she was dead inside. But what 'appened? Did somebody break in?"

"They couldn't have. Everything was locked. It could only have been somebody to whom Miss Mansbridge opened the door."

"But she wouldn't let anybody in. She was scared of burglars."

"Probably she wouldn't let any stranger in, no."

Barry considered for a minute, his eyes wary.

"She must 'ave. Someone told her a tale and got inside, and then meant to quiet her and lost his top and dun it too hard, must a' bin that." He added, "Poor old girl," in a tone which to Corby sounded perfunctory. His voice rose again to a shrill note.

"But why've you brought me in? I got nothing to do with it. I couldn't have done her in; why should I? She's been good to me. She was my best friend. Is Mr Holdsworth here? He was on the doorstep with all of them. He'll speak for me. He knows what she did for me. He knows I bin going straight ever since I got out. He's bin sending me my cheques from her."

"The allowance she made you? Were you due for another cheque just now?"

"No. Mr Holdsworth paid me for her on the first of the month regular. I just had one, last week. What should I want to murder her for? It's always the same. Once you bin inside you're the one the police pick on for everything. I swear I didn't touch her."

"I'm not accusing you of murdering Miss Mansbridge, nor at the moment of anything else."

"Then what they brought me in for? I 'aven't been inside this house for several weeks."

"How was that? You've just said that Miss Mansbridge was your best friend and always doing kindnesses to you. Didn't you come and see her sometimes?"

"Yes o' course I did, but I bin busy and I told you I bin sick. By rights I shouldn't be out today in this weather, but the old girl wrote and asked me to tea and I didn't want to let 'er down."

"Have you kept her letter?"

"No, I threw it away."

"Well now, I want to put a few routine enquiries to you. Your name?"

"Barry Slater."

"And your address?"

"16, Lawnswood Road, Islington, N.1."

"How old are you?"

"Twenty-two."

"And where do you work?"

Barry shifted in his seat.

"I bin driving a van."

"Who for?"

"Garstang and Waitley."

"Who are they?"

"Wholesale grocers."

"And their address?"

"There's no point in me giving you their address."

"Their address?"

"Crossway House, Fewston Road, Kennington." He added, dragging the words out of himself, "But I left there."

"When?"

"Middle of January."

"About three weeks ago. Did you give notice or were you sacked?"

Barry burst into a tirade about managers who tried to take the micky out of you, and the unjust natures of employers generally.

"I see. You were sacked? Did Miss Mansbridge know?"

"I told you, I bin sick. I 'aven't seen 'er."

"What have you been living on since you were sacked?"

"On the Exchange, and the money Miss Mansbridge sent me. She gives me a bit extra to pay for evening classes and that."

"Do you go to evening classes?"

"I 'ave bin," Barry said non-committally.

"That's a very fine leather coat you're wearing. Did Miss Mansbridge give you that?"

Barry hesitated for several seconds.

"No, I got it cheap off a man I met in a pub. He was a big man, see, it was too small for him across the chest, like, and the shoulders. I took it off him."

"What was his name?"

"I didn't ask him. No business of mine, was it? He got the cash and I got the coat, see. A man's got a right to buy a coat in a pub if he likes, 'asn't he?"

"Of course, if the coat was honestly come by. Have you been seeing any of the people you used to go about with before you went to prison?"

"No, I kept out of all that, like I promised Miss Mansbridge," Barry said virtuously.

"Have you talked about Miss Mansbridge at any time to the people you meet in pubs? Have you told anyone about your rich friend, and the things she did for you, and her big house and so on? Think carefully. You see somebody knew that Miss Mansbridge would almost certainly be alone in this house between two thirty and four on Sunday afternoon."

"Well they didn't 'ear it from me. I'm not one to go shooting my mouth off."

"Now let's hear where you yourself were between 2.30 and 4.00 this afternoon."

"I knew you were trying to pin it on me! I wouldn't touch nobody. I'm not such a mug. That last time I didn't touch nobody, did I? I shouted to Ron not to hurt the old man. The old man gave evidence for me, di'n't he? They knew that was true in the court. I only got six months and Ron got eighteen."

"Calm down: we're not talking about that time. Where were you between 2.30 and 4.00 this afternoon?"

Sullen and suspicious, Barry muttered, "I was on my way here."

"Did it take you an hour and a half to get here from Islington?"

"Nah. I went into a pub on the way for a drink to warm me up. No law against that, is there?"

"None. Which pub was it?"

"I didn't notice the name. Well I mean to say, you don't, do you? I just saw one and went in."

"What street was it in?"

"I didn't notice. It was one of those behind King's Cross Station. I got off the tube and I was going to get on the bus, see, and I 'appened to pass this pub."

"If you were on your way from King's Cross to the bus you wouldn't have gone through the streets behind the station. What time would this be?"

"Near a'past three. I looked at the clock so I shouldn't be late for Miss Mansbridge."

"How did the pub come to be open so late?"

"They don't all keep the same hours, do they?"

"Come on now, Slater, what were you really doing at 3.30?"

Barry looked cornered. He fidgeted in his seat. Corby could feel Newstead's growing certainty that this was their man, and could not have defended his own conviction that it was not. But

Slater was uneasy about something connected with his afternoon's activities.

"Well? Where were you?"

"With a friend."

"What friend? Where?"

"I was in a caff in Trout Street in Camberwell, with a pal I 'adn't seen lately."

"What is his name?"

Slater hesitated. "Fred—er—Smith."

"And his address?"

"He's moving about like."

"Where do you get hold of him when you want to see him?"

"They generally know at the caff where 'e is."

"So do you," Corby said at a venture. "Come on now."

With obvious reluctance Barry muttered, "He's stopping with his uncle at No. 16, Robins Yard, N.1."

"And you were with him in this café at 3.30? You're sure of that?"

"Certain sure." Slater sounded more cheerful, as if he had rounded a difficult corner. "I said 'Look at your watch Fred,' I said, 'and see if it's 3.30 because I must get off, the old girl doesn't like anybody to be late.' And then I ran for the bus."

"All right. You can go home. But you mustn't go away from home. I may want to see you again."

CHAPTER XIII

ANTHONY WAS SITTING IN THE HALL WONDERING IN A DAZED way what, if anything, he ought to do next. He knew of no precedent for such an occasion. Lisa had gone off home remarking that there was no point in her staying, and that anybody who felt like arresting her could come after her. There would have been a point in her staying if she had realized how much Anthony wanted her, or if she had cared whether he did or not. As it was he shared the hall with a uniformed policeman who sat on a chair by the front door with his helmet on his knees. Albert Mansbridge looked down out of his heavy gilt frame with his confident stare as from a world in which he would not have allowed such things as murder to happen.

Nobody seemed to need Anthony, but since he was the nearest thing to a son of the house he felt he ought to stay there. His mind swung about as if dangling from a rope over a cliff. Who could have done it and why? He wished he had bothered more about the dead woman; because he hadn't, he felt as if this was in some way his fault. Would his mother come? Would his father have another stroke when he heard the news? Had it been terrifying and awful for poor old Alberta? She was more vivid to him now than she had been in her lifetime. He saw her as he first remembered her, coming into his nursery with presents at Christmas and on his birthday; taking him to see the Works, and not pleased when he pulled his hand out of hers and bolted away from the clang and orderly bustle of the engineering shed. "Most boys like machines," she said reproachfully. He saw her again at what she had called his hole-and-corner wedding, sitting on a chair in the registry office, erect and rigid in a large fur hat. He saw her dead body as he had seen it when he went across the room behind Dr Musgrave.

And then that awful wait in the dining-room with the policeman there so that he could not ask any of the older men what they thought. Being interrogated was not so bad, routine questions the Inspector said, and he did not speak to him as if he thought he could be a murderer. Would he now get some money and would that make things better with Lisa or worse? He was ashamed to be thinking of it and ashamed too to find himself aware that Lisa liked to feel that she was making a success of things when he wasn't. It was with relief that he saw Inspector Corby and Sergeant Newstead coming downstairs.

He got up to meet them.

"Do you want me any more, Inspector? Is there anything else I can do here?"

"No thank you, Mr Seldon. I should go home if I were you. If anything occurs to you or to your wife when you have time to think and talk things over, anything unusual that either of you have noticed lately about your aunt or anyone connected with her, will you ring me at Blent Street Police Station."

"Yes I will, and I'll ask the Baxters, the people living in the flat above us, if they heard me go out, shall I?"

Was there a faint twinkle in the Inspector's eye?

"Don't bother about that. One of our men will be making a routine check."

"Oh!" So he was still suspected? How appalling!

"The Bramleys will be all right here tonight. They seem a sensible couple and we shall keep an eye on the house. I'll let you know of the inquest."

"Yes, thank you. I'll be there."

*

There were lights on in the basement flat in Brittany Street. This relieved a half-fear in Anthony that Lisa might have gone out with somebody. He tramped down the steps, his pulses quickening with a mixture of desire and nervousness, as they always did when he came home to her.

He saw as soon as he pushed open the door of the big room, which was sitting-room, dining-room and at the far end kitchen, that she had made efforts. The room which in the middle of the day had been strewn with various garments and with magazines and patterns was now tidy. The table was laid with a red checked cloth. There was a half-bottle of red wine on it and cheese, bread and a jar of chutney. Lisa, who had changed her purple dress for slacks and a scarlet jersey, was busy at the stove.

"Hulloa! They've let you out at last have they? There's some whisky over there. I stopped at the off licence. Luckily I had some cash on me. Help yourself to a drink, and bring me one."

He opened the bottle of whisky, poured two drinks and took a long swig of his own. It made him feel as if a hundred little tight strings all over him had been cut. He carried Lisa's drink across to her.

"I'm making a huge curry. I thought you'd want warming up after all that."

Dizzy with sudden joy at the kindness of her welcome, the warmth of the whisky and the smell of her skin and hair, he put an arm round her and pulled her towards him.

"Come on, darling. Leave that for a few minutes."

"Not now. I'm starving. I can't think of anything beyond food." But she leaned her head against his shoulder for an instant, then raised it and gave a vigorous shake to the pan of rice. She pointed to a dish.

"Hold that—with a cloth, stupid, it's hot."

He held the dish while she poured the pearly grain on to it.

"Put a dab of butter in it and take it across. I'll bring the curry."

These were the times when he felt married. He happily carried the dish to the table. Lisa followed him with the casserole full of steaming curry.

"I put everything that was left in the fridge in here. By the way a policeman has been to this house, to the Baxters. I saw him going up the steps. He was only there about five minutes."

"He would be checking my alibi, asking them if they knew what time I went out. I wonder if they did?"

"Of course, you must be suspect No. 1."

"*I* must? I don't see why."

"Fool, you're Alberta's nephew. You'll get something out of her dying and you need it. I don't suppose for a minute the Baxters will have noticed what time you went out. It's a pity we didn't have time for a word with them before the copper came."

"Then I really should have been in trouble." He had realized that much if she hadn't. "We'd have been jugged for tampering with evidence. Anyhow have *you* got an alibi?"

"I shall have when they find the taxi I took from the Savoy."

"Oh, that's where you were, was it?"

"Yes, that's where I was."

"Who with?"

"Oh, bugger it, Anthony, that's a historical novel now. It seems half a century since lunchtime. It's odd."

"I don't see anything odd about that, seeing what's happened."

"Well, what has happened? One old woman has died a violent death a few years before her time in a world where violent deaths are happening every day, in Ulster, in Vietnam, in Africa. One old woman has died a few years before her time and nobody is going to miss her much except one or two people who were getting something out of her."

"You didn't see her. You didn't go into the room."

"Yes I did, I was just behind you; but that's got nothing to do with it. I really doubt if it's worthwhile for the police to spend so much time trying to find the murderer."

"Of course it is."

"Why? If you look at it realistically."

He said with confused passion,

"Looking at things realistically is only another word for lies. But even looking at it realistically, somebody who has done one murder may do another. Besides, if you didn't track down the murderer and punish him, there wouldn't be any more meaning in civilization."

"There isn't much. It's only a charade."

"That's another realistic lie. Civilization isn't a charade, it grew out of feelings just as much as war and violence do."

"It's nearly finished now anyhow. It's no use trying to hold on to it."

"Yes, it is."

"We don't belong together, do we, really?"

"Oh we do, we do."

There was a minute's silence; wanting to surface he said, "This is a super curry."

"No, I think I've made it too hot."

She suddenly pushed her half-finished plateful away. She got up unsteadily, said, "Oh damn, oh blast," and vanished into their bathroom, slamming the door behind her. Anthony heard the sound of violent retching.

He put down his fork, but he knew she would want him to take no notice. When the sounds were over he went on with his dinner.

A few minutes later she came out of the bathroom, very pale, her hair hanging limply.

"Leave me alone. I'm going to bed."

He was still hungry and, as generally seemed to be the case today, there was nothing he could do. He ate more than half her lavish provision and a hunk of bread and cheese. He left the rest of the wine in case she might feel like having a glass later on. He was sorry that she had been so sick, but he was also relieved in some way that he did not examine.

When he had cleared up everything he went softly into the bedroom without putting the light on. From the bed he heard faint sounds that surprised him. He went across and knelt down by the side of it.

"Darling."

She did not answer; he slipped his arm under her shoulders, and eased her body round towards him. He kissed her damp cheek.

"Don't cry any more, darling. I didn't know you were so much upset."

"I have *some* human feelings."

He was still holding her when their doorbell rang. The ring was followed at an indecently short interval by loud knocking.

"Oh Christ! What *now*."

What came now was a brisk, plump, middle-aged man accompanied by a figure, half visible in the dark, who seemed to be carrying a camera.

"Am I speaking to Mr Anthony Mainsbridge?"

"My name is Anthony Seldon."

"But you are the nephew of Miss Alberta Mainsbridge?"

"Mansbridge."

"Mansbridge, is it? Well anyhow the old lady who was murdered at 31 Porlock Square this afternoon in the middle of a tea party?"

"She wasn't. I mean she was murdered but the tea party hadn't started."

"Is that so? I'm from the *West London Echo*. I think if you wouldn't mind answering a few questions our readers would be very much interested to read your account of it, and I'm sure they'd like a picture. May we come in?"

PART II

NEWS FROM THE SQUARE

CHAPTER XIV

"AT THE MOMENT," CORBY SAID, "WE'VE GOT DAMN ALL. EIGHT improbable suspects who came to tea, or somebody out of the whole wide world whom none of the eight have heard of or even seem able to imagine. And of course the Bramleys are on the list, I suppose, until we get their alibi confirmed."

"We've got that," Newstead said. "Croydon have just rung through. There's no doubt at all about it. The married daughter lives in one of those council estates where the houses are built round an open green space. At least ten people who knew all the family affairs saw the Bramleys arrive, and one couple knew the exact time as they were watching for some relation of their own coming down from London by the same train."

"It's a good job somebody's got an alibi." Corby pushed a paper across to Newstead. "Look at that. No-one saw Myra Heseltine leave her block of flats; the hall porter at the York and Lancaster doesn't know what time Armistead handed in his key; at the tobacconist's shop in Putney the girl who does Sunday afternoon was new and doesn't know any of the customers; the house in Harley Street was empty until the housekeeper and her daughter came home at seven; the house in Camden Town where Signor Bartolozzi-Fospo lodges was empty until the family came home at bedtime. Sunday's a good day for crime! The people who live in the flat above young Anthony say they would never have noticed the Seldons' door slamming in the daytime. They'd only asked them, without much hope, to try to remember not to bang it when they came home in the small hours. The photographer and his friend can't remember anything about the end of the lunch party at the Savoy: they say frankly that they were stoned. I've no doubt we shall find the girl's taxi and Slater's friend. He doesn't want us to, does he? He'd almost as soon be suspected of murder. I'd say he picked up his pre-nick chums again, doesn't want us to know, was keeping it dark from Miss Mansbridge."

"Which would be a reason for killing her if she was beginning to find out."

"You've still got your money on Slater, haven't you?"

"I don't see anybody more likely," Newstead said woodenly. "He's been sent down once for breaking and entering. There *was* violence: the night watchman was hurt, although he seems to have cleared Slater."

"But of course what Slater said was true. If there are eight possible suspects and one has been inside he automatically becomes suspect No. 1."

"I don't say that's right in every case, sir, but it's generally probable. At least that has been my experience."

And mine too, Corby thought, so it's not reasonable to be irritated with this young man because he puts his words one before the other as if they were feet walking along a white line.

"Hasn't the report come in from Dabs?"

"I have the D.F.I.'s report here, sir. It doesn't give us any help so far as I can see. Only two sets of prints in the big sitting-room, the deceased's and Mrs Bramley's. Mrs Bramley's were all over everywhere. There were several sets of prints on the landing, on the settee, and on the banisters. Armistead's, Seldon's, pretty well all of them. They were all shuffling about there until Rothery moved them downstairs into the dining-room. Holdsworth's prints in the bathroom where he went to get some water when Miss Heseltine fainted. In Miss Mansbridge's bedroom only her own prints and Mrs Bramley's."

Newstead added rather unwillingly, "There are no prints of Slater's anywhere in the house. Of course the murderer would keep his gloves on."

"We may get something from the Square. Even on a day like this one or two people may have looked out of the window. But nine people out of ten haven't any eyes. You might see if Rothery and Bates are back, will you?"

Alone, Corby heard the hum of the Blent Street traffic coming as a subdued bourdon through the double window. After sitting through so many interviews he felt restless. He got up and walked across to the radiator, holding his hands over it.

What was going to become of that overheated house in Porlock Square? Who was going to benefit most by the death of Alberta Mansbridge? Young Seldon? Probably, even if indirectly. Could so open-faced and innocent seeming a young man be a murderer? Armistead might also benefit indirectly, but that he would have killed for it was hard to imagine. Holdsworth—what good could it do him to lose a client who probably paid him well? The doctor? The doctor's nerves were taut, he felt threatened in some way. But why should he want to lose a valuable patient and old friend? He was probably worried about something in his private or professional life totally unconnected with Alberta. Neither Myra Heseltine nor Lisa Seldon seemed to Corby to be probable murderers, and the Italian was sitting pretty so long as his patroness was alive. Unless, unless she had left a lot of money to one of them. Or unless she knew something incriminating about one of them. As soon as possible after the inquest he would go to Hithamroyd.

There where the first half of Alberta's life had been lived, the half that was so important to her, he would surely learn something. Young

Seldon clearly knew no more about his aunt than one would expect a not particularly perceptive young man to know about an elderly relative. But the half-sister, Anthony Seldon's mother; Armistead, who had known Alberta from childhood, when he had had time to think; the lawyer who had cut the two dances but had still drawn up Alberta's will; Corby felt convinced that one of these people would be able to tell him something even if, as so often happened, it was something that they did not know themselves.

Newstead came in again.

"Rothery and Bates are back from the Square. They've brought in three people. One is a young boy, and his father is with him."

"We'd better have the boy first and let him go home to bed."

"He was in bed but Rothery made them get him up. Not that he minds; his father is a bit stiff about it."

The boy whom Newstead ushered into the room certainly did not show any signs of reluctance. His cheeks were bright red either from the cold or from excitement. His stout little overcoat was buttoned to his chin and the collar turned up to the lobes of his rather large ears. He was recognizably like his father who, without the brightness of eye and cheek, had the same round face, and the same blue eyes behind horn-rimmed glasses.

"Mr Haverstock and Humphrey, sir."

"Sit down there, will you, Humphrey. Please sit down, Mr Haverstock. I am sorry to have had to ask you to bring Humphrey out so late."

"I should certainly have thought it would be time enough in the morning, Inspector. I thought your officer a little over-zealous."

"Impressions are apt to get blurred very quickly, you know. A night's sleep can make a lot of difference to the immediacy of a story. I won't keep you long. Now Humphrey, how old are you?"

"Nearly twelve."

"Did the policeman tell you what you were coming here for?"

"He said I was coming to help you with your inquiries."

"You misunderstood him," his father interjected.

"No I didn't, Dad. Other people help besides the murderer."

"Who told you anything about a murder?"

"Bryce and Duncan—they..."

"Mr Haverstock, will you let me talk to him? Humphrey, I am hoping that you are going to be able to help me. What were you doing this afternoon?"

"Building a snow-house in the Square garden."

"Have you any idea what time you first went out there?"

Humphrey looked doubtful. Corby glanced at his father who said,

"He went out about three. I fetched him in just before four when his mother was getting tea ready. There were some other boys playing in the garden after that but your officer does not appear to have brought *them* here."

"It was Bryce and Duncan," Humphrey explained. "They came out just when you brought me in."

"They don't cover the time that matters to us. Now Humphrey, I expect you told P.C. Rothery about something you saw, didn't you, or he wouldn't have bothered you to come here so late?"

"It will be midnight before I get into bed again," Humphrey said with satisfaction.

"It will be morning," his father grumbled, "if you don't be quick and tell the Inspector what he wants to know."

"Did you see anybody going into No. 31?"

"I didn't see her go *in*."

Newstead's pencil jerked on his pad.

"It was a woman you saw, was it?"

"Yes. She came in a Triumph and stopped it outside our house, so that I thought it might be Aunty Peggy, only she has an Austin."

"So you went to see? Can you tell me at all what this lady looked like?"

"Like an animal."

"Humphrey," his father said indignantly. "Don't talk nonsense."

"I'm not, Dad, she *was* like an animal. She had a striped fur coat on and a furry thing all over her head, and fur gloves. She was like the cat in the pantomime."

"Did you see her face?" Corby asked.

"I didn't look much," Humphrey added carelessly; "she was very old."

"How do you know she was old if she was wrapped up in furs and you didn't look at her face?"

Humphrey hesitated, at a loss to define or account for his impression.

"I don't know; she *was* old."

"What did she do?"

"She got out of the car but she forgot to lock it. She walked up the pavement, but she kept on stopping. Then she went back and got something out of the car."

"What was it, do you know?"

"It was a big envelope."

"Yes. What did she do next?"

"She went to No. 31 and went up the steps."

"Did she ring the bell?"

"I don't know. I didn't see her any more. I went back to my snow-house."

"You didn't happen to see this woman or anybody else come out of No. 31?"

"No."

"And you don't know how long the car stayed in front of your house?"

"No." Humphrey sounded disappointed. He brightened as he added, "It wasn't there when I went in."

"Can you remember anything else at all about this woman or her car?"

Humphrey frowned in intense concentration. At last he produced,

"She had red boots on, with fur tops."

"And you didn't—think very carefully—you didn't, after you had stopped looking at her and gone back to your snow-house, hear a door bang or shut? You didn't, without noticing it, hear her walking back towards where she had left her car? You didn't hear her drive off?"

"No."

"Well, never mind. What you have been able to tell me has been most useful. Now do you mind waiting a few minutes while Sergeant Newstead gets your evidence typed out, and then we will ask you to sign it."

"You can have my fingerprints if you like," Humphrey offered.

"That's very kind of you, but unfortunately the Divisional Fingerprint Officer has gone home. We'll send you back in a car, Mr Haverstock, at the first possible moment."

Left alone, Corby added a paragraph to his notes. He tilted his chair back against the wall, raising his arms above his head. Sleepiness after the previous week of short or interrupted nights was beginning to creep over him. I wonder if I shall get to Tilly's birthday party? That was an observant boy, pity he didn't go on watching a little longer. Nothing interesting in it for him, of course; we were lucky that he saw as much as he did. It was the Heseltine all right, red boots and all. She lied about sitting in the car in St Stephen's Square. It was rather a clever lie, odd enough to sound true, but not too odd. I'll see her again in the morning.

He brought his chair to the ground again smartly as the door opened and Newstead ushered in a woman with a lot of grey hair flopping over her face.

"Mrs Severing, sir."

Mrs Severing shook back the hair, uncovering a low forehead and a pair of protuberant blue eyes. She gave the Inspector a beaming, almost roguish smile.

"Good evening, Inspector. It is nice and warm in here after the cold outside, although we seemed to get here in no time. I have never driven in a police car before."

She began to unwind one or two voluminous garments in which she was wrapped. She looked, Corby thought, as though she had hastily put on everything that she could find, including something that might be a bed-spread... but then so many people's clothes might be that nowadays.

"It's very good of you to come. May I have your full name?"

"Daphne Severing, Mrs. But my husband and I are separated. On perfectly friendly terms, you understand. We often meet and go to an exhibition together, or have a meal together—not in my flat, I think it better to have our meetings on neutral ground. We did go on one foreign holiday together after our separation, we went with an advanced drama group, but it was not a success. There is no doubt that since our separation my husband has become susceptible to other more commonplace influences. In fact he left the drama group party in the middle of the tour with a young woman who should never have been there at all; she was not serious, her apprehension of anything beyond the visible surface was negligible. But I did not allow that to affect my relationship with my husband. I simply sent out feelings of forgiveness and understanding towards him. I am sure you know, Inspector, how much can be achieved by sending out waves of feeling."

"Were you going to tell me about something you saw in Porlock Square this afternoon, Mrs Severing?"

"Yes." Daphne Severing paused to give her statement full effect. "I saw the murderer."

"How did you know it was a murderer?"

"I didn't exactly *know* at the time. But I must explain to you that I am extremely psychic. I have been told that I ought to have that faculty trained. But I am doubtful; I know that if you cultivate a flower it loses its scent. Where was I?"

"You told me you saw the murderer."

"Oh yes. I began to have uneasy feelings directly after my lunch. Little shivers of cold were running up and down under my skin. This is a sign that I have learnt to recognize. It means that there are evil influences approaching. I made myself a cup of dandelion coffee and filled a hot-water-bottle and went to lie down on my bed."

"Do you know what time you went to lie down?"

"After lunch," Mrs Severing said vaguely. "After I had washed up. Not that that took long, because I just had a cheese and lettuce sandwich and a piece of cake. I was going out to supper with a friend who is a very good cook, so I knew I should be victualled for the day." She broke into a trill of laughter and then turned her head.

"Is your colleague writing down everything I say?"

"Some of it. Could you tell us what you saw?"

"I am coming to that. I fell into an uneasy sleep, from which I woke up with a jerk and with an even stronger sense of approaching evil. I saw that it was snowing. I got up and looked out of the window, but there was nothing to see except a taxi, empty with its flag up driving along the far side of the Square, and the little boy from No. 28 playing in the garden."

"What time was this?"

"I do not have a clock in my bedroom, Inspector. I have never been able to sleep well with a clock ticking in the room. And I had left my watch in the kitchen. I found it afterwards by the sink. No, I am not time-bound."

"In my profession we sometimes have to be."

Mrs Severing gave him a glance of compassionate understanding.

"Naturally, you can't help it. Well, I lay down again on my bed, and tried to go to sleep again, but my sense of approaching evil was too strong. I got up and it was while I was tidying my hair at my dressing-table that I looked out of the window and saw the murderer."

"What was he like? What was he doing?"

"He was coming out of the door of No. 31."

"What did he look like?"

"He was wearing a dark overcoat. Directly I saw him all my antennae began to quiver."

Corby said patiently, "What did he look like?"

"I never saw his face, Inspector. How could I? He put his umbrella up as soon as he came out of the door. I was looking down on him from above."

"Can't you tell me anything about his appearance, Mrs Severing? This is very important. You have no idea whether he was tall or short, young or old? What kind of umbrella was it?"

"Just a large black one such as men have. No, I really can't tell you anything about the man except that his aura was evil."

"Where did he go?"

"He walked round the corner into Cheriton Street, I expect, or of course he may have turned up Porlock Mews that runs just behind these houses."

"I suppose you have no idea what time this was?"

"Let me see." With a near-kittenish gesture, Mrs Severing put one finger up to her cheek. The finger was thick and red and there were chilblains on it. It passed through Corby's mind that she was lonely, a bit dotty and getting old.

"I am trying to help you, Inspector. I think I can make a guess. I went back into my sitting-room, and into the kitchenette which opens off it, and put the kettle on. I then went to put a little tea-tray ready, and to get out some sweet biscuits. I suppose that it must have been about ten minutes before I had everything ready, and then when I had settled down and was drinking my tea cosily in front of the fire I heard the church clock strike."

"What did it strike?"

"It struck the four quarters, and then of course the hour, four o'clock; it is a sweet chime and I always like to listen to it. It's company for me."

"So it would be about a quarter to four when you saw this man leaving No. 31?"

"You have such an accurate mind," Mrs Severing said in a tone between pity and admiration.

"And you can't tell me anything else at all about him?"

"I am afraid not."

"Did you see or hear anything else?"

"Oh yes, Inspector. A little later on there was a terrible noise of somebody knocking over and over again with one of those old-fashioned iron knockers. I am peculiarly sensitive to harsh noises. I looked out of my window. There was a group of people on the doorstep of No. 31 and one of them was making this disturbing noise. I wanted to call out to them to ring the bell. I opened my window but so much snow came in on me that I shut it down at once. I don't know what happened. The noise stopped and I went back to my fire."

"Well, thank you very much, Mrs Severing. We shall get your statement typed out, and ask you to sign it."

"I am so glad that my instincts have been of use to you, Inspector. I always feel that we are not given such gifts for nothing."

As Newstead ushered Mrs Severing out of the door the first glance of real sympathy passed between him and his chief.

Corby added a paragraph to his notes.

When Newstead came back he said,

"All the same, you know, she did give us something. Some man came out of No. 31 at about a quarter to four. Armistead, Holdsworth and the doctor were wearing dark coats; that blue thing Bartolozzi had on would look dark against the snow; Seldon's dufflecoat was dark blue. Like the dabs it points away from your favourite Barry Slater, who was tastefully dressed in light-brown leather. And of course any unknown might be wearing a dark coat. Damn the weather; without the man's perishing umbrella we might really have got somewhere. Well, anybody else?"

"A lady Bates brought in who says she didn't see anything but there is something she thinks she ought to tell you."

"Right, have her in."

"Miss More, Chief Inspector."

Miss More, a comfortable, sensible-looking woman of about fifty, said at once,

"I thought I ought to come round, Inspector, because it seems to me I must be the last person who spoke to Miss Mansbridge before she was killed."

"May I have your name and address, please?"

"Josephine More. I live in the first-floor flat at No. 72 Porlock Square with my brother, who is a Professor at the Purcell School of Music."

"And you saw Miss Mansbridge this afternoon?"

"No, I didn't see her. She telephoned to me at seven minutes past three."

"You are very accurate about the time."

Miss More smiled. "My brother and I particularly wanted to listen to a programme of chamber music on sound radio which was due to start at 3.15. When we heard the telephone bell we looked at the clock and he said to me, 'Finish them off before the Mozart, whoever they are.' So I was very glad that it was Miss Mansbridge because she was always brief and to the point."

"Will you tell me what the conversation was about?"

"I must explain that I am trying to raise some money for the Organists' Benevolent Fund. I had undertaken to arrange a series of coffee mornings throughout the year. Perhaps you don't know what those are. The hostess invites a number of her friends, serves coffee and specially delicious cakes, and she usually has on sale home-made cakes or sweets or flowers. The guests pay for their entrance.

"Miss Mansbridge had undertaken to give a coffee morning in July. She rang me up to say that her plans might change and she could not be quite sure of doing this, so she was sending me now a cheque to cover what coffee mornings generally make."

"A cheque!" Corby exclaimed.

"Yes. She was a most generous person."

"Did she talk about anything else?"

"We just commented on the weather and Miss Mansbridge said she had people coming to tea and hoped the snow would not be too thick before they had to make their journeys home. That was all; we were in plenty of time to switch on the Mozart."

"Thank you very much, Miss More. That is extremely clear and helpful. Did you know Miss Mansbridge well?"

"Not intimately, but I have known her over a period of years."

"Can you make any guess at all as to why anybody should want to murder her?"

"None at all. I think most people who knew her better than I did would agree that she was very just and very kind. I suppose it must have been somebody mad."

"I am most grateful to you, Miss More. I needn't keep you after you have signed your statement."

To Newstead when he came back Corby said,

"Well, the Square has helped us quite a bit. She was alive between 3.07 and 3.15. A man wearing a dark coat and hidden by his umbrella came out of her house, probably at 3.45. Myra Heseltine was in the Square earlier than she said and has lied to us for some reason. And there seems to be an ordinary explanation of the cheque. After her telephone conversation Miss Mansbridge evidently sat down to write it before the guests arrived and was interrupted by the murderer. Directly after the inquest, if we haven't run anybody to earth by then, I shall go to Hithamroyd."

CHAPTER XV

"THEY HAVEN'T FOUND SLATER'S ALIBI," NEWSTEAD SAID, as they waited next morning for the lift in the hall of Lyveden Court, "and he's missing from his lodging, didn't sleep there last night. His landlady says he was going to leave today anyhow. She'd given him notice, she said she couldn't do with him coming in at all hours, and she didn't like the sort of company he brought in. He hasn't taken his things. I've got a call out for him. I've had the ports and airports alerted."

Corby grinned.

"Isn't that right?" Newstead asked stiffly.

"Quite right, of course. But I don't see Slater leaving the country. I don't think he'd know where to go. Much more likely he's gone to ground in London somewhere with this pal he was so cagey about. He must be pretty badly scared to have left his things. We must trace him, of course. My guess is that he's coming our way again, qualifying for a spell inside if he hasn't already qualified. But, again my guess, not for murder."

Newstead folded his mouth in the way that meant he did not agree, but wasn't going to say so. Bob Randall would have said so. Corby pressed the bell again impatiently.

"This is one of those damned lifts that always gets called back again to floor six just when it's nearly at the bottom. Ah, here it comes. She'll be in. I rang and asked her if she'd rather we saw her at home or at Gamlins."

Miss Heseltine opened her door to them, looking, Corby thought, as though she had not slept for a week. Her careful make-up could not hide the ravages of shock and anxiety. Her flat was very warm; there was a large electric fire burning in the sitting-room to support the central heating. The room was too full of furniture and objects, and had somehow a look of temporary quarters. Corby guessed that all the contents of the large upstairs flat in Porlock Square had been crammed in, and that, whether consciously or not, their owner hoped one day to take them all back there again.

"Do sit down," she hesitated and then said with an air of bravado, "I suppose I mustn't offer you anything, not even coffee?"

"No, thank you."

She glanced at Newstead, who was slipping the elastic off his notebook.

"Do you always hunt in couples? It's so much easier to talk to one person. No, of course I shouldn't have said that, it was silly of me. You have to have a witness." She gave an unreal laugh. "I don't know what more I can tell you. I've been thinking about it most of the night, but I can't get any nearer to understanding it. I haven't any more idea at all who could have murdered poor Alberta."

"Miss Heseltine, why did you lie yesterday about the time at which you arrived at the house?"

"What do you mean? I didn't lie. I told you I sat in the car in St Stephen's Square until just before four. I daresay you don't believe me; it was a silly thing to do, I know."

"I don't think you did it, though. I think you drove into Porlock Square much earlier, sometime between half past three and four. I think you stopped your car at the end of the Square, got out, and began to walk towards the house. You went back to the car to fetch something, and you were seen on the doorstep of No. 31."

The colour which she had put on her cheeks suddenly stood out against livid skin.

"I didn't go in. If anybody says he saw me go in he's lying."

"You admit that you were in the Square at that time, earlier than you originally told us, and that you walked towards the house and were on the doorstep?"

She bent her head. He saw how thin her carefully waved grey hair was on either side of the parting.

"What were you carrying, Miss Heseltine?"

"I don't remember carrying anything."

"In a large envelope. I think you can remember."

She said bitterly, "Your spies notice everything." Then quickly, "No, I'm sorry. Of course you are only doing your job. I suppose somebody in the Square saw me. I did lie, partly, though it was perfectly true that I sat in the car in St Stephen's Square till nearly four. I drove back there after I had been seen in Porlock Square."

"But you admit that you had been in Porlock Square first, and that you went anyhow as far as the doorstep of No. 31. What exactly did you do?"

"I daresay you won't believe me if I tell you. Why should you when I have already lied? But this, I swear, is the absolute truth. I went early to Porlock Square because I had some private papers that I wanted to show to Alberta, before the others arrived. At least I half wanted to and half didn't. I couldn't make up my mind. It was all very difficult, you see. I hadn't spoken to her since I left her house last August. Even at Christmas we didn't send cards. So when I got as far as her doorstep I suppose my nerve went and I just couldn't ring the bell. I couldn't do what I meant to do. I went back to my car and drove to St Stephen's Square and sat there as I told you."

"What did you mean to do? What were these private papers? I think you must understand that there can be no privacy about anything connected with murder."

"I suppose you can see them, if you want to."

She crossed the room walking so unsteadily that she looked almost as though she might fall. She jerked back the lid of the bureau, took out a large square brown envelope and half threw it to Corby.

"I told you I employed a private detective to find out about Marcello Bartolozzi. This is the gen. I wanted very much to show it to Alberta, for her own sake, really, but at the same time it seemed such a mean thing to do I couldn't do it. I don't know whether I would have if she'd lived longer. I think I would after we'd met again. I wouldn't have been able to bear to see that charlatan making a fool of her. But it seems a shabby thing to do to show it to you."

"You haven't any choice. But you may be quite sure that we shall respect anything confidential if we can. I suppose you wanted to show this to Miss Mansbridge before Bartolozzi moved into the flat upstairs?"

"Before he moved completely into my place in her life."

Corby could see the tension in every line of her body. The thought crossed his mind that perhaps she and Alberta Mansbridge had been lovers, and she knew or believed that Marcello was going to succeed to that place, but this possible piece of the puzzle did not seem to him quite to fit the pattern; it was not in keeping with his slowly growing image of the dead woman.

Meanwhile he realized that the living woman in front of him was on a rack.

"If I answer your question it will make you all the more likely to think that I killed her."

"If you didn't kill her, nothing that you tell me can do you any harm."

"I knew Alberta had left me the house and ten thousand pounds. She told me when she made the will. I was afraid that after he moved into my flat, this adventurer would get so much influence over her that she would transfer all that to him. I have only what

I earn; at present I earn a good salary, but I am getting near to retirement age."

She bent her head and covered her face with her hands. Corby said with some gentleness,

"I don't see why you should be so much ashamed of feelings that anybody would have, whether they admitted them or not."

He saw Newstead look up from his notes with an air of faint surprise as at something not in the book.

Myra Heseltine raised her head, scuffled feverishly in her bag and fished out a cigarette and a lighter.

She said more calmly, "I daresay you won't believe me, but I really did want, too, to protect Alberta from an unscrupulous adventurer. She would have found him out in time, I think, but not soon enough to prevent her from feeling that she had made an awful fool of herself. That was why I let Marcello know what I had found out about him. I thought it might scare him off."

"You let him know? When?"

"About a fortnight ago, when I got the information from the private eye. I wrote to him and said I had found out all about him and that he had better clear out because I would send all the particulars to Miss Mansbridge. I didn't of course know then that she was going to ask me to tea; when she did I thought it might be easier to bring them with me."

"Did Marcello answer your letter?"

"No."

There was a pause so long that Newstead glanced up at the Inspector. Corby got up.

"I don't think I need trouble you any longer for the moment, Miss Heseltine."

With a painful attempt at jocularity she said,

"You're not arresting me now?"

"We're not in a position to bring any charge against you. You were in the Square between 3.30 and four. You were on the doorstep of No. 31. You tell me that you did not ring the bell but changed your mind and went back to your car with Bartolozzi's dossier. I know that it is true that you didn't leave the papers in the house because they would have been found when our men searched it."

She said suddenly, "I wish I *had* rung the bell."

"Why?"

"Because the murderer may have been inside then, and it might have frightened him and prevented him from doing it."

"Or her."

"Oh no, it must have been a man. Alberta was strong, and still vigorous. I don't think a woman could have done it."

It was Corby's own opinion. As he and Newstead left the flat, he glanced back and saw Myra Heseltine standing on the threshold. She looked, he thought, battered but relieved, as in his experience people sometimes did when they had come out with the truth at last.

CHAPTER XVI

THE CORONER'S COURT ON MONDAY AFTERNOON RETURNED, as everyone had expected, a verdict of murder against a person or persons unknown. As he walked away from the Court with Newstead, Corby heard hurrying footsteps behind him; Russell Holdsworth and Anthony Seldon, who had been sitting together, caught up with them.

"I thought you might like to know," Holdsworth said, "that I have been in touch by telephone with Herbert Clough, my fellow executor, and Miss Mansbridge's lawyer in Medford. He has opened the letter of instructions about her funeral which she left with him. There is to be a service in St Stephen's Church here on Saturday for relatives and close friends, followed by cremation at Golders Green. Her ashes will then be taken to Hithamroyd by her nephew, Anthony here..."

"Good God!" Anthony exclaimed. "How does one take ashes?"

"The undertakers will arrange all that," Holdsworth reassured him. "The ashes will be placed in her father's grave, and there will be a memorial service in Hithamroyd Church, for which the whole firm of Albert Mansbridge will be given time off to attend. The office, the drawing office and the Works will be closed for half a day." Holdsworth allowed himself a discreet smile. "The instructions are entirely characteristic; Miss Mansbridge apparently explained in her letter that she would prefer to have the memorial service in Yorkshire so as to save expense for the many Hithamroyd people who would want to come to it, and also to prevent the employees of Albert Mansbridge Ltd from taking two days off instead of half a day.

But I thought you might like to know, Inspector, that Mr Clough is coming down on Thursday evening so as to talk over various things with me. You may want to see him."

"I shall see him before that," Corby said. "I am going up to Hithamroyd on a sleeper tonight."

"Are you? I had hoped to save you the trouble of a long journey in this weather."

"No, there are things I want to go for," Corby said vaguely. What he wanted to go for was to follow his nose, as he had already explained to Newstead, who had registered respectful disapproval. Corby knew that his senior officers sometimes thought that he followed his nose too much, and was inclined to wonder whether they had attached this very correct and logical sergeant to him as a steadying influence.

Dr Musgrave passed them, walking with long strides towards his car. He nodded to Holdsworth and Anthony, but seemed undecided whether to include Corby and Newstead in his greeting or not. He looked, the Inspector thought, strained and ill, as if he had taken the shock hard. But he and his wife, by his own account, were really fond of Alberta Mansbridge, the godmother of their first child. Corby went up to the doctor as he was unlocking the car door.

"Did you want to speak to me, Dr Musgrave?"

"I just wondered whether I might ask if you have got any further with your inquiries?"

"Not yet except that we have cleared away a few misapprehensions. I suppose nothing more has occurred to you?"

"Nothing. My wife and I were talking about it half the night. She is greatly distressed. We have had so much kindness…" He broke off as if he felt his control giving way. "But neither of us can imagine anybody except a psychopath wanting to murder Alberta Mansbridge. Is anything arranged about the funeral?"

"Mr Holdsworth can tell you about it. I must get back to the Station."

"I must get to work too," Anthony said. "I'm very late."

The idea of doing anything so normal as going back to work late revived Anthony's spirits, which had been further dashed that morning by Lisa's attitude. After her collapse she was at her most hard-boiled. Anthony had been further subdued by a long telephone conversation with his mother, from which he received the impression—one that he was at all times too ready to receive at any contact with his family—that he had been inadequate. Though how he could have been expected to protect Alberta from a completely unknown murderer, or to know exactly what the detectives were doing now he could not tell. But there was nobody who ever thought that he was efficient and sensible, so he inclined, while asserting that they never gave him a chance, to think that they must be right.

Still the inquest anyhow was over, and nobody had arrested him. He pushed open the door of *Evelyn's*, the boutique where he had been working for the last four months. The shop ran back from the street to a large and beautiful mirror which occupied more than half the wall at the far end. Curtains of pearly grey velvet screened the built-in wardrobes that lined the walls. A rich, deep-piled carpet of purple covered the floor.

Evelyn himself was at the far end of the shop, helping a young man to try on velvet coats before the mirror. The young man was very pretty, with chestnut hair falling in Cavalier curls to his shoulders. He shrugged himself into a coat of bronze velvet and looked at his image with the rapt attention of an artist contemplating a work of art.

"It's the *One*," he said reverently.

"It's *perfect* for you," Evelyn said with equal reverence. "Oh Anthony, darling, there you are. Meet Charlot. Charlot, this is Anthony, who is ever such a great help to me. He's just come from an inquest, poor Anthony. His old aunt was murdered yesterday. Was it terribly frightening, Anthony darling?"

"No it wasn't. It was more... businesslike. They brought in a verdict of murder against a person or persons unknown."

"And just think," Evelyn said to Charlot, "that could be Anthony. It wasn't, of course. Anthony's sweet, he wouldn't hurt a wasp. But he's a suspect. He inherits an estate in Yorkshire from his aunt."

"I don't. She didn't have an estate in Yorkshire."

"Well you told the *Echo* that she did."

"I didn't. I didn't tell them any of that rubbish they printed."

"Where did they get it from, then?"

"Out of their own bloody minds I suppose."

What the *Echo* had made of his straightforward answers to simple questions was inconceivable. He felt that he would never again be able to face anyone he knew, and Lisa had laughed at him. There had even been a twinkle, he thought, in Inspector Corby's eye, when he said dryly,

"Better leave the Press to me. Tell them you've got no comment."

Evelyn was looking at him now with malice, his curled grey head—he had gone grey at the age of thirty—on one side. Evelyn could be very kind, as Anthony had found out on more than one occasion, but he loved to tease. It was Charlot who came unexpectedly to the rescue.

"The Press," he spat out, "will say *anything*." He began to wail about a review of some play in which he had been acting with a company touring the provinces. "And then in Wolverhampton they said I was amateurish and didn't know my words. I knew my part, every syllable of it. It was only because I had had this *terrible* row with Trevor, and he'd been *absolutely* beastly to me for days, so that I couldn't sleep and had a splitting headache. Now a friend of mine, a very sensitive, intelligent person, came to Lincoln to see me in that very part, and *he* said…"

Evelyn and Anthony had both stopped listening. Evelyn made a movement to help Charlot to take off the bronze coat, but Charlot did not co-operate. He only turned sideways and looked at himself over his shoulder. Evelyn exchanged glances with Anthony. This made Anthony feel better; so often when one of the bunch came into the shop he was at once made aware that he was outside their charmed circle. He did not want to belong to it, but he liked Evelyn and wanted to be liked by him.

"Darling," Evelyn said to Charlot, "let's take that off. I want to see you in the olive green."

"No," Charlot said emphatically, "this is perfect. It would be a waste of time to try on any of the others. This is the one I would have… now… if I wasn't so damnably hard up."

He made no movement to take off the coat. He said plaintively,

"I don't suppose you send in your accounts straight away, do you—not to friends?"

"I don't send accounts. This is cash-and-carry. Pay for what you want on the spot and take it away with you. It's so simple, you see. It saves all sorts of administrative costs. It means that Anthony and I can run this place without any more staff."

"If you want more help at any time," Charlot said eagerly, "I'd come in and give you a hand while I'm waiting for my next engagement. I expect I could bring you quite a lot of customers." He jerked his arm towards Anthony. "Or if he's going to leave you to look after this estate…"

"I told you, there isn't an estate." Anthony picked up Charlot's own jacket which was hanging over a chair. "Here's your coat. Let me help you out of that one." He laid a firm hand on the bronze lapel.

"Oh Evelyn darling, he is a great big he-man, isn't he?"

But Charlot shrugged himself out of the velvet coat and allowed Anthony to thrust him into his own. He said to Evelyn, "Let me know if I can be any use to you. Bye!"

He kissed two fingers to Evelyn, ignored Anthony and walked out of the shop.

Evelyn sighed. "He would never have paid for the coat. He hasn't a penny. He's a very bad actor. Oh, very bad. It's a pity because he did look delicious in the coat, didn't he? I believe if you hadn't been so firm I might almost have been tempted to let him walk off in it."

"Then I saved you £40."

"You're such a good businessman!"

So, Anthony knew, was Evelyn. He did not give away £40 coats to impoverished charmers. But there were times when he liked to think he would have done if Anthony hadn't been there.

Evelyn's real kindness showed itself a minute later. He said, "All this, your aunt's death and the inquest, and everything, must have been very trying for you. You look quite peaky. Why don't you take a few days off?"

"I was going to ask you if I might have Friday afternoon to meet my mother when she comes down for the funeral."

"I suppose you have to make all the arrangements?"

"No, my aunt's executor does that, a man called Russell Holdsworth."

Evelyn gathered up an armful of velvet coats.

"How do you think poor Charlot would do here, suppose at any time you wanted to leave? I mean, estates in Yorkshire apart, you probably will have something coming to you, won't you?"

"I don't know."

And, he thought, I wouldn't myself trust poor Charlot to sell a row of washing-up cloths. But Evelyn fancies him, I saw that. Has he had enough of me?

"I'll tell you what, Anthony. You take the rest of this week off for the funeral and all that and I'll get Charlot in to help me just for the few days. A bit of money will be very useful to him."

"He'll be able to buy the bronze coat."

"Don't be stuffy, my lamb. I'm not going to pay him £40 for making me long to have you back again."

"All right," Anthony said after a minute. "Thank you. I'll be here on Monday morning first thing. I shall be glad of a day or two to turn round in. It's been very upsetting for my wife."

"Of course, of course," Evelyn said hastily. He did not want to hear about Anthony's wife. At first Anthony had tried to talk about her sometimes in the boutique because she occupied two-thirds of his mind, and because he always vaguely hoped that somebody would be able to give him some advice that would help him to deal with her. But although Evelyn had never said anything that you could call crushing or heartless, he had made Anthony realize that between these grey velvet curtains chatter of wives was not wanted.

Anthony was pricked now by a suspicion that not only would Charlot rather like his place but that Evelyn might prefer Charlot to have it. But Anthony also recognized with a distant flicker of surprise that he himself did not much care.

"Well, thanks a lot, Evelyn. See you Monday."

CHAPTER XVII

THE LONDON RUSH-HOUR WAS AT ITS WORST THAT EVENING. The snow had changed to a cold, sleety rain that gushed down as if every pipe in the heavens had burst on to the heads of the coughing, sneezing bus-queues. Anthony pulled the hood of his dufflecoat so far forward that he could only see the dripping hem of the mackintosh worn by the man in front of him; he thrust his bare, froggy hands into his pockets, and stepped forward doggedly whenever a few people from the front of the queue managed to get on to a bus.

All this made Anthony long more intensely for Lisa and the warmth of their flat. He did not know what she was doing this evening, he never did know what she was doing. He was afraid she might be out with some of her new friends, and he would have to scratch up a meal for himself out of the cold remnants in the fridge. In that case, he decided, he would take any money he had and borrow any of Lisa's that he could find lying about, and go round to the local and get stoned. After all, he was under suspicion for murder; he had a feeling that his job, which was not much of a job anyway, was precarious; he had rejected the world he had grown up in without being able to find a real foothold in another one; and his wife seemed to be drifting away from him. Nothing would be any use but oblivion.

As he went down the area steps he saw a light shining through the red velvet curtains that they had bought in the Portobello Road. He fitted his key into the lock and heard voices, Lisa and a man talking… now for God's sake who? He felt in his present mood that he couldn't stand any of her friends. Another red curtain covered the doorway into the room. He pushed it aside, and saw Lisa lying across a chair, her long legs in violet velvet trousers hanging over the arm. One embroidered Turkish slipper lay on the floor, the other dangled from her big toe. Anthony looked quickly to see who the man in the chair opposite hers was, and saw with surprise, immediately tinged with resignation, that it was Inspector Corby. The Inspector with his hard, compact body, and his bright, probing brown eyes seemed inevitably to have become part of their lives. Anthony noticed that Lisa had a half-full glass, but that Inspector Corby was not drinking. He felt a small shiver of apprehension.

"I'm acquitted," Lisa said.

"I came round to tell Mrs Seldon that we have found her taxi. The driver remembers picking up a young lady in a black cloak at the Savoy and driving her to Porlock Square. He remembers seeing some people standing on the doorstep of No. 31, and wondering why somebody didn't let them in. He knows she arrived there after four because it was his last fare of the day—he packed it in and went home to tea. I shall have to ask you, Mrs Seldon, as a matter of routine, just to come to Blent Street Station tomorrow at twelve to let the driver identify you. I hope that won't be very inconvenient?"

"No, I can make it."

"Thank you for coming," Anthony said. "Of course I knew she couldn't have done it, but I'm very glad she's definitely in the clear."

"And now," Lisa said lightly, "we want an alibi for Anthony."

"The best alibi for you, Mr Seldon, would be for us to find the murderer and prove his crime."

"Well you will, won't you?"

"I expect so, if everybody co-operates with us by telling us every scrap of everything that they know. For instance, what did either of you know about Marcello Bartolozzi?"

"He made a few passes at me," Lisa said, "when we first met. No, don't be a fool, Anthony. It was only because he thought it was due to himself, and I wasn't interested. As soon as he found out that I was in Alberta's black books, he sheered off and never came near me again. He's very practical. But it's no use you thinking that he murdered her, Inspector, because she was far more good to him alive."

"I see." It was Corby's own opinion. Newstead had promoted Bartolozzi-Fospo in his list of probable suspects because he might have been afraid that Alberta Mansbridge either knew his record or soon would know it and would then expose him.

"It must have been somebody connected with Alberta's past," Anthony opined.

Lisa said, "People like that don't have a past."

"Oh nonsense. Everybody has a life. And probably secrets in it. Don't they, Inspector?"

"Yes, although the secrets are not often of the kind that lead to murder. But in this case something has. Can you remember anybody connected with your aunt, at any time of your life, whom she had thwarted in any way, or about whom she might know something?"

"I didn't really know her private life at all. She bossed a lot of people about but she generally helped them at the same time. Mr Holdsworth could tell you more about them. He used to do the money part of it for her. I got into a bit of a jam before we were married. The bank stopped my overdraft and I couldn't pay my rent and I had a few debts. I didn't want to tell my own people at home, because my father was still very ill after his stroke. So I had to tell Alberta." He made a wry face.

"She was bloody, I suppose," Lisa said with sympathy.

"Well, she had given me some money for a start when I first came to London, which was good of her because she was furious with me for ditching the firm at Hithamroyd. She hoped up to the last minute that I would go into it. So she said a good deal about my not doing a man's job, and playing about down here when there was real work waiting for me at home. But she did send Holdsworth to settle the bank and to find out all my debts and start me off clear again. He was much easier to deal with, he was just businesslike and quite kind, and I think he did that sort of thing for her with other people. You could ask him if he knew of any queer characters in her life."

Corby, who had already drawn a blank there, nodded and got up to go.

"Whether he's got an alibi or not," Lisa said, "it would be ridiculous to suspect Anthony. You've only got to look at him to see that he couldn't murder anyone."

At the implied contempt in her tone Anthony reddened to the line of his pale hair.

"There's nothing admirable in being capable of murder," Corby said sharply.

"Oh, I think there is in being *capable* of it. You needn't do it."

Corby looked down at her sprawling gracefully across her chair with her empty glass precariously poised on one knee. He said,

"I don't know whether you are a proper little bitch or just want to make yourself out to be one."

"Is that the sort of thing detectives are supposed to say on duty?"

"No it isn't, so I'm going before I say any more."

Anthony came back from letting him out.

"He's all right. I like him and I don't believe he really suspects me."

"I've told you why he doesn't, my Lily-white Boy."

"Don't call me that. You know I hate it."

"But it's just right for you. It describes your face. And people are like their faces."

"You think you know everything, don't you?"

"Not everything. But I've got my eyes open a bit more than you have."

Anthony swooped over her, seized her under both arms, and lifted her bodily out of the chair. There was a tinkle of broken glass. He shook her as hard as he could, with enjoyment. She slapped his face, and tried to scratch it; she tried to kick him in the crotch. They reeled backwards and forwards across the room, but though she fought like a fury Anthony could feel with rising joy that he was too much for her. At this game he was the master. He shook her again until he felt her giving up all attempt to fight. Then he threw her down on to the settee.

She gasped for a minute, struggling to get her breath back. Then she began to laugh.

"If ever I murder anyone," Anthony said fondly, "it will be you."

CHAPTER XVIII

I N HIS ROOM AT THE STATION, CORBY FOUND NEWSTEAD METHODI-
cally noting the salient facts of Berto Fospo's shady career. He
looked up.

"Fospo's father was a clerk in the offices of the Fiat works near
Turin. The boy did well at school and his father got him into the
drawing-office of an engineering works. Fospo was sacked for being
always off work. He got a girl with child and went away from Turin.
Found a rich woman in Rome and lived with her for a year. She
seems to have set him up in a sort of architect's office of his own.
But he evidently counted on his luck too far; he started taking a girl
out and his patroness got to know it, so she threw him out of her
house, and gave up financing him. He decided to cut his losses and
come to England, where he lived by scrounging and doing odd jobs
until he had the good luck to meet Miss Mansbridge. And of course
he knew from Miss Heseltine that his luck there was coming to an
end. He hasn't so far reported here today with his passport. We'd
better bring him in for further questioning."

"Oh yes, do that," Corby said with a palpable lack of interest.

"Anyhow we could charge him, hold him for obtaining money
under false pretences."

"Yes, he's done that all right, apparently."

"We now know from Miss Heseltine that he had a motive for
the murder, to save himself from exposure. And so now has she, if
she thought the will was just going to be altered and she was going
to be cut out of it."

"Yes," Corby said absently, "but they didn't do it, you know."

"Sir?"

"No, they couldn't have brought it off, either of them. Well now, I'm going home to dinner and to fetch a bag. I'll ring you from Hithamroyd some time tomorrow. I expect to come back tomorrow night. Two bloody nights in sleepers—the one place where I never can sleep. Can't be helped."

There was a knock at the door and a young policeman put his head in.

"A Miss Josephine More, sir, who was here last night, would like to have a word with you on the telephone."

Corby sat down and put the receiver to his ear.

"Yes, Miss More, Inspector Corby here. What can I do for you?"

"I hope I'm not wasting your time, Inspector, but I thought I should let you know that the cheque which Miss Mansbridge promised me arrived this morning by the second post. I have only just come in and found it. I thought she said that she was *going* to send it, but evidently I mistook her, she already had. It will not be viable now of course. Shall I send it to her executors? If you could give me an address?"

Corby turned over his notes and gave her Holdsworth's address. Then he flipped back the later pages and crossed out a paragraph.

So far as the unwritten cheque was concerned, back to square one.

PART III

HITHAMROYD

CHAPTER XIX

THE MANSBRIDGE ARMS AT HITHAMROYD, ACCORDING TO A framed notice in the hall, had been the Roebuck for three hundred years before it was rechristened when Albert Mansbridge bought the property between the two wars.

"Crazy for his own name that man was," Corby reflected crossly as he waited for his breakfast by the fire which had not yet burned up, while the central heating, evidently a slow starter in the mornings, laid only a thin film of warmth over the snow cold.

The thaw had not yet reached the West Riding of Yorkshire. The young constable who met Corby with a car at Medford Station had skidded at what seemed to him a reckless pace over the slippery hill-roads. But they had arrived safely and in a way the Inspector was coming home. His grandmother came from Huddersfield and he had known this country as a child. He was struck again by the beauty of the long valleys clotted or strung with lights that made a dazzle of the snow. Now, always an impatient man, he wanted to get started on the day's work, in which he might find after all that he was chasing wild geese. Newstead thought so, and he did not want Newstead to turn out to be right.

Good hot coffee and crisply cooked bacon and eggs restored his temper, and his conviction that somewhere in the place where Alberta Mansbridge had grown up he would get on the track of her murderer.

It was unlikely that either Herbert Clough or John Armistead would arrive at their respective offices much before ten, but Mrs Seldon might be stirring. The housewife's day began earlier and ended later. She was stirring; she answered the telephone herself. It was a light, pretty voice, young in timbre; when she heard who was calling her she said at once in an agitated tone,

"Oh! It isn't about Anthony, is it?"

"I want if I may to have a talk with you about Miss Mansbridge. I am hoping you may be able to help me. I am sure you must know more than anyone else about her life and the people who came into it."

"I don't think I do, now. She had been living in London for so many years. Of course she often came up here, and before my husband became an invalid I used to go and stay with her in Porlock Square. But there must be a lot of her life down there that I don't know. I can't imagine how this terrible thing can have happened to her. I keep on thinking it's a bad dream and I shall wake up from it."

"I do understand what a shock it has been to you, Mrs Seldon."

"Yes and then Anthony…" Her voice began to quiver. "He isn't really in trouble, is he? He *can't* be suspected of having had anything to do with it. I couldn't make out what he was saying. He told me he had no alibi for the time of the murder. But why should he have? Nobody could think… surely?"

"Plenty of innocent people have no alibis for the time when a murder was committed. We have to make routine inquiries from anybody who could by any remote possibility have been around at the time."

"But Anthony never could… wherever he was…"

"He has not been charged with anything at all," Corby said firmly. "What time can I come and see you?"

"I think it would be easier if I came into Hithamroyd. My husband had a stroke last year. He has partly recovered but he is easily upset. He knows that Alberta was murdered, of course. I had to tell him because he reads the papers. But he has no idea that Anthony… that Anthony could be… I'd better come in and see you this morning. I have some shopping to do in Hithamroyd. Are you at the Mansbridge? Would half past eleven be possible?"

Corby said that it would do splendidly and rang off.

He decided not to wait for Herbert Clough to arrive at his office but to contact him at his home address. A search in the Medford part of the telephone book revealed that he lived at The Towers, Cawston Road. A minute later a man's voice, plummy and pompous, announced, "This is Herbert Clough speaking."

"Chief Inspector Corby here from the C.I.D., Blent Street Police Station, London. How soon can I see you, Mr Clough? I want to make some inquiries of you about Miss Alberta Mansbridge. What time do you get to your office?"

"My usual practice is to arrive at ten. But the office is open from 9.30, and if that would be more convenient for you I can be there by then."

"I should be very grateful if you could. I have a lot to get through today. I want to go back to London tonight."

"Very well, Inspector. My offices are in Bolton Street, at the back of the Town Hall."

"I have a police car coming for me, thank you."

The police car when it arrived was driven not by the young constable who had fetched Corby from the station but by a middle-aged sergeant with a firm sensible face and a pleasant smile. Corby got in beside him, glad that he was not Newstead, but glad that Newstead was there in London looking after things—a careful, reliable chap whom he could appreciate at a distance.

"Do you come from these parts?" he asked the sergeant.

"I was born and bred in Hithamroyd, sir, but I did my first ten years in the Force in Leeds."

Corby could see as they drove up the steep main street that Hithamroyd was a town that ran up the slope from the canal in the valley below to the higher sweeps of snow which must be moors.

"Where are the Albert Mansbridge Works?"

"Down yonder in the valley. You'll see them when we turn the corner. They run alongside the canal for the best part of half a mile." The sergeant added, "It's a shocking thing this about Miss Mansbridge. If I may ask, sir, have you any idea yet of who the murderer was?"

"Nothing at all clear, not yet. What is that large house behind the trees?"

"That's the Albert Mansbridge Memorial Home for Orphans. It was called the Old Hall when Albert and his family lived there. We had a bit of trouble there at the Orphanage a two-three years ago."

"What happened?"

"Some of the bigger boys ganged up and locked the matron in her sitting-room and wouldn't let any of the maids go near to get her out. They'd cut the telephone wires—right little bucksticks some of those boys are. They said she kept the place freezing cold and didn't give them enough to eat. We had to go up there and let the matron out and put a constable in to keep order. Miss Mansbridge and Mr Holdsworth, he's the treasurer of the Orphanage, they came down from London, and Mr Holdsworth found out that Matron had been mismanaging the money; well I think they thought she'd been sending some of it to her own relations. Mr Holdsworth found out that she was going a bit queer with her time of life, and he persuaded Miss Mansbridge not to prosecute her. They sacked her at once, and got Mrs Gracey. She seems to be a nice woman by all accounts. She reckons a lot to that orphanage, does Miss Mansbridge. She was here about ten days ago visiting it."

"Oh *was* she? I didn't know she'd been up here as recently as that."

"She wasn't here only the one night. She stayed with her sister Mrs Seldon out at Kirby Waterlow."

They were driving now along the main road into Medford between warehouses and offices, some of them old buildings of soot-blackened red brick or yellow-grey stone; some of them new erections of glass and concrete. Dirty snow was banked up on either side of the street, which near the centre of the town was so narrow that it seemed to run through a canyon, dark between the high walls and under the threatening sky. It was a relief to come out into the wide square in front of the Town Hall, where more of the unpromising sky was visible. They turned off to the right and right again into a street of old eighteenth-century red-brick houses that had somehow not been obliterated by the tide of heavy Victorian buildings nor by the new wave of clinical erections.

All the houses in this street had brass plates by their doors. They stopped at one which was inscribed with the name of Herbert Clough and Son, Solicitors, Commissioners for Oaths. Clough must have startled his office by arriving so early, for a woman who looked like a cleaner came out of the door with an indignant expression on her face, and the girl in Inquiries was still busy attending to her make-up in front of a mirror over the old fireplace. She relinquished this occupation to say that Mr Clough had just arrived, and to take Corby up to the first floor to a door marked 'Private'.

CHAPTER XX

"AH NOW," HERBERT CLOUGH SAID. "THE WILL... OF COURSE, the will."

Corby was relieved that they were coming to it at last. Since Sunday afternoon he had heard a number of people say that they could not believe that Alberta Mansbridge had been murdered, and that they could not imagine anybody wanting to murder her, but none of them had said it at such length or with such rotundity of phrase as Herbert Clough, who appeared to be making something between a funeral oration and an after-dinner speech.

He now began slowly to draw the folded parchment from its envelope.

"When did you draw up this will, Mr Clough?"

"Two years and three months ago. Miss Mansbridge was up here for the celebration of her nephew Anthony Seldon's twenty-first birthday. Since this meant that the youngest of her sister's three children had come of age, she instructed me to draw up a new will, which as you see I have—I have it here."

"Yes, yes."

With the parchment halfway out of the envelope Herbert Clough paused and fixed his slightly opaque eyes on the Inspector.

"You understand that this is strictly confidential? Entirely confidential. I shall be reading the will to the family after the funeral. I have already arranged that we shall go straight back from the cremation on Saturday to Mr Holdsworth's office, where he is placing a room at our disposal. But I understand that you think it necessary to be informed of the terms now?"

"Yes, please. Time is very important in getting on the track of a murderer."

"Quite so." Clough looked as though he wanted to add some other comment but could not think of one. He repeated, "Quite so." He added, "You may be interested to know that Miss Mansbridge evidently intended to make some alterations to this will."

"Did she? When did she tell you so?"

"She did not tell me in so many words. But she was up here for one night recently staying with her half-sister, Mrs Seldon, and she telephoned to me in the morning and asked me if I should be coming to London before long, and if so whether I could call in to see her and bring her will with me."

"Do you suppose she mentioned this to anyone else?"

"I think it highly improbable. She may have mentioned it to Mrs Seldon but I should think it highly improbable. Miss Mansbridge was extremely secretive. For instance she never told *me* anything about the various affairs that Mr Holdsworth transacted for her." The lawyer blew out his padded cheeks, and his face, already purplish, became suffused with deeper colour. "Miss Mansbridge considered it necessary, since she now lived in London, to have somebody at hand there to attend to her private business. Seeing that I am always to be reached on the telephone, and that fast trains from Medford to London only take just over three hours, some people might not have thought it necessary. But she did, she did; she was—I will not say an eccentric woman, because I would never speak ill of the dead—but she was certainly a woman who had her own ways of doing things."

All on account of two dances cut forty years ago at a girl's first ball, Corby thought; how can we hope to know about anyone?

"Well, the will, Inspector. I need not trouble you with the legal phraseology. I will give you a brief résumé."

Wondering if Herbert Clough could be brief about anything, Corby took out his notebook and pencil.

"Miss Mansbridge left the house in Porlock Square, and ten thousand pounds, to Miss Myra Heseltine. I should explain that Miss Heseltine is…"

"Yes, I know her."

"Oh, you know her? Very well, then we can go on. Miss Mansbridge left her shares in the firm of Albert Mansbridge Ltd to be equally divided between her nephew, Anthony Albert Mansbridge Seldon, and his sisters who are both married. Their names are Pamela Brackley and Philippa Aldridge."

"May I have their addresses?"

"Their addresses? Oh certainly, certainly."

Corby wrote them down.

"Miss Mansbridge left a special legacy of £10,000 to be given to her nephew Anthony Seldon on the day that he joined the firm of Albert Mansbridge Ltd. If he joined it in her lifetime she would make him a gift of the £10,000 and the legacy would be expunged from her will. If he never joined it the legacy would be included in the rest of her estate."

"Do you think that Anthony Seldon knew about this legacy—or gift?"

"I am certain that he did not. Certain. Miss Mansbridge particularly wished it to be a surprise for him."

"You don't think she may just have mentioned it to his mother?"

"I should think it most unlikely. If she did, it would be under the seal of confidence."

"Yes, no doubt, but how many people can be trusted to keep a secret?"

Herbert Clough looked shocked.

"I am confident that Mrs Seldon, who is a very honourable woman, would not commit such a breach of confidence, supposing any such confidence to have been made to her, either directly or indirectly. She has always been inclined to take her son's side about the question of his joining the family firm. Miss Mansbridge in this very room spoke with some bitterness about her sister's weakness in her dealings with her son. But at that time Miss Mansbridge still believed that her nephew would give up trying to earn his living in London without any training for anything. 'Scratching a living like a hen on poor soil', was her expression. She thought that in a short time he would be glad to come back to Hithamroyd."

"But so far he hasn't."

"No. No, he has not."

"Probably a good deal of defiance mixed up with it," Corby mused.

"Possibly. Shall I continue the will? There is a legacy of £5,000 to the Orphanage. There are one or two small legacies to old servants of the family, to her present servants, the Bramleys if they are still with her at the time of her death. There is a legacy of £1,000 to Mr Holdsworth, who is her other executor besides myself. The rest of her estate, which includes a good deal of land that Albert Mansbridge bought in and around Hithamroyd, is to go into a trust for the nieces and nephew, but Mrs Seldon is to have the use of the income during her lifetime."

Corby shut his notebook and slipped it back into his pocket.

"I should think that the legacy to the Orphanage is much needed nowadays. So many of the old endowments are inadequate. There was a bit of trouble there a year or two ago, wasn't there? Can you tell me anything about that?"

"I have nothing at all to do with the Orphanage," Clough said stiffly. "Miss Mansbridge chose to make Mr Holdsworth treasurer of the trust fund, and to leave all the pecuniary affairs of the place in his hands." Again the large face was suffused with uncomfortable colour.

"There are, I believe, people up here who have said that the affairs of the Orphanage would have been better managed by somebody on the spot—on the spot. But this is a subject on which I cannot make any comment. I heard, of course, that an unsatisfactory matron had been dismissed about two years ago. The present matron, Mrs Gracey, appears to be a pleasant and capable person. My wife knows her and I have met her socially, but as I say, I have nothing at all to do with the management of the Orphanage and I make a point of leaving it entirely to those who have."

"I've taken up too much of your time," Corby said getting up. "I'm very grateful for your help."

"I hope you will succeed in tracking down the criminal. It must, I imagine, have been somebody who broke into the house with intent to steal."

"No, I don't think so," Corby said vaguely. "I must be off. Mrs Seldon is coming into Hithamroyd to see me this morning."

"Then I hope, Inspector, that you will be able to reassure her. When she telephoned to me to tell me the terrible news she seemed to have an idea that her son Anthony was under suspicion of having had something to do with the murder. I assured her that it must only be that the police had been making some inquiries of him as the nearest relative on the spot. Or else she herself must have misunderstood something that Anthony had said on the telephone. I told her that it would be unthinkable that he should have been in any way involved in the murder."

You a lawyer in your sixties, Corby thought, and you haven't realized yet how many unthinkable things happen. But he only said, "I'll do my best not to alarm Mrs Seldon. Thank you very much for your help."

In the car he was silent, thinking over what he had heard. Of the eight people who were on the doorstep of 31, Porlock Square on that Sunday afternoon, Myra Heseltine and Anthony Seldon were the two most likely to benefit by the death of Alberta Mansbridge. Myra suspected it. Anthony may have guessed it. Both of them were out of favour with Alberta. Did either of them know or guess that she had asked her lawyer to come up to London soon and to bring her will?

CHAPTER XXI

I T WAS JOHN ARMISTEAD, CORBY REMEMBERED, WHO HAD SAID that Evie Seldon had come home from her finishing school in Switzerland "as pretty as a primrose". The conventional phrase had evidently suited her, for she was small and delicately shaped, still pretty, though at the moment she was pale, her eyelids pink and swollen with crying: but her blue eyes were unfaded, her fair skin hardly lined, and the blonde hair showing under her fur cap was still only touched with grey. As she came into the lounge of the Mansbridge through the swing doors she looked cold and nervous, but resolute.

The Inspector went to meet her.

"Mrs Seldon? I am Inspector Corby. It's very good of you to come in on a day like this."

"Oh, I don't mind the weather. I'm used to it, and I wanted to see you."

Corby pulled two chairs close to the fire which was now roaring up the chimney, and ordered coffee. As she pulled off her gloves, she began at once.

"Please, may I ask you first about Anthony?"

"Of course."

"It's not only for my own sake. It's for my husband's. People come in to see him, and very often they talk to him about the one thing you hope they won't mention. Of course he knows that Alberta has been murdered; the shock has upset him dreadfully. But he has no idea that Anthony…" She stopped as if to get her breath. "You see, Anthony told me on the telephone that he was one of the people who were under suspicion because he had no alibi for the time when the murder was done. It can't be true that he is suspected, can it? He must have misunderstood something. I suppose he was confused by the shock; nobody could really think that he could do such a dreadful thing?"

"I expect he told you that he was one of eight people invited to tea on Sunday by Miss Mansbridge?"

"Yes. I knew he was going to tea with her. I happened to ring him up the night before; he's not good about writing home and I always like to keep in touch with him. I was very glad that he was going, I wished he went to see her oftener. I know of course how young people feel now about that sort of thing, as if being nice to old ones was letting the side down. At least I knew that Lisa, Anthony's wife, felt like that, or anyhow behaved like it. But Anthony isn't that sort of person really."

She looked hard at the Inspector and said with a directness that he could also imagine in her father and sister,

"You don't really suspect Anthony, do you?"

Corby answered carefully,

"As a matter of routine we have had to question all the people whom Miss Mansbridge had asked to tea that day."

"I don't see why."

"Because nobody broke into the house. Your sister must have pressed the spring that opened the front door herself. So the presumption is that somebody whom she knew rang the bell and spoke to her up the tube."

"I always thought that thing wasn't safe. It meant leaving the front door unlocked. Anybody could speak to her and walk in."

"Would she have opened the door to anybody?"

"No. I don't think she would. She was always nervous when the Bramleys were out. That was why I was so glad she had Myra Heseltine in the flat upstairs... I thought it was a great pity she moved out. I hoped they would make up the quarrel. And of course Sunday afternoon the Bramleys would be out."

"Yes, they had gone to Croydon. They have complete alibis."

"But Anthony must have had one. Didn't he and Lisa arrive at the house together?"

"No, she had gone out to lunch alone. She arrived after all the others were there."

"But," she smiled faintly, "I don't suppose Anthony was all that punctual. He hardly ever is. Weren't some of the others there when he turned up?"

"Yes, they were. But you see, Miss Mansbridge was killed about half past three. The guests arrived at her house at four. We have to consider the possibility that one of them, who would have known that she would be alone in the house, might have gone there early, killed her and slipped out again."

"What a terrible idea—her own friends!"

She added positively, "Well it couldn't be Anthony. Even if he could ever have done such a dreadful thing, he wouldn't have had the nerve to come back afterwards. Oh no, I can't believe any of them did. Anthony told me who was there. Of course... I don't know. I was never quite happy about that boy she met when she was prison visiting, but why should he want to kill her anyhow? She was help-ing him. No, I don't think it could have been any of them. But I am absolutely sure it couldn't have been Anthony."

"We haven't charged him with anything," Corby said. He added, "And at the moment we're not thinking of charging him."

Thank God Newstead didn't hear that, but I shall never get any-thing out of her until we've disposed of Anthony. Well! Lucy would be just the same about one of ours.

They had not disposed of Anthony yet. The waitress put the coffee tray down on a table between them and Corby poured a cup and handed it to Evie Seldon. She took it mechanically. He realized that she was still half anaesthetized by shock.

"I want to explain to you about Anthony, about his background here. My father married my mother a few years after his first wife died, partly because he so much wanted a son. There was only Alberta from the first marriage, and it was for the firm you see, a sort of Dombey and Son thing.

"When I was born I was a great disappointment. I don't think my father ever forgave my being a girl. I don't mean that I was ever unkindly treated. I was given a lot of things that Alberta didn't have, an expensive boarding school and a finishing school and so on. But I knew from the time when I was quite small that my father didn't love me as he loved Alberta.

"My mother died when I was three."

Albert Mansbridge, Corby reflected, seemed to have had a habit of being too much for his wives.

Evie paused and looked at him as if she had suddenly realized that she was talking to a stranger.

"Am I wasting your time by telling you all this?"

"Not at all, but won't you drink your coffee while it's hot?"

She drank some mechanically, put the cup down and pushed it away from her.

"You see all this explains about Anthony.

"Alberta was thirteen when my mother died. She brought me up." Evie smiled. "She was a bit bossy with me, she has always been a bit bossy. But she was very good to me. I don't think I knew much about her, what she herself thought and felt. I was rather frightened of her and very frightened of my father. I was much happier when I was away from home at my schools. But," her eyes filled with tears, "I was very fond of Alberta and we've grown closer together as we've grown older. I haven't half realized yet... I can't realize it." The tears spilled over. She wiped her eyes and blew her nose. "I'm sorry."

"Please don't be sorry, Mrs Seldon."

She put her handkerchief away and said in brisk tones,

"But I want you to understand about Anthony.

"Of course as soon as I got married, my father and Alberta wanted me to have a son. I was a disappointment to them again when first I had two daughters. Aubrey and I were delighted with our little girls, and indignant because the others wanted them to be different. It made a slight coolness. They never exactly said anything, but we felt it.

"Then when the girls were eight and seven I had Anthony."

"And that made everything all right?"

"Not altogether, because from the beginning he was under pressure and we tried to prevent it. It even started at his christening, poor child!

"Alberta and my father were set on his being christened Albert Mansbridge—nothing else. We were determined that he should have a name of his own. There were a lot of arguments about it. Alberta insisted on being his godmother, although she was already godmother to our elder girl. I didn't mind that at all, but I was so nervous that if Alberta held him at the font she really would leave out his first name and just say Albert Mansbridge. So although she wasn't pleased, I insisted on holding him and saying the names myself. Once a long time afterwards Alberta said that giving him a silly unnecessary name like Anthony was the beginning of all the trouble."

"Was there a lot of trouble?"

"No real family quarrels, not anything like that. My father and Alberta were good people. But all the time pressure on Anthony as he grew up; they took him round the Works, they let him sit and draw on blue paper in the drawing office; they gave him model cranes on his birthday, that sort of thing. And from quite early on he pulled against them.

"We were determined not to let him be forced into a career he didn't want, but it would have been so much easier for us if there had been something he did very much want. If he'd been set on being a doctor or a lawyer, or if he'd had some special talent for music or painting we'd have had a definite thing to fight for. He says he wants to write plays but I really think that's because he hasn't so far very much wanted to do anything else. And then he got married so young, and I don't want to be unkind about Lisa but I don't think she's the sort of girl to make him grow up, if you see what I mean."

Corby did. He waited a minute while she looked in sad perplexity into the fire, clearly still preoccupied with Anthony, who had in Corby's opinion been brooded over by his family far too much. It could be that Lisa's unashamed egotism was a welcome change.

"Mrs Seldon, you've given me such a clear picture of your own family, I wonder if you could help me by telling me something about Miss Mansbridge's friends, the other people who came to the tea party. I expect you know them all?"

"Yes. I don't know the two young men, her new Italian friend or Barry Slater, very well. But of course the others I've known for a long time. I'm perfectly certain none of them would have murdered her. Why should they? It's just unthinkable."

"The more I know about Miss Mansbridge's immediate circle the more quickly I shall be able to clear all the innocent people and get on the track of the killer."

"Oh I see. Well I'll tell you anything I can."

"What can you tell me, for instance, about Dr Musgrave?"

CHAPTER XXII

"EWAN MUSGRAVE? HE'S ONE OF OUR OLDEST FRIENDS." EVIE Seldon's face had cleared, her voice lifted as if she thought that she had settled his mind about Anthony and was glad to be dealing with somebody with whom she was not deeply involved.

"Poor Ewan! Anthony told me that he went into the room first after the policeman, and found Alberta… like that. It must have been a terrible shock for him. After Myra—and of course that had gone wrong—Ewan and Elaine, his wife, were really closer to Alberta than any of her other friends."

"He came from Hithamroyd, didn't he?"

"Not really, no. He's Scottish; his family lived near Edinburgh. But this was his first practice after he'd finished walking the hospital. He came here as assistant to our dear old Doctor Lawson, with the idea that later on he would become a partner. It would have worked out very well if Ewan hadn't made such an unfortunate marriage, his first marriage that was. Elaine is his second wife. She's absolutely charming. We've all been so glad for him. He had such an awful time with Brenda for years."

"Were they divorced?"

"No. She died in Australia. She was a nurse at the hospital where he was a house physician. She was very pretty. She had beautiful auburn hair and great big greenish eyes. He was tremendously in love with her, and she seemed to be with him. But she must have been unstable even then and I suppose she just couldn't stand married life.

"The trouble began only a month or two after their wedding. She started having dreadful fits of depression, and she began to fly into terrible rages for no reason.

"She hated Hithamroyd. They had a nice little house, just right for a young couple, but she took a violent dislike to it. She wouldn't do anything in it. Everything would have been in a mess if Ewan hadn't cleaned it in his spare time. I think he used to do most of the cooking too. It was very uncomfortable going there. Brenda made you feel that it had been a nuisance getting a meal ready for you, and she didn't want to see you, and Ewan would try to coax her into being welcoming. If you praised a dish she would say, 'Oh, Ewan made that. He doesn't mind doing that sort of thing.'

"Then she took to wandering off and spending the whole day alone on the moors. If she didn't do that she lay in bed all day and refused to speak to anyone.

"Ewan was at his wits' end. He was very young, at least he seemed young, then. Now, of course… I do so wish that Anthony hadn't married before he was twenty-three. I wish he'd given himself time to look about for a more… more comfortable sort of girl. Though I don't want to be unkind about Lisa. She's only nineteen…"

Recalling her from the inevitable Anthony, Corby asked,

"What happened to the young Musgraves?"

"It went on like that for several years. I didn't see so very much of them. But Alberta and my father liked Ewan and tried hard to help in any way they could.

"They asked them to the Old Hall often and had them to stay there for a few days now and then to give Brenda a rest… though she didn't have much to rest from. Alberta used to take her to matinées in Leeds, and for drives in the country and on shopping expeditions in Leeds and Harrogate, anything to cheer her up.

"They took her to see a psychiatrist that Dr Lawson found for them. Talking to him about her troubles seemed to make Brenda happier for a time; then she began to drink.

"She took an overdose of sleeping pills, leaving a note to say that she couldn't stand life any longer. But Dr Lawson, who was a very wise old man, had been afraid of something like that. He'd given her weak pills on purpose, so she only made herself ill for a day or two.

"After that she started telling everyone, even strangers she met in the street, how unkind Ewan was to her. He was still very much in love with her. I could hardly bear to see his face sometimes when he was watching her and didn't know anybody was looking at him.

"At last my father and Alberta and Dr Lawson persuaded Ewan to let Brenda go to a very good private nursing home for mental cases in York. I think my father was going to pay for it, but she was only there a week, then she ran away from it and came back home. She tried to manage better for a time after that. I think she was frightened of having to go back. She did a few things about the house and she took trouble to make herself look nice again.

"But she still complained all the time about Hithamroyd. She said it was always grey and cold, and if she could only live in some warm, sunny place she would feel quite different."

Evie added with a touch of resentment, "It isn't cold and wet here all the time. We have lovely weather here sometimes. You should see what it's like when the spring comes, and how beautiful the moors are in the summer."

"I know. My grandmother came from Huddersfield; I used to stay up here when I was a small child."

For the first time she smiled brilliantly. "Oh, well, of course you understand, then. That must be why I don't feel as if you were a stranger. But we all came to the conclusion that Brenda would never be happy here. We thought she would end up in a mental hospital. She was beginning to drink again too. Ewan kept all drinks out of the house, he kept her very short of money, although he hated doing it. But it was no use, she got hold of drink somehow."

"Yes. They do."

"So in the end he applied for a hospital appointment in Melbourne where Brenda would get the sunshine she longed for and a complete change. He hoped she might be able to make a fresh start among people who didn't know anything about her."

Evie Seldon paused and glanced at the watch on her wrist.

"Am I keeping you too long, Mrs Seldon?"

"No, I needn't go yet. It's only that my cleaner, Mrs Caley, can't stay after half past one and I don't like to leave my husband alone in the house for long. But I needn't start back for another half hour."

"What happened to the Musgraves in Australia?"

"At first we gathered that the move had been a success. Ewan had a very good job and was enjoying it. He wrote that Brenda was delighted with the sun and the novelty. She was sleeping and eating better, had put on a little weight. He said she was beginning to make friends with the wives of his colleagues, and was talking about doing a part-time job helping one of them who was running a children's clinic.

"We were all delighted. We thought she had really turned the corner. Only Dr Lawson was doubtful.

"I can't remember how long it was before we began to realize that Brenda was slipping backwards again. Ewan always wrote regularly to Alberta. I think at first he asked her not to tell anyone. Later we knew that Brenda had given up her job at the clinic, and that she had taken a dislike to Melbourne. Her depressions had come back and she was starting to drink again. Then Alberta told us that Ewan had been obliged to put her in a mental hospital.

"She kept on going in and then coming out again for a few months, and then having to go back. I think Alberta knew more than she told us about what Ewan was going through. She talked of going out to Australia to see them but then my father's health began to fail, and she no longer thought of leaving him."

Evie stopped. "I'm talking far too much. I am sure you don't want to hear all this old history."

"Yes, please, I do."

You had to listen always to what might be irrelevancies; you never knew when the pointer would appear.

"What happened to Brenda Musgrave in the end?"

"It was very tragic. Ewan heard of a new mental hospital up country, on the edge of the Bush, where they gave people like Brenda light work to do in the gardens or on the farm, and let them feel perfectly free, although they kept a close watch on them. At least they said they did, but Brenda was too cunning for them. She disappeared.

"Of course they sent for Ewan, and he came and they searched for a fortnight. Apparently Brenda had asked one of the nurses questions about the Bush and said she longed to go there.

"They had police and other people on the search, but they never found her body, only the remains of her shoes, and her handbag with just her powder case and lipstick and two dirty handkerchiefs in it.

"Ewan had a breakdown after that and was in hospital for weeks. As soon as he could he came home to England and began to do awfully well. And two years ago he married Elaine. She is absolutely sweet, so pretty and warm-hearted and intelligent: her father is a distinguished surgeon, so she belongs to Ewan's world, and now they have this fine baby boy, Alberta's godson, and it's all perfect. I do hope it has wiped out all the unhappiness."

Corby thought it hadn't; something was not perfect, the doctor looked hag-ridden.

"You don't know of any troubles or difficulties that Dr Musgrave has had lately?"

"No. I haven't heard of any. I think he's had his share. Now I must go."

"You've been most kind and helpful."

"I don't quite see how, except that I hope you understand now about Anthony. If you want to know more about Alberta's affairs the person you ought to see is John Armistead. He always had so much to do with her about the business of the firm."

"I'm going to see him at the end of the afternoon. Are you in favour of this take-over or merger, Mrs Seldon?"

"Yes. Because I think it would be better for Anthony. There wouldn't be any more question of him going into the firm or feeling he ought to go into the firm, and if that was right out of the way he might be able to settle down properly to something else. Besides, I want it for the Armisteads' sake. It might save Mary Armistead's life."

"Mrs Armistead? I hadn't heard anything about that."

"Oh, hadn't you? She has been ill now on and off for about two years. She developed chronic bronchitis, and the doctors say that the only chance of controlling it would be for her to go to a warmer climate. So John wants to retire now and take her out to some cousin in South Africa to see if that suits her, and if they could stand living there. If not they'd come back to Cornwall or Devon. Yes, I do want the take-over for them as well as for Anthony. Mary Armistead is a dear and they are absolutely devoted."

"There is just one more question I should like to ask you. Your sister's lawyer, Mr Clough, told me that she was up here for a night about a week ago, staying with you. Did she come up for any special reason?"

"Yes. She was worried about the Orphanage."

"In what way?"

"I don't know. She didn't tell me. I knew that Mrs Gracey had been
finding it very difficult to make the money go round and I knew that
Alberta had been supplementing it for some time. She cared very
much about the Orphanage."

"Was she satisfied with the way things were going there?"

"I don't know. I didn't see her again after she'd been there. I drove
her over after breakfast and left her there, and she was going straight
on to Medford to catch the midday train to London. I didn't hear
from her afterwards except just a note to thank me for putting her
up for the night. I should think the trouble was that the money still
didn't go round in spite of the extra Alberta was sending. All those
boys growing out of their clothes and eating like horses! I can't think
how Mrs Gracey manages."

"I'm going to see her after lunch."

"Oh well, then she will show you everything and tell you all about
it. Alberta was always so proud of it, I was sorry that it had become
an anxiety. Now I really must go. If Mrs Caley doesn't get her bus at
1.35 there isn't another one till three."

CHAPTER XXIII

THE BIG IRON GATES OF THE ORPHANAGE WERE OPEN. THE half-thawed slush on the drive was already beginning to harden again. On the round lawn in front of the house were a score of snowmen. Some were elaborately finished off with old hats, pebble eyes and moustaches made of twigs: others, whose makers had tired sooner, were roughly outlined figures with curious planes and shadows and looked, Corby thought, something like a display of sculpture by Henry Moore. The orphans had evidently been enjoying themselves.

The house, which would certainly have been much uglier when not covered by snow, was solid, imposing, crenellated. Corby pulled the old-fashioned bell chain and heard a distant clangour. He was just going to pull it again when the door opened. A Pakistani girl in dark jeans and a thick, high-necked sweater stood there wiping a running nose and looking disconsolate.

"Can I see Mrs Gracey? I am Inspector Corby from London. She is expecting me; I telephoned for an appointment."

"Oh, yes. Please come in."

The hall felt dank; the heavy handsome Victorian furniture looked as though it belonged to the time when this had been the Old Hall and not the Orphanage. Above the fireplace, whose wide grate was stuffed with logs and with crushed handfuls of red paper, there was another photograph of Albert Mansbridge, this time in middle life and in mayoral robes, with an elaborate gold chain of office.

The Pakistani girl sneezed mournfully once or twice into a paper handkerchief, and said,

"This way, please. Mrs Gracey is in her room."

Mrs Gracey's room was pleasant, with pale grey walls and a big sofa and armchairs covered with tweed linen in a bright rose red. There was a good fire burning in the grate. Two small boys were squatting on the hearth rug in front of it watching television. Mrs Gracey, who got up from her desk to meet the Inspector, was comely and fresh-faced, wearing a pretty sugar-bag blue woollen dress.

"Come in, Inspector Corby. Do sit down. Bill, Cuddy, you'll have to run away to the play-room now."

As she switched off the T.V. set she explained,

"They've both been in the sick bay with mild 'flu. This is their first day up, so I let them sit by my fire—it's warmer in here than the play-room. It's rather early for tea, isn't it? Would you like some coffee?"

"No, thank you. I've just had some."

"You're staying at the Mansbridge, I think Mrs Seldon said? She rang me up after lunch."

"I'm only here for the day. Mrs Seldon kindly came in to see me this morning."

"Yes, she told me. I am so glad you were able to set her mind at rest about Anthony. It's a terrible thing. It's been such a shock for them all. I thought Mrs Seldon looked very ill when I saw her yesterday. Well, Mr Corby, what can I do for you? Would you like to see over the Orphanage?"

"I would rather you told me about it first. Miss Mansbridge was very much interested in it, wasn't she?"

"Yes, indeed she was. You know that her father, Albert Mansbridge, was left an orphan at the age of seven? He went to live with an uncle and aunt who had six children of their own and didn't really want him, or anyhow he thought they didn't; he felt left out. It was something he never forgot, so when he made his will, as neither of his daughters wanted this house, he left it for a home for forty orphan boys who were to be taken in here at the age of seven. I'm glad to say his executors haven't insisted on this too strictly: if there's a child of six or eight in real need they've let him come in, but on the whole we have them from seven till they leave school and go to work."

"Forty of them must be quite a packet to look after. Do you enjoy the work?"

"Yes, very much. I like boys, I have one little girl of ten myself... my husband died four years ago. Polly lives here with me and very much enjoys having forty brothers to play with. Yes, she and I both like being here. It's cold in winter but it's healthy, the moors are beautiful and the people are very kind and friendly." She smiled. "They know you can't help being an 'incomer'."

Not a woman, Corby thought, to make grievances where there were none. But when she was not smiling there were two sharp, vertical lines of worry between her eyebrows. She said now,

"Of course there are difficulties."

"Staff, I expect?"

"Yes, that always. The local girls don't dream of going into service, they work in the mills and factories. Other girls don't want to come to Hithamroyd: there's nothing for them to do here in the evenings and in winter the last bus from Medford leaves at ten. We have mostly foreign girls and they don't stay with us. For one thing we can't pay them enough. We're very hard up."

"I suppose Albert Mansbridge endowed the Orphanage?"

"Yes, he made a trust fund. He endowed it handsomely for those days, but of course he couldn't foresee, nobody could, how the value of money would go down and the cost of living go up. My monthly cheque from Mr Holdsworth doesn't cover running expenses; it's impossible to renew anything or to keep the place in repair. The blankets are threadbare; the boys are short of clothes; the central heating is old-fashioned and some of the pipes are worn out, anyhow we can't afford enough coke to keep it running all day; the whole thing needs replacing by a modern plant. Then the roof wants repairing in several places: and all the kitchen equipment is out of date."

"Does Mr Holdsworth know all this?"

"Of course he does. I keep him informed of everything and from time to time he sends me an extra cheque from Miss Mansbridge. Only…"

She stopped as if she had been going to say more and had changed her mind.

Corby prompted, "Only what?"

Mrs Gracey still hesitated.

"I am entitled to ask you to speak freely, Mrs Gracey."

"Yes I know, but I don't know how far I ought to discuss my employer's concerns."

"Your employer has been murdered. It's your duty to answer truthfully any question I ask you. I think you are puzzled about something to do with the finances of the Orphanage? What is it?"

"Well then I am. You see I don't know—didn't know—Miss Mansbridge very well myself. I've only been here two years and of course she's been up here a few times, not for very long at a time, but she always seemed so much interested in us, she seemed to care so much about the place. And then I know her reputation round here; everyone says she's very generous, I've heard of people and societies and so on that she's helped in the district. What I can't understand is why, when she knew about it, she sent so little help here and kept this place so short."

"You are sure she did know all about it?"

"She must have done. I sent all the receipts to Mr Holdsworth. I wrote to him last November and sent him the plumber's report on the central heating with his estimate, and the builder's estimate for repairing the roof, and I told him we need an extra blanket for each of the boys' beds and new sweaters for them… but all I got was the money Miss Mansbridge always sent for Christmas so that the boys could have a Christmas tree, and an extra £20 'for running expenses'."

"A disappointment?"

"Yes, it was. But we went on for a few weeks managing as best we could. Then about three weeks ago I had half the boys in bed with 'flu. Of course there was a lot about and it runs through a household of children, but I could *smell* the damp in one of the dormitories where the roof leaks. Then three of my staff gave notice; the central heating failed entirely, and when I got the plumber to it he didn't know if he'd be able to patch it again.

"So I did a thing I wasn't supposed to do. I sat down one evening and wrote an account of the whole thing and sent it direct to Miss Mansbridge. I even sent her the menus for the week. I don't think the boys are getting the meat and fish and fruit they ought to have when they're growing. I've had to fill them out too much with rice and spaghetti and potatoes. I let her know everything, and asked her what was to be done. I had an idea in my mind that they might open a subscription list in the neighbourhood, or get the Council to help with running the place, though of course I didn't suggest that in my letter."

"Did Miss Mansbridge answer you?"

"Yes, by return. She thanked me for my letter and said that I should be hearing from her again. Then last week she suddenly turned up here at 9.30 in the morning.

"She was very nice. I said I'd been sorry to bother her but she said 'You did quite right', and she asked to see everything.

"I showed her the lot, the blankets that are so thin you can't darn them any more, and the holes in the roof and the faulty pipes, and the menus I'd drawn up for the week. She said at once, 'Do they only have roast meat on Sunday? That's not enough for growing boys.' I said I could hardly manage the butcher's bill anyhow."

"Did Miss Mansbridge seem surprised to find that you were so short?"

"She seemed very much upset by the whole thing. I half wished I hadn't started it all when I saw how it distressed her, but I had to put my duty to the children first.

"While we were waiting for the car to take her to the station I brought her into my room and made her drink some hot coffee. She seemed to me as if she had had a shock. I said how sorry I was to bring her up here in such bad weather, but she said again, 'You did quite right, Mrs Gracey. I blame myself...' Then she didn't say any more about that. 'I want to think this over,' she said, 'but you'll be hearing from me. I can assure you there will be a difference, a real difference.'

"And now of course I don't know what will happen. I must just carry on here as we are for the moment."

"Yes," Corby said absently, "that's all you can do."

"Perhaps you'd like to see round the place?"

"I'm afraid I haven't time, Mrs Gracey. Did you know your predecessor, the matron they sacked?"

"Miss Hawkhurst? No, Inspector, she had left before I arrived. Mr Holdsworth sent away the under-matron, too; she was young and going to be married a few months after that anyhow, and he said that Miss Hawkhurst would have got her into bad ways, and it would be better for me to start clear and choose an assistant of my own."

At that moment there was a noise outside the door as if a herd of bullocks had stampeded into the house.

"That's the boys home from school," Mrs Gracey observed placidly.

"I won't keep you any longer."

"I do hope I've been some help to you," Mrs Gracey said, looking as if she would have liked to know how and why.

"You have, you have indeed." Corby said good-bye to her, shouldered his way out through a rabble of boys who, however cold and undernourished, appeared to be in tearing spirits. He walked out of the house into the frosty late afternoon.

CHAPTER XXIV

D USK WAS FALLING AS CORBY TURNED OUT OF THE GATES OF the Orphanage and walked down the steep road into the town. The mill chimneys in the valley below, the yellow-grey stone buildings, the cold heights, were gradually veiled: lights sprang out everywhere in shops and offices and factories, clusters of lights in the valley, long single lines where the roads went up over the moors.

In the steep main street of Hithamroyd boys and girls just released from school were crowding into the sweet shops; the younger and more casual housewives were going in and out of self-service stores for things that they had forgotten earlier in the day. When the Inspector passed the uncurtained window of a living-room the unknown interior looked so warm and inviting that he was pricked with nostalgia for Lucy and a quiet evening at home. But this had been a good day, a very good day. He had been right in thinking that he should find a key in Hithamroyd.

Down at the bottom of the hill, beyond the stores and the super-markets, there was less light and bustle; the air was even colder with the chill of nearby water. Lights streaked the dark surface of the canal, until it was blocked from view by the complex of the Albert Mansbridge buildings. Corby skirted the wall, and came to the big main gates. As he crossed the yard, where the trodden slush was freezing again, he stopped to look in at the doorway of one of the sheds. It was full of light and noise, a crane moving overhead, wheels turning, the beat of metal on metal, the rush of water; men in blue boiler suits, the younger ones with their long hair confined in the compulsory nets, were guiding, turning, stopping, starting the complicated machines. Corby thought that for what was supposed to be a running-down business it all looked remarkably active, but of course that was an outside view. He passed the shed and went in at the doorway of the offices, an imposing cluster of red-brick buildings with an ornate portico over the front door.

The girl in Inquiries had evidently been told to expect him. She looked at the detective from London with open curiosity and took him to a room at the end of a long passage. John Armistead rose to meet the Inspector from behind a well-polished mahogany table. On the wall above his desk was another copy of the photograph of Albert Mansbridge standing in the doorway of the engineering shed. On the opposite wall a photograph of some kind of office celebration at the Old Hall presented Albert Mansbridge in the centre of his employees, an old man sitting in a wheeled chair with a tall, middle-aged woman standing protectively behind him—Alberta in the days when she kept her father in the saddle.

"Sit down, Inspector," Armistead said. "Would you like a cup of tea? The canteen's closed now but we have a pantry in the office and I told the girl to have the kettle boiling."

"No, thank you, I shall soon be eating on the train."

There was a pause while Armistead lowered his bulk into the chair. He put his broad hands one on each arm and looked across at the Inspector.

"Well? Have you found out anything yet, then?"

Was there any personal anxiety behind the question? Here on his own ground, in a suit of good grey worsted instead of the dark London clothes, Armistead looked younger, a man who might well have several more years of hard work in him before he need think of retiring.

"I've learnt more about Miss Mansbridge's background up here," Corby said. "I haven't had time to fit the pieces together."

"I was glad to hear from Evie Seldon when she rang me up this afternoon that young Anthony was cleared. Not that I ever thought he could seriously be suspected."

"I told Mrs Seldon that he hasn't been charged with anything." And I suppose, he thought, that she's telling everyone that I said he wouldn't be. I should have brought Newstead.

"Tell me, Mr Armistead, did you want young Seldon in the firm? Were you one of the people who were putting pressure on him to come in?"

"I was not," Armistead said emphatically.

"Did you feel it was unfair to him?"

"Nay, I felt it would be unfair to Albert Mansbridge Ltd. Not that I've anything against the lad. But I didn't want the firm to carry a passenger. I've seen it happen often enough, a firm paying out good money to someone who had no qualifications except being related to the management. There's no sense in that."

"You don't think he might have learnt the business?"

"He might, if he'd wanted to. If I'd seen him take a degree in engineering at a university instead of in English, which he knows how to speak and write well enough anyhow, I might have thought something about it. But he's never wanted to work here and if they'd forced him in, he'd only have wasted his time and ours, and in a few years he'd have got out with nothing to show for it except that he'd have been older for training for anything else. A young man's got to be in at the start nowadays if he's to get anywhere."

"Did you say this to Miss Mansbridge?"

"I did more than once, but it made no difference. It was the name, you see. He was to stop calling himself Anthony, he was to be Albert when he came in here, and I think she had some idea he was to drop Seldon too. Another Albert Mansbridge, that was what she cared about, and it was as difficult to argue with her on this as it was about the take-over."

Corby leaned forward.

"Mr Armistead, why did you not tell me that you had another reason for wanting the take-over… a strong personal reason?"

If Armistead was disconcerted he did not show it.

"I see," he said; "Evie Seldon's been talking."

"She did not know that you had told me nothing at all about your wife's health, and your wish to take her to live in a warmer climate."

An angry red flush went up Armistead's face to the short tufts of grey hair.

"And you think I'd planned to sell Albert Mansbridge to get my wife away?"

"I am bound to think that it may have influenced you, all the more so because you kept quiet about it."

"I kept quiet about it, as you call it, because it had nothing to do with what I was after. I never have and never should let my private affairs influence any decision I took about the firm, and that's the truth, believe it or not, Inspector. I reckon in your job you have to deal with so many crooks and twisters that you forget there are still some honest men left in the world."

"What would you have done about your wife if Miss Mansbridge was still alive and still refusing to consider the take-over?"

"I told Alberta last Saturday, the last time I saw her alive, what I was going to do. I was going to resign. I've got a good man that's been working as my deputy for ten years: the firm wouldn't suffer because I left it a year or two before I meant to retire."

"But wouldn't you personally have left on less advantageous terms? Wouldn't Morchard Williamson either have retained you as managing director of this place to the end of your time or given you a handsome compensation if they put somebody in your place?"

The angry red colour spread again up Armistead's neck and ears.

"I don't know what they'd have done. I hadn't gone into my own position with them. But if you think…" He paused, ran a hand over his face and resumed more calmly.

"I've never been feckless, Inspector. I've been paid a good salary, and I've saved and invested all my life. Even when the children were young and I was earning less I always put by a bit. We've a good pension scheme in this firm that covers everybody in the office and the Works. I could have drawn mine three years ago when I was sixty, but I waited till I was ready to retire. I'll be frank with you, I daresay I might be better off if the take-over bid went through—as it will do now—but I've enough to keep my wife and myself in reasonable comfort. All my children are out in the world and don't need help; in fact my eldest son could help me if I asked him, but I shan't need to. So if you're thinking that I was going to hand over the firm to make a bit more for myself you're wrong."

He looked hard at Corby and added,

"And if you're telling yourself a cock-and-bull story that I murdered Alberta Mansbridge because she was standing in the way of the take-over, you'd better forget it."

He added more calmly,

"I've read a lot of these things that people write nowadays and call it psychology or something like that, about how there's a murderer in every one of us. They may be right. I daresay there wouldn't be wars without they were right. But if there is a murderer in each of us, Inspector, in nine hundred and ninety nine cases out of a thousand he doesn't come out. Not even nowadays."

"Of course that's true."

"In my opinion you'll find that Alberta was killed by some half-crazy person that she'd been trying to help without anybody knowing. She was a great one for keeping things to herself. She did most of her charities through Holdsworth, but I shouldn't be surprised if there were one or two that he knew nothing about: people he thought it would be no use helping or she guessed he would think that."

Corby said, "I've been to the Orphanage this afternoon and had a talk with Mrs Gracey."

"Ah, it's badly run-down that place. There's not enough money in the trust to keep it going nowadays. What they want to do is to get the Council to come in on it. They'd keep the name, they'd have to do that of course because they'd be using the trust fund, but they'd supplement and run it on the same lines, only they'd get the place done up, and pay proper salaries. I said to Holdsworth about a year ago that that was what would have to be done and he agreed with me, but he said Miss Mansbridge wouldn't hear of such a thing. It'll happen now most likely."

"Miss Mansbridge seems to have been an obstacle to progress all round."

"We all get to be as we get older. Alberta Mansbridge was slow to come round to anything new, but she did come round in time. She'd more or less accepted that Anthony wasn't coming into the firm, and she'd have come to see about the Orphanage one day. Getting through her prejudices was like getting through a thorned break, but she had a good heart and a real wish for other people's good and that generally came out on top in the end."

"You'll be up in London, I suppose, Mr Armistead, for the funeral?"

"Yes, I'm coming up on Thursday with Herbert Clough, and we'll be seeing Holdsworth on Friday. Those two are the executors, and there are one or two things they want to talk over with me."

"When you were talking to Miss Mansbridge last Saturday, did she say anything about changing her will?"

"Not a word."

"Did she seem worried about anything?"

"I thought she was looking ill, but then she was so put out by my going against her over the Morchard Williamson offer. I had the impression that she knew at the bottom of her mind that she would be driven to accept it in the end. I'd shown her all the accounts; she could read a balance sheet as well as I could."

"Could be," Corby said absently. "Well thank you very much for speaking to me so frankly. If I want to get hold of you in London, where will you be?"

"At the same hotel where you sent to ask about my alibi," Armistead said grimly. "I've got my car and my man here, Inspector. Can I drop you at the station?"

"Thank you, I've got a police car coming. It will be here in five minutes."

"Oh, by the way, there's two personal letters that came this morning for Miss Mansbridge, addressed to her c/o the firm. Shall I send them on to the executors, or do you want them?"

"I'd better have a look at them."

Armistead swung his chair round, took two letters out of his desk and passed them over.

Corby slit open the first. The Hithamroyd Antiquarian Society begged to remind Miss Mansbridge that her subscription was now due, and ventured to ask whether in view of the rising costs of running the society she could see her way to increase it. Corby handed the letter back.

"I don't want this one."

"I'll send it to Herbert Clough, then."

The other letter was in an airmail envelope with an Australian stamp.

The intercom on Armistead's desk buzzed. He answered it and said to Corby,

"Your car's here, Inspector."

There was no answer. Corby was intent on the letter. It was written on a sheet of thin paper jaggedly torn off from a cheap block. The handwriting straggled across the page, the lines sometimes far apart and sometimes nearly running into one another.

"Your car, Inspector. And with the roads in the state they're in and all the traffic there is on the Medford Road at this time of day you'd best be off."

Corby still did not answer. His whole attention was focused on the letter. The address at the top of the page was a number in a street in Sydney. The signature at the bottom, written more clearly than the rest of the letter, was Brenda Musgrave.

PART IV

THE MAN IN THE DARK OVERCOAT

CHAPTER XXV

CORBY LET HIMSELF IN TO HIS OWN HOME AT A QUARTER TO eight the next morning to the smell of coffee and bacon and the shrill voices and scampering footsteps of three children getting ready at the last possible minute for breakfast and school. They plunged at him in vociferous welcome shouting various items of news, then were swept off to finish dressing by Lucy, looking warm and pretty in her padded crimson housecoat.

"Did you have a good day up there?"

"Excellent."

If he told her any more about the case than she could read in the papers, it would be at the end. At present, in spite of an affectionate greeting, she knew that he was not with her, his mind was wholly occupied with the case. She said,

"The bath water's hot. I didn't let the brats take it all. There was a letter from your mother for us both yesterday but nothing urgent. Kidney and bacon for you and I'm just grinding some fresh coffee."

The C.I.D. room at Blent Street was another home. Corby liked being out on the trail, but always came back with pleasure to the long room with its light-coloured wooden desks, its typewriters that were constantly being carried across from one desk to another; and its three telephones on the end table, where as usual one or two people were waiting impatiently to use the one in the sound-muffling hood. The Inspector walked past the file cases and the notice boards with their list of Divisional Fingerprint Officers and their hours of duty; the

identikit pictures of wanted men looking stiff and improbable; the
list of official interpreters. Corby nodded to those of his colleagues
who were at their desks or leafing through the files and beckoned to
Newstead to follow him into his own small room shut off at the end.

"First of all," he said, "read that."

He flipped the airmail envelope across the table to Newstead, and
watched him carefully extract the two sheets of thin paper covered
with irregular lines of handwriting.

Corby went over to the window and stood looking out with his
hands clasped together behind him. Down here the snow had melted
away except for a dirty crust here and there in a corner. It was a grey,
lightless day, the streets greasy. Half the people passing below the
window wore mackintoshes; most of them looked depressed. They
had the look of dogged endurance that belongs to the latter end of
an English winter.

Corby swung round and saw Newstead, with no change of expression, folding the letter.

"Well? A surprise packet, eh?"

"It looks as though the doctor was our man."

"I don't know; it certainly provides him with a strong motive.
We must see him. Ring up his house and find out where we can get
hold of him today."

While Newstead was making the call, Corby took Brenda
Musgrave's letter out of its envelope, spread it out on the table, and
read it again. The address was 41 Taverner Street, Sydney:

Dear Alberta,

I don't know where you live now, perhaps not in the Old Hall,
but if I send this letter to the office I expect it will reach you. I expect
it will give you a shock, because you probably thought I was dead,
nobody would tell you anything different.

You were always a good friend to me, and I think you will help me now. I saw in an old English newspaper that somebody left in the café where I work, that Ewan has a son born and has a wife called Elaine, only of course she is not his wife, and the child is a bastard.

I am working as a waitress in a café here, it is very hard work, my feet are so swollen at night that I can hardly walk home. It isn't right that I should be working like this when I have a husband who should be taking care of me. I have written to him twice since I saw his address and the last time I said I should write to you if he did not answer, and you would make him write to me.

He ought to have stayed here in this country till he found me. Some people picked me up in the Bush for dead. I was ill for a long time and I didn't remember my name. When I did remember it I didn't tell anyone because I didn't want them to send me back to the hospital.

I am better now and I have done some work in different places but I am not fit for this hard work, it will kill me in the end.

I think Ewan must have got both my letters. He should be ashamed of himself not to answer when I am his real wife and this woman is his mistress and the baby is a bastard. I told him if he didn't answer I should write to you and you would tell him what his duty is, to send this woman and her child away, and take care of me. Please help me, there is nobody else alive who could help me, but you were always my friend. I think you will MAKE HIM COME.

WITH LOVE FROM

BRENDA MUSGRAVE

Poor woman, Corby thought, probably a great pity that they found her in the Bush.

Newstead came back.

"Dr Musgrave has consultations at the hospital all the morning. He's expected home for lunch at about 1.15, then he's seeing patients at his place in Harley Street all the afternoon."

"He'll have to see us in his lunch hour. Is that his secretary you've been speaking to?"

"No, his wife."

"Ring her back and tell her we'll come and see him at 1.45. Tell her we want to ask him for a little more information."

"I suppose he must have got the two letters from the first wife?"

"I should think so and that's why he was looking hag-ridden. Evidently he's been keeping it to himself and not telling the present wife. Perhaps he's been trying to make up his mind what to do. He may have hoped that if he didn't answer the first letter Brenda would give up. When he heard that she was going to write to Miss Mansbridge he must have felt driven into a corner.

"He wouldn't be sure what Alberta would do. She seems to have been very fond of him and his present wife and the child, but by what I heard yesterday up at Hithamroyd she had always been very concerned about the first wife and protective towards her. I think she would have felt that he had a duty towards her too, and she'd have tried to make him do it. She might even have been capable of reporting him to the police if he didn't. She seems to have had an uncompromising side to her."

"So that his way out could be to kill her before she got the letter?"

"Could be. We've certainly got to look into it. I wonder whether he had Brenda legally 'presumed dead' before he left Australia or whether he just took it for granted?"

"Without that he might land up inside?"

"I don't know. I'm not sure about the bigamy laws. It hasn't come my way before. He can probably get a divorce under this new Act and remarry the second wife."

But even so, Corby thought, when this came out it would tarnish the second marriage, which by all accounts had so far been one of idyllic happiness. Who could tell what the second wife's reaction would be: sympathy for her husband in his predicament? Compassion for her forlorn predecessor? Anger because, even if not deliberately, she had been deceived? Certainly she would not like discovering that her son was illegitimate. Even in the much talked-of permissive society, there were still plenty of people in all stations of life who would mind that very much.

"We'd better get the Sydney police to find out what they can about Brenda Musgrave, and let us know at once. Will you get somebody on to that."

When Newstead came back Corby said,

"That's not the only thing; it may not even be the most important thing that turned up at Hithamroyd. It looks as if Russell Holdsworth has been fiddling the accounts of the Orphanage, and I think that Alberta had just tumbled to it.

"The old man's endowment isn't enough for these days. The last matron had trouble because the money wouldn't go round. Holdsworth sacked her. This matron can't make the money go round either. She has appealed to Holdsworth several times and he hasn't sent her any substantial increase. But Mrs Seldon thinks that her sister provided a lot of extra money. We must have a look at her bank account, and at the bank account of the Orphanage."

"Didn't Miss Mansbridge look into it at all?"

"Yes she did, lately, when Mrs Gracey, the matron, wrote direct to her. Alberta went down and saw the whole thing for herself, the state the place was in and the shortages. Mrs Gracey said she seemed very much upset. We'll go round and see those accounts this morning.

"If Alberta discovered somebody cheating the Albert Mansbridge Memorial Fund, she would have been ruthless. She may have been slow at finding out but once she did understand I'm pretty sure he couldn't have talked her round."

Newstead, his fair skin flushing, said with an effort,

"You guessed right, sir, about Hithamroyd."

"It was a lucky shot. One other thing: Armistead had a strong personal motive for wanting the take-over. He wants to retire now because of his wife's health, and if this deal went through he would retire on much more advantageous terms. He says he didn't mention this to us because personal considerations would never weigh with him in any decisions he took for Albert Mansbridge Ltd. I think that is probably true."

"He ought to have told you all the same."

"Yes, of course he ought, but people have a way of partitioning things off in their minds if they don't want to talk about them."

"It means that he had a stronger motive than we knew for wanting the old lady out of the way."

"Yes. We can't rule him out. What's your news?"

"Nothing to help from the forensic people. They think it must have been done with a stocking, or a strip of strong material. Two pairs of stockings found in the dustbins of the neighbourhood, one pair discarded because they were stained with something that wouldn't come out; one pair because they were laddered by the owner's cat. Several strips of strong material, but all accounted for: nothing on her clothes or her skin, and they've been over the room and drawn a blank.

"I saw Mrs Bramley again yesterday. I spent a long time with her asking her about everybody who came to the house and whether she could remember Miss Mansbridge talking about anybody she'd known before who might have turned up again in her life. I got a list of all the people who came or telephoned but they're not a promising lot. The vicar, his wife, the deaconess who works in the parish, the matron of the nursing home where Miss Mansbridge had an operation, an old cousin living in Brighton and coming up occasionally—that sort of thing. I've got all the names and addresses. Did you get anything more on young Seldon at Hithamroyd, sir?"

"Only that his mother said he couldn't possibly have done a murder, which is hardly evidence. Under the will he now comes into some shares in the firm, and his mother will have a larger income; but he will have no claim on it in her lifetime unless she chooses to give him some. Which by her way of talking about him I should think she would."

"So we've got to keep him in mind. Mrs Bramley told me one little thing that might be a pointer. She said that on Sunday morning when Miss Mansbridge came in from church she asked her if any of the tea party had rung up. When Mrs Bramley said they hadn't, Miss Mansbridge gave a great sigh and said, 'They're all coming then'. She said—Newstead consulted his notes—'I'm not a good judge of people, Mrs Bramley. I used to think I was but I'm not, or else it's this world we live in nowadays. It's too much for all but the strongest; only the very best can stand against its temptations.'

"Mrs Bramley thought she had Barry Slater in mind, but she didn't pay any particular attention—only when she was talking to me it came back to her."

"Is there any news of Slater?"

"No report so far. We've got a call out for him to all stations."

"And Signor Bartolozzi-Fospo?"

"The same. As he hadn't been in with his passport, I went round to his lodging yesterday afternoon and had a talk with his landlady. They're a Greek family with a shop and a cheap restaurant in Soho. She was careful to tell me it was very respectable, shuts at 10.30 every evening she says. They liked Fospo, said he was very pleasant and well-behaved. They had a bit of difficulty getting his rent sometimes, but that was before he was taken up by the rich old lady in the West End. He told them that she was going to adopt him and make him her heir. They didn't know whether this was true but he never seemed so short of money after he met her and she did come once in a car and bring a big oil stove and have it taken up into his room. He'd always told them he might be going to live with the old lady. They didn't know her name and hadn't connected her with the account of the murder in the papers, in fact they don't bother with papers much, only look at television when they have time.

"They said that 'Mr Bartolotsky' left yesterday afternoon. He'd paid up the rent for the week before. They found he'd taken all his belongings except a lot of drawings and printed things, which were thrown away in the corner of his room. They thought he'd gone to live with his old lady. They've never looked at his passport, they had no idea that his name might not be the one he gave; they don't know his address in Italy. They said 'ask at the Italian Club'. I did, but no-one there knew very much about him either, though they had an impression that he had gone up in the world lately. He had more money in his pocket and a lot of new clothes.

"Then I went after Slater's alibi. The woman at the café vaguely remembered two young men sitting there for a bit on Sunday afternoon, and she thought that one of them might have had a leather coat on. She didn't know the name of either of them, or said she didn't. I pressed her because I'd got an idea she did, but I didn't get any more from her. I found the friend's uncle, who said Fred hadn't been there lately and he didn't know where he was."

"So those two have vanished, and London's a large place to hide in; but I daresay some Station will turn them up sooner or later. Before we go round to the bank let's get an appointment with Holdsworth for this afternoon, after we've visited the doctor. Have him put through here. I'd like to speak to him."

But the call to Holdsworth's office only produced a polite secretary.

"I'm sorry that Mr Holdsworth is not in the office today. He has taken a day off to drive Mrs Holdsworth and their daughter down to Mrs Holdsworth's mother's in the country for a week's holiday. Mr Holdsworth will be here tomorrow. Can I make an appointment for you or give him a message?"

"Not at the moment, thank you."

"There seems to be a high rate of disappearance among the invited guests at this tea party. She says Holdsworth's only gone off for the day. I wonder. Get Daly to go out to Putney and find his garage and get the number of his car. We won't use it at the moment but I'd like to have it. And we'd better, I suppose, alert the passport offices at the ports and airports. Though I incline to think he will come back—except that he knew I was going to Hithamroyd. Yes, alert them, just to be on the safe side. We'll probably go out and call on him at his house tonight."

CHAPTER XXVI

Alberta's bank was the York, Lancaster and London; her branch was in the City, in Threadneedle Street. Small, with a good many branches in the North of England and only one or two in London, the Y. L. & L. had so far resisted any merger. Its premises in Threadneedle Street, though not large, wore an unmistakeable air of grandeur. The atmosphere inside was solemn, the two cashiers behind the counter seemed to be on the point of retirement, and a couple of long-haired girls in bright jerseys working at the back looked as though they might have got in there by mistake.

The manager received Corby and Newstead with courtesy and underlying distaste.

"Yes," he said, "we have had Miss Alberta Mansbridge's account here since she came to live in London. Before that she banked with our branch in Medford."

"What about the Albert Mansbridge Orphanage? Do they bank in Medford too?"

"No, Miss Mansbridge had their account transferred to this branch some years ago at the time when Mr Russell Holdsworth became the treasurer of the trust fund.

"Miss Mansbridge often came here, she liked the City. I simply cannot understand how this dreadful thing can have happened to one of our most valued clients."

"Since that's what we are trying to find out, sir, you won't mind if we examine Miss Mansbridge's account and the account of the Orphanage?"

"You must do whatever you think necessary," the manager said regretfully. "I will place a room at your disposal."

The room was very small with extremely high walls so that Corby and Newstead felt as though they were sitting at the bottom of a well. The manager had the two ledgers brought in and went away and left them to it.

"I'll take hers," Corby said. "You take the Orphanage. What we want to find are any cheques drawn by Alberta to the Orphanage during the last two or three years, and any entries in the Orphanage accounts corresponding to them. Let's work backwards."

They were both silent for a few minutes, their heads bent over the ledgers. Then Corby said, "Ah, here we are. On December 10th 1971 Alberta paid a cheque for £250 to the Orphanage Fund. See if you can find an entry in their account."

"Yes, here it is, paid in on December 12th, £250."

"Is it, now? Mrs Gracey said that all the extra she got for Christmas was £20 besides the usual money for the children's Christmas treat."

"That's right. There's a cheque here for £40 paid on December 14th to Mrs Gracey."

"So what's happened to the rest?"

"There's a cheque here for £210, which would be the balance, paid out to Shadburn's Supplies and Services."

"Oh, is there? Well let's go further back. I've got a cheque for £150 which Alberta paid out on September 1st last year to the Orphanage fund. Have you got a corresponding cheque paid to Mrs Gracey?"

"No. There's a cheque for £30 paid to her on September 4th and a cheque to Shadburn's Supplies and Services for £120. I suppose Holdsworth bought supplies in bulk for the Orphanage?"

"Then if so why are they so desperately short of supplies and services? The blankets are threadbare, the boys' clothes are worn out. Let's go on."

Newstead turned a page.

"Shadburn's Supplies and Services comes in again in April last year. A cheque for £250 was paid into the Orphanage account."

"Yes, I've got it."

"Twenty went to Mrs Gracey, the rest to Supplies and Services."

"Mrs Gracey has been there for two years. The Orphanage was short of money before that, and the last matron was sacked for mismanagement with a hint of embezzlement covered up out of kindness because she was supposed to be affected by the menopause. But let's go on. I'm keeping a list."

The ledgers showed eight payments during the last two years made by Alberta Mansbridge to the Orphanage fund; eight small payments at corresponding times made to Mrs Gracey; on each occasion a much larger payment to Shadburn's Supplies and Services. In the year before that the name of Hawkhurst appeared instead of Gracey and two cheques had been drawn by Alberta Mansbridge, of which again the much larger proportion had been paid out to Supplies and Services. Corby totted up his figures and dashed a line under them.

"So, during the last three years, Miss Mansbridge contributed £4,000 of her own money to the Orphanage. The two matrons received, apart from their salary cheques, £450 in small payments. All the rest went into the account of this Shadburn's Supplies and Services. Newstead, ask if we can borrow the S-Z telephone book. And if it would not be taking too great a liberty in this establishment, ask if we can use the telephone. Ring up Blent Street and tell them to see if Shadburn's S.S. is on the Industrial Register. My own guess is that Shadburn's S.S. is Holdsworth's pseudonym."

"If so he's taking a great risk for a few thousand pounds."

"Think what a lot of secrets have been betrayed for chicken feed. Besides, as we said, this isn't the only Trust that Holdsworth handles. He may be playing the same game all round. Let me have the telephone book while you ring up the Station."

Corby ran his eyes down the names beginning with S.

Of course it may not be in the London area, he said to himself, but somehow I think it will be, if it's anywhere. More questions asked about anybody setting up a business outside. Ah…

His pencil stopped at a number. With growing excitement he read the name and address: "Shadburn's Supplies and Services, 18 Shovel Road, N.W.3."

Newstead came in again.

"They'll ring us back in a few minutes."

Corby pushed the telephone book across to him.

"Here they are."

"I know where Shovel Road is, it's near Primrose Hill."

Newstead was summoned to the telephone. Corby, too much excited to sit still, jumped up and began to walk backwards and forwards across the small floor space.

Newstead returned.

"Yes, Shadburn's Supplies and Services is on the Industrial Register, a private company."

"It will be less private this afternoon. We'll go and visit it as soon as we've seen the doctor."

"Shall I get an appointment, sir?"

"No. I think we'll take them by surprise. And now let's relieve the manager of our undesirable company and go and get an early lunch in a pub before our appointment with Dr Musgrave."

CHAPTER XXVII

Myra Heseltine could not have said exactly how she spent the first twenty-four hours after the detectives had left her flat.

She telephoned to Gamlins that she was ill and asked them to postpone till later in the week an appointment with the manager of an enterprising young firm near Oban who was bringing a selection of tweeds and knitted clothes to show her. That telephone call was her last link for the time being with her ordinary life.

Part of the time she lay face downwards on her bed either crying or half stupefied; part of the time she walked up and down the room with a glass of whisky in her hand. The pile of stubs on the ashtray grew and spilled over; her mouth was dry and her throat sore from chain smoking.

Vivid memories of her life with Alberta kept on coming back to her with the intensified value of something lost. There had been irritations, plenty of them, before the quarrel that separated them, but there had been a home; warmth and kindness in a world running short of them; someone to come back from work to, someone who wanted to hear what she had been doing; and there had always been the sense that her future would be looked after.

She began to realize that she had never expected the quarrel to be permanent; half her possessions were still in suitcases and boxes. She had never bothered to redecorate this flat which she hated, yes, *hated*. Its small rooms, the feeling of so many other people living all round her, of being such a long way from the ground, stimulated the claustrophobia that had always been one of her secret troubles.

During the long sleepless night she was assailed by terrors from beyond the border of reason. The detectives knew now that she could have had a motive for murdering Alberta. If this man Corby could not find out who had killed Alberta, he might fasten on her. She was sure she had read somewhere that they had to get a conviction for the sake of their own reputation in the police force; she had been seen in the Square at the time of the murder, approaching the house. She would not be able to prove herself innocent; she would be shut up in prison, locked into a small cell, she would go mad with claustrophobia, she would scream, and scream, and scream...

But she was a brave woman: late on the Tuesday evening she began to crawl out of the abyss. She had a bath, surprised to find herself so weak that it was an effort to climb out of it. She boiled an egg and made some coffee. She even glanced at the patterns of tweed that the young man from Scotland had sent in advance. She made her bed, filled two hot-water-bottles, one for her feet and one for her back, took two of her sleeping pills and sank into the heavy sleep of exhaustion.

She got up in the morning fully determined to have no more of "this nonsense". She dressed and made up carefully, and put what she would want for the day's work into her briefcase.

She was ready before it was time to start. She longed to talk to somebody who knew all about Alberta and the fatal tea party. The person she would really like to talk to was Mrs Bramley, who had been so much part of the shared life; she had so often talked to Mrs Bramley about this and that, but not, of course, lately; not since the quarrel. Mrs Bramley would know everything about the quarrel, she would have sided entirely with Alberta, she had always preferred her. She might even suspect Myra—no, not Mrs Bramley. Dr Musgrave was not Myra's doctor and would be far too busy for idle conversation; Russell Holdsworth would be going to work, and was anyhow too dry and self-contained a character to understand anybody wanting to talk just to relieve a tension.

Anthony, now; surely it would be quite natural for her to ring up her dead friend's nephew in this crisis and take him out to lunch? His boutique was not far from Gamlins. If she made it a quick lunch in the middle of the working day for the two of them she need not ask that girl, Lisa, who was always off-hand with her. Myra dialled the Seldons' number.

Anthony, when the telephone bell rang, was walking about their flat in his pyjamas with a cup of coffee in his hand. He went reluctantly to the telephone because he thought it would be his mother ringing up again. She had telephoned three times the night before, once to tell him all about her conversation with the detective; once to ask him to order a wreath of flowers for her for the funeral; and again to remind him that Aunt Alberta did not like freesias so there mustn't be any.

He was surprised that it was Myra asking him to lunch, and showed his surprise. Afraid of not getting him, she hastily changed the venue from Gamlins to a trendy pub which was probably more the sort of thing he would like. He did brighten at the sound of it, and accepted with an approach to grace. He had nothing else to do that day; he was still on holiday from Evelyn's and surprised to find how much he wished he wasn't. Lisa was going to Brighton to model some Regency-style dresses at the Pavilion. Anthony was uneasy because the photographer who was going with the party was a new young man, Claud something, whom Lisa had described as "a dish" and with whom she had already been out to dinner once on her own.

Lisa now drifted into the long room, wearing a short scarlet poncho and her Turkish slippers.

"Is there any coffee left? I've got to get my hair curled and get to the station by 11.30. Who was that who rang up?"

"Myra Heseltine to ask me to lunch today."

"Whatever for?"

"I suppose she wants to see me. People do sometimes."

"She never has before, has she? She must want to find out something, whether Alberta left her any money perhaps."

"If so I should think she would ask Holdsworth to lunch."

"No, because she'd know he wouldn't tell her anything. She thinks you're easy game."

"I can't take your cheap cynicism at this hour of the morning. And I can't think of anything more ridiculous than you will look with your hair in curls wearing muslin dresses outside the Pavilion with the remains of snow on the ground."

"I'm going to be photographed *inside* the Pavilion in the Music Room. Claud thinks he will get some wonderful pictures; he says I have a Regency type of beauty."

"Probably doesn't even know who the Regent was."

"Well it doesn't matter, does it?"

"Oh no. Oh, not at all. Any ignorant fellow can buy an expensive camera and set up as an authority on anything."

"Oh, shut up, Anthony. I'm glad the old bag's asked you to lunch because we shall both get a good lunch and we needn't bother about cooking anything tonight. In fact I don't know when I shall be back."

"Are you dining with Claud again?"

"I daresay I shall, if he asks me. It's no use, Anthony. When there are so many fantastic men in the world I can't spend the rest of my life only going out to dinner with you."

At which he swore, and Lisa ran into the bathroom and slammed the door with such violence that the doorknob, always shaky, came off and rolled across the floor to Anthony's feet.

Half past twelve found him waiting outside the trendy pub with mildly pleasurable anticipation. He was hungry; since Lisa had decided that all they needed for breakfast was a cup of coffee, Anthony was usually ravenous halfway through the morning. He hadn't been to this place before; it looked all right.

Myra was punctual, and as always very smart in a short, light-coloured fur coat and her red boots. She greeted Anthony cordially, said that she had booked a table for a quarter to one, and bought him a double Scotch at the bar. It was not until they were sitting at the table in the restaurant and Myra was pressing smoked salmon on Anthony in spite of its being much more expensive than the other starters, that he suddenly noticed how ill she looked. He felt sorry for her and said, "No thank you, I'd really like potted shrimps, they're my favourite starter." He added, "You do look tired. I expect all this has been very upsetting for you."

He was horribly afraid for a minute that she was going to burst into tears.

But she didn't. She said, "Potted shrimps then. And steak *à la maison*. I wonder why they have to try and put things in French in a solidly English pub, don't you? Yes, it's been very upsetting—but no more for me than for anyone else."

"Oh, I don't know. You lived with her for such a long time."

"And then had that stupid quarrel, which I couldn't regret more. But for that…"

But for that she would probably have been with Alberta waiting for the tea party, and there would have been no murder.

"Quarrels don't matter if people don't die after them."

Anthony imagined how he would feel if Lisa was killed in a railway accident on the way to Brighton. Better, far better, that she should live to go out to dinner with Claud, or any number of fantastic men.

"Your work is to do with clothes, isn't it?" he said. "When you first began on it, did it sort of go to your head?"

"No, it did not. I began when I was eighteen making tea and answering the telephone in the office of a fashion magazine which was run by a totally incompetent couple, husband and wife, who often couldn't pay me at the end of the week and went bankrupt after a year and a half."

"No, I meant were there times after that when you thought about yourself wearing the clothes and looking beautiful in them so that almost everything else bored you?"

"I never did modelling. I was too beaky and too tall. Anthony, after I left No. 31, did Alberta say anything about the quarrel to you?"

"No, I don't think so. I don't remember anything."

"I wondered lately since she asked me to tea again. Did you ever hear her say something about wanting to be friends again; did she perhaps laugh about the whole thing a bit, anything like that?"

"I haven't seen her lately, not since Christmas Eve."

"She might have mentioned me then, perhaps?"

"No, I don't think she did."

Having failed to give any satisfaction to each other about their separate preoccupations, they munched their steaks in silence for a minute or two, until Myra roused herself.

"Have you seen the detectives again or heard anything more about what they're doing?"

"Inspector Corby came round to our flat. Lisa's in the clear; they found her taxi. Yesterday Corby was up at Hithamroyd and seems to have told my mother they didn't suspect me—at least my Mama thought he did. What he actually said, so far as I could make out, was that he hadn't charged me with anything, and she says he told her that he wasn't going to. Sounds a bit unlikely to me, him saying that, but I didn't do it, so I don't really think I shall get run in for it. I think Corby's very clever, I expect he'll find out who did."

"They came to my flat to see me. They didn't charge me, but I'd told them some lies about what time I came into the Square and they'd found out."

Anthony said uncomfortably,

"I expect you didn't remember. I don't see how people can remember exactly what time they did things. I never know."

"It wasn't that I didn't remember—oh well, never mind. But I think I'm still on the list of suspects."

"That's absurd. You were one of Alberta's greatest friends. The quarrel wouldn't have lasted."

"No, I don't suppose it would."

She could not tell him about putting the private eye on Marcello. She felt that he would recoil—that it would offend the often misguided tolerance of wrong-doers that was one of the few principles of his generation. And most certainly she could not even begin to mention to him her secret fears about Alberta's promised legacy.

She said, "It must have been somebody whom Alberta had dealings with without any of us knowing it. She did like to keep things to herself."

"I think she told a lot of them to Holdsworth and got advice from him. I've been wondering if I could ask him for some advice."

"What about?"

"About what to do. I'm sick of the boutique, I don't think Evelyn wants to keep me. And I don't want to have anything more to do with clothes anyhow. Not as a job, I mean. I'm sick of them too. I want something solid."

Indifferently she suggested,

"What about the firm in Yorkshire?"

"Oh no. Lisa would never live up there."

Myra's impression had always been that Lisa would not live anywhere with him for very long. She was too apathetic and too much absorbed in her own feelings to achieve any empathy with him. He was reaching out for it because he wanted somebody to understand how often Lisa humiliated him and how he needed to make something of himself that both he and she could respect—only perhaps they didn't respect the same things.

"If you like," Myra offered unenthusiastically, "I could ask at Gamlins if there's anything there. In the office perhaps or… but you don't want to sell clothes any more. I don't know, perhaps you could sell gramophone records—or carpets. I expect you'd soon learn about them. I don't know that there'd be much future in it."

He did not feel vitally interested in any future there might be.

"It's awfully kind of you to suggest it, Myra. I think I won't do anything until I've had a talk with Holdsworth."

And until I know whether Alberta left me any money, but that I don't like to say.

It did not enter his head that Myra was wondering the same thing on her own account.

"By the way did you know that Holdsworth has a secret life?"

"No, has he? He seems to be trustee of so many things I should have thought he had enough with other people's secrets."

"I didn't mean that kind of thing. Lisa went out one evening with some friends to one of the riverside pubs, and she saw him just going out of the bar with a glamour girl."

"Not Mrs Holdsworth in her best?"

"I don't know. Lisa doesn't know Mrs Holdsworth. She said this one had long dyed golden hair and a red trouser-suit and was all tarted up with fashion jewellery. She was pretty-well stoned."

"No, not Mrs Holdsworth certainly. Well I suppose the most buttoned-up men have an evening out sometimes. Anthony, I must

go, I'm afraid. I've got a tweed man from Scotland coming to see
me with some samples."

"Thank you tremendously for this super lunch."

"It's been a pleasure."

It had not really been anything and she did not know exactly what
she had hoped it would be.

"Bye bye, Anthony, we'll keep in touch," she added perfunctorily;
"love to Lisa."

He answered quickly, "She sent hers, of course."

She hadn't, and wouldn't, she had no time for that sort of nonsense, but Anthony so much wanted everybody to like her that when
she wasn't there to hear it he often filled in the gaps.

"Bye." He held the swing door open for Myra. "Thanks again
so much."

She went off towards Gamlins thankful that there was work to
go back to; and he, forgetting all about her, swung off towards the
other end of the street.

CHAPTER XXVIII

THE DOCTOR'S HOUSE, A COMPACT RED-BRICK VILLA OF GOOD proportions, stood back a little way from Chestnut Tree Avenue, and was sheltered from it by a closely-clipped box hedge. The white paint of window-frame and door was freshly shining; the circle of gravel in front of the house was clear of weeds. The door of the garage at the side was open; a small car stood there in a space which could easily accommodate two cars.

"I should think that's hers. He hasn't come back yet."

Corby rang the bell. The door opened at once and a young woman stood there with a baby a few months old over her shoulder. She was more than pretty, near beautiful, with large grey eyes, a clear forehead, and light hair flowing round a long neck. She did not look in the least disconcerted when Corby told her who they were.

"Oh yes. Do come in. I am sorry my husband is not back yet. He telephoned a few minutes ago and asked me to tell you that he had been unavoidably detained at the hospital, but he should be here any minute now. He has postponed his first two patients at Harley Street until the end of the afternoon so that he will have plenty of time for you. Will you wait in his study?"

She turned and walked ahead of them; the baby studied the strangers with solemn interest over her shoulder.

The study was warm and comfortable with deep blue paper on the walls, shelves of books, some medical; a collection of beautiful white china on top of the shelves and two or three good pictures. Elaine Musgrave offered them coffee which they refused; she opened the cigarette box, and pushed it towards Corby. She said again, "I'm sure he won't be long. I think I hear his car now," and went out. She evidently had no idea that her husband had been touched by suspicion.

The doctor when he came into the study a few minutes later was not unconstrained. He looked fine-drawn, as though since Sunday the flesh had melted off his face leaving the skin stretched more tightly over the bones.

"I'm sorry," he said. "I was called urgently to one of my cases in hospital."

"I am afraid we are preventing you from having lunch."

"It doesn't matter. I don't have much at midday." He sat down in the chair at his desk. "May I ask if you have found out anything more about Miss Mansbridge's murder?"

"I can't answer that question at the moment."

Ewan Musgrave glanced at Newstead, who had taken out his notebook and pencil.

"I am still completely at a loss. I can't think of anything more I could tell you."

"Perhaps you will be able to, Dr Musgrave, if you read this letter."

As his eye fell on the unsteady writing on the thin paper the doctor's start was visible.

"God!" he exclaimed. He went white round his mouth. He jerked a packet of cigarettes out of his pocket with the hand not holding the paper, opened it and spilled the cigarettes on the floor. He ignored them. Corby offered one of his and leaned forward to light it.

"So you know about this!" Musgrave added quickly. "My wife, my present wife, Elaine, knows nothing at all about it."

"Read that, please."

In the silence while the doctor's eye ran quickly down the page, Corby heard the sound of footsteps on the stairs and the young woman's voice softly talking to her baby.

The doctor handed the letter back.

"Did you get those two letters addressed to yourself to which Mrs Brenda Musgrave refers?"

"Yes. We moved in here just before my son was born. As we had not had time to send change-of-address cards round we put the new address in the notice of his birth in *The Times* and *Telegraph*. Brenda wrote to me at this address."

"Had you any idea before you got the letters that she was still alive?"

"None, I assure you."

"Did you take legal action in Australia or here to have her presumed dead?"

"No. It never occurred to me that there was any doubt about it. I think I was half crazy at the time. I was ill; all I wanted was to get away from Australia as soon as possible. Then when I got back here I was so busy it seemed worlds away. I was working very hard, I was lucky, I got a good appointment, I began to build up my private practice and I met Elaine. Oh God!" He sank his head into his hands.

"Did you keep the other two letters from your first wife, Dr Musgrave?"

"Yes. They are in the hidden drawer in that old desk."

"May I see them, please."

The doctor looked at Corby and past him at Newstead with his pencil and notebook. He seemed to be about to say something, but shut his mouth on it. He unlocked the desk behind him, pulled out a drawer in what appeared to be only the carving above one of the pigeonholes, took out several sheets of airmail paper and handed them to Corby.

The doctor said bitterly, "I don't suppose you will believe me when I say how much ashamed I am that I haven't answered them."

The first letter said much the same as Brenda had written to Alberta. She was alive, working as she ought not to be when she had a husband to look after her; he must fetch her home and send away the other woman and her child. The second letter repeated this, but added,

> If you don't answer this letter I shall write to Alberta Mansbridge. She was always kind to me, she understood how much I suffered. She will make you get rid of your mistress and her bastard and look after your own wife.

Corby handed the two letters to Newstead.

"I must ask you to let me keep these, Dr Musgrave. I will give you a receipt for them, and they will be returned to you later. As with everything confidential we shall not use them unless we are obliged to."

"Use them? I suppose you may have to run me in for bigamy?"

"I don't think you fully realize your position, Dr Musgrave."

"I've only just become aware of it. I don't know how the law stands."

"I'm not talking about bigamy. We are investigating a murder. You knew that your first wife was going to write to Miss Mansbridge and ask for her help. Whatever Miss Mansbridge decided to do, your secret would no longer be a secret. Miss Mansbridge was murdered before the letter from Brenda Musgrave could reach her."

"Oh God!"

"You knew Miss Mansbridge's habits very well. You knew that she would be alone in her house for a couple of hours before the other guests arrived for the tea party. You of all the guests have the knowledge of the human body that might make killing easier…"

"And you think that… that I murdered Alberta to keep my secret from her?"

"It's up to you to prove to me that you didn't."

"No, it is up to you to prove that I did."

"Ultimately, yes. I am only asking you at the moment to help us with our inquiries."

"That sinister phrase," the doctor said bitterly. "But as it happens I can prove that I didn't kill Alberta. I showed her the first two letters on Thursday last week."

"Because in the second letter to you, Brenda Musgrave said that she was going to write to Miss Mansbridge?"

"You don't leave me much self-respect, do you? Yes, I suppose so. I also told her because I wanted advice, I wanted to tell her the whole thing. It was an unspeakable relief. People used to think Alberta bossy and interfering. She was, I suppose, but whenever you got to the core of anything with her you realized how kind and wise she was. I'm not a very strong character, and about this I hadn't been honest, not even, I see now, with myself."

He looked at Newstead. "Is all this going down in your damned notebook?"

"Only what is essential," Corby said. "And that will only be used if necessary."

The doctor resumed more steadily.

"Alberta had known the whole story right from the beginning of my first marriage. She was the only person I could talk to about it without having to make all sorts of explanations.

"Alberta said to me at once that I must tell Elaine. I didn't want to. I wanted to keep it from her as long as I could. She has been so happy; especially since the boy was born. She has a special gift for it, it's wonderful to see her. I said to Alberta that I couldn't bear to destroy that, that perhaps she would never be quite as happy again after the shock.

"Alberta said to me, 'My dear, you *must* tell her: sooner or later Brenda will write to *her*.'

"She talked to me about Elaine. She said that she thought in spite of being so devoted to her I was in this underrating her. Elaine was not a child. She would want to share any troubles that I had.

"Alberta told me that I must see my solicitor and if necessary get the name of the best counsel for dealing with these cases. Brenda must divorce me. Of course she must be looked after and provided for. 'I can help with that,' she said. She said, 'You and Elaine will have to be remarried, and the boy legitimized; you can find out all about that.' When I was going she said again, 'Now promise me, tell Elaine at once.'"

"And did you, Dr Musgrave?"

"No, I haven't yet. On Friday I was up to my eyes all day and then there was a medical dinner at night to which I had to go. On Saturday we were going out to dinner with friends. I was working hard all day. I thought when I got home I would ask Elaine to ring up and say I was too tired to go at the end of a thick week, but when I got home she had a new dress on and was looking so pretty... I left it for Sunday. Then on Sunday the baby wasn't well so I went to Alberta's alone... and then I thought when Elaine had just had the shock of hearing that Alberta had been murdered I couldn't give her the other one immediately.

"Of course I must now, and we must face whatever comes. At least I have been able to satisfy you that I could have no motive whatever for murdering Alberta."

"No, Dr Musgrave," Corby said abruptly. "You haven't."

"But I had no reason to be afraid any more of Brenda writing to Alberta. I had told her everything there was to know."

"Have we any proof but your word for it?"

The doctor sat in shocked silence. Newstead's whispering pencil stopped. Corby waited. There was no sound in the room. From the road came the sudden menacing squeal of brakes applied too quickly. Somewhere else in the house the child could be heard crying.

Corby repeated, "Can you prove that you told Miss Mansbridge anything at all about your first wife's letters?"

Swellings had appeared on the doctor's cheekbones so that his fine dark eyes seemed to have sunk in and looked smaller.

"No, I can't. But do you imagine I could have made all that up?"

"It's not a question of what we think but of what can be proved. Did you make an appointment with your solicitor?"

"No, not yet. I had several very full days ahead of me. I was going to ring him up on Monday, and then again Alberta's death put everything else further off."

"Do you think that Miss Mansbridge might have mentioned your predicament to anybody?"

"No. She would respect my confidence."

"She might have said to someone, 'I am so sorry for Dr Musgrave, he's in serious trouble.' Something like that?"

"I doubt it."

"To whom would she be most likely to say it?"

"I should think to Mrs Bramley. It would have been to Myra Heseltine once, but since the quarrel she probably talked most confidentially to Mrs Bramley, or to Holdsworth."

"We can ask them if she gave any indication. You see the importance of finding any proof of your statement that you had told your story to Miss Mansbridge."

"Yes, I do indeed," the doctor said dejectedly. "But there's nothing more I can say, except that I didn't kill Alberta, and it's not the slightest use my saying that. What are you going to do? Are you going to arrest me? If so for God's sake let me ring up my father-in-law and get him to come to Elaine."

"I am not charging you with anything at the moment. You can go on doing your ordinary work. But if you can remember anything that would help to prove that you did tell Miss Mansbridge about your first wife's letters will you please ring up Blent Street Station at once and let us know."

CHAPTER XXIX

"WE'LL DROP IN AT THE FIRST STATION WE PASS AND RING Blent Street, and have the doctor tailed."

"Did you believe all that story, sir?"

"Yes, most of it. It fits in with what I heard about his first marriage at Hithamroyd."

"It doesn't seem likely he'd forget to have her legally presumed dead."

"I think he may, without being aware of it, have doubted whether she was. Perhaps he felt guilty, though God knows he seems to have done his best for her. But of course he must often have wished her dead. And I think he's an idealistic type. So no wonder he had a breakdown and wanted after that to put the whole thing behind him."

"He's been behaving in a very shifty way since he found she was still alive."

"I think he was half-paralysed by the shock. He would have had to do something sooner or later if she hadn't threatened to write to Miss Mansbridge, but that threat put him in a blinding panic."

"And of course it gave him a very strong motive."

They called at a police station and Corby telephoned his instructions.

"Now," he said, "for Shadburn's Supplies and Services."

Shovel Road proved to be a short street of terraced houses which ended at the bottom of Primrose Hill.

The small front garden was well cared for; a boy was playing with a toy car on the square yard of lawn. There were two bells beside the front door, a neat brass plate inscribed with the name Shadburn by the upper one. Corby rang the bell. It was a minute or two before they heard footsteps inside and the door opened.

A woman wearing slacks and a bright blue sweater stood in the doorway. Her shining golden hair covered so much of her face that the first fleeting impression was of a girl, the second that the face half hidden by hair was older and sharper than her poise and manner suggested. She had made up her eyes heavily but had not bothered with the rest; she looked tousled as though she had been having a nap.

"We are looking for Shadburn's Supplies and Services, madam. May we come in?"

"Certainly. I am Mrs Shadburn. Did somebody send you to me?"

"No. We saw the name of your firm in the telephone book."

"Oh, of course. I'm not really widely known yet, that was what made me ask. Will you come up? Shall I lead the way."

They followed her up a well-carpeted staircase. She stopped on the first landing.

"I have all the top part of the house, a maisonette it is really, quite spacious."

She turned towards a door on which was a brass plate inscribed "Shadburn's Supplies and Services. Registered Office."

"Do come in. It's a bit untidy I'm afraid. I was busy all the morning and I was just having a spot of shut-eye. Won't you sit down?"

There was a roll-top desk against the far wall, but otherwise nothing about the room suggested an office. There was an electric fire filled with glowing artificial logs, a shining cocktail cabinet well filled with bottles and glasses, and a colour television set across whose screen figures were still moving. The small table by the sofa bore an empty coffee cup, a brandy glass, and a pile of women's magazines.

Mrs Shadburn switched off the T.V., moved her cup and glass to a side-table, sat down and waved them to chairs opposite to her.

"Would you care for a drink? No? Well, what can I do for you?"

Corby took out his card.

"We are police, Mrs Shadburn. This is Sergeant Newstead from the Blent Street Station C.I.D. I am Inspector Corby."

If she was startled she did not show it.

"Oh, I suppose you've come about the other day when I left my car too long behind Selfridges."

"No, that has nothing to do with us. We want to make a few inquiries about Shadburn's Supplies and Services."

She said sharply, "Well, what about it? It's registered in the Industrial Register." Then with less sharpness, "There's not much to tell you about it. It's a new firm. I only started it three years ago after my marriage broke up. I'm building up a connection gradually. I don't want just any sort of client. We give a very special kind of service, and it takes time to get known."

"How do you do it, by advertising?"

"Well no, more by word of mouth you know. You satisfy one client and then she or he tells someone else."

"What do you do for your clients?"

"Whatever they ask for, within reason. I buy things for people living out of London, and I try to find staff for private houses or hotels. It's not easy, as I am sure you know, in these days. And I make arrangements for baby-sitting and shopping for old ladies or people living in the country... that kind of thing. But of course there's competition; there are other firms of the same kind in the field who started before I did. As I say, you need time to make a connection."

"You have made one very useful one, haven't you, with a client in Yorkshire... the Albert Mansbridge Orphanage?"

Watching her closely, Corby thought he saw a slight movement of her eyelids.

"Yes, they are among my best clients. Are you sure you won't have a drink, or let me make you some fresh coffee?"

"No, thank you. What do you do for the Orphanage?"

"I buy things for them, furniture and linen and clothes for the children, and so on. And I engage staff for them—when I can. These foreign girls don't want to go up North; they all want to be in London. That place up there is too quiet for them."

"You've been there, have you?"

"No, never. They order what they want by letter or telephone."

"But they don't get it, do they?"

"I don't know what you mean, Inspector. I get what they want for them if I can. I can't work miracles."

"You charge them plenty, don't you?"

"Everything, as you must know, is very expensive and these agencies for the foreign girls charge high fees."

She took a cigarette out of a packet on her table, and lit it. As she snapped her lighter shut she shook her hair further forward over her face. Her hands with their long sharp nails varnished with silver did not tremble. She sat back and looked at Corby with a boldness that he could not help admiring.

"Why have you come to see me, Inspector? What are you accusing me of? Has there been any complaint of overcharging against me? People are not obliged to pay my fees. The Orphanage knew my terms before they started dealing with me three years ago when I first opened this business."

"Were you introduced to them by Russell Holdsworth?"

"Yes. He is their treasurer. He pays my accounts and sometimes when he has been up there he rings me to order things for them."

"How did you come across him?"

"He was a great friend of my father's."

"Where are your files?"

"Oh well, I have notes and odd letters all over the place. I am afraid I am not a very tidy person, Inspector."

"I should like to see the books of the Company, please."

Was there a flicker of something in her large blue eyes? She answered calmly.

"I am so sorry, I haven't got them here. They have gone to the auditor."

"The address of the auditor?"

Iris Shadburn leaned back against the sofa cushions and let out a trill of rather unreal laughter.

"You will think me a perfect fool, Inspector. I haven't got it here."

"But I suppose you know it?"

"I know this sounds absurd, but I don't remember it. I told you my marriage came to an end three years ago. My husband, to whom I was absolutely devoted, went off with someone else. I had a serious breakdown. My memory has been very uncertain ever since. I have to make notes of everything. I keep all the addresses I am most likely to use in my diary, and, would you believe it, I lost that two days ago."

"No, Mrs Shadburn."

"No what, Inspector?"

"No, I don't believe it."

"Well I can't help that, it's true. My diary isn't here. You can search my flat if you've got a warrant."

Corby, who hadn't and who guessed that she guessed it, nearly laughed. If she hadn't been a crook she would have made a good policewoman.

"I think I know where I lost it. I was shopping this week in the Oxford Street stores, and when I sat down to lunch I looked in my bag for my diary and it was missing. So I must have dropped it in one of them. Let me see, I went to Marshalls and to D. H. Evans and to Selfridges. I must try their Lost Property Offices. I am absolutely sunk without my diary."

"I'm sure you are. But if you don't know the name of the auditor who has your books at the moment, supposing always that there are any books, I imagine that Russell Holdsworth must know it."

"Why should he? He is an old friend, and one of my most valued clients, but he has nothing to do with the management of my business."

"If there is a business."

"What do you mean, Inspector? You've seen the name on the door and in the telephone book, haven't you? You can look it up in the Industrial Register."

She was still perfectly cool but she threw a sudden glance over her shoulder at the door as if she wanted to get out.

Corby leaned forward, a hand on each knee. "What is your relationship with Russell Holdsworth?"

"I told you, he is an old friend of my father's."

"Are you his mistress?"

"Really, Inspector, is that your business?"

"I am investigating a murder. Everything that might be even distantly connected with it is my business."

"I can assure you I have never murdered anybody."

Corby sat back.

"Have you seen in the papers that a woman called Alberta Mansbridge was murdered on Sunday afternoon at her house in Porlock Square?"

"I think I did read something about it."

"Did you not know that Alberta Mansbridge was closely connected with the Albert Mansbridge Memorial Orphanage?"

"I suppose I may have heard that, but it didn't matter to me who was connected with it."

"But you knew that Russell Holdsworth was her man of business?"

"I may have heard it, but it was nothing to do with me."

"Did you know that he went to her house on Sunday afternoon?"
For the first time he saw her look startled.

"I don't know what all this is about. I've never been to this woman's house. I didn't know where it was."

"Perhaps not, but he did. What is your relationship with Russell Holdsworth? Are you his mistress?"

"If I am there's no law against it, is there?"

"No. But there is against receiving money diverted from its proper purpose. I suggest to you that Shadburn's Supplies and Services exists in name only. That Holdsworth has been paying into its account, for you, money diverted from the Albert Mansbridge Memorial Trust Fund, and probably from other sources of the same kind. Isn't that true? Answer me."

"I shan't answer any more questions without having my solicitor present. I ought never to have answered at all without him. If he'd been here you wouldn't have dared to make all these false accusations against me."

"You can send for your solicitor to the police station at Blent Street where I am now going to take you for further questioning. Will you go up to your room and pack a small bag with things that you will want for the night."

She rose with some alacrity, and Corby said at once,

"There's a telephone extension in your bedroom, is there? Sergeant Newstead will go with you and stay there while you pack."

"Can I put through a call to my mother?"

"Yes. If you give Sergeant Newstead her number he will get her for you."

"On second thoughts I won't upset her about nothing. You will have to release me as soon as my solicitor arrives."

Corby did not answer. As Iris Shadburn was going out of the room with Newstead behind her she stopped in the doorway. In a voice that sounded for the first time uncertain, she said, "What did you mean? Why did you say that Russell, that Mr Holdsworth, was at Porlock Square on Sunday afternoon?"

"You are the one, Mrs Shadburn, who is going to answer questions."

CHAPTER XXX

Mrs Bramley was not a nervous woman. When her husband was out at work she did not mind being alone in the house where a murder had taken place a few days ago.

"Whoever tried to burgle this house," she said to Mr Bramley, "isn't going to try again after what's happened, not if it was the last house in London."

"I should be afraid," her sister-in-law said to her, "that the old lady might walk."

"She wouldn't do a thing like that," Mrs Bramley replied. "She was too considerate, Miss Mansbridge was. Anyhow I don't believe in ghosts."

But she did find it depressing to be alone all day in the big empty place.

"I'm sure I shall be very glad when we get out of here," she said to her friend Mrs Dixon, who on Wednesday afternoon had dropped in for a cup of tea with her. Dixon was the porter for the block of flats which had been made out of three large houses at the end of the Square. Mrs Dixon did a certain amount of cleaning in the flats of those tenants whom she felt inclined to oblige. What with the rent-free basement flat, and nothing to pay for heat or light, and Dixon's salary, and the tips he got for doing anything extra, and Mrs Dixon's pay, they were as well off for their way of living as any couple in England. When Mrs Dixon said, "What you two want is something like what we've got," Mrs Bramley nodded agreement.

"That's true. We might look for something like that. Mr Bramley wouldn't mind leaving his job before his time. What with the other men slacking and putting things on to him and then the shop stewards dropping down on him if he does what they leave, it's just not worth it; it takes too much out of him. He's been bad with his nerves since Sunday, it's been a great shock to him. We want to get out of here as soon as we can. But of course we've got to see what they're going to do with the house, it can't be left empty yet. When Mrs Seldon comes up for the funeral at the end of this week I expect we shall have some idea. We shan't have any difficulty in finding what we want as soon as we start looking for it."

"No, of course not."

Secure in the knowledge of having something to offer for which people were queuing up to pay well, the two women sipped their tea for a minute in contented silence.

"Have the detectives found out anything more yet?"

"I don't think so. The sergeant, Newstead, was round here, Monday it was, asking me to try and remember all the people who had ever been to the house. But there wasn't one of them that would have done such a thing and so I told him. He's a nice fellow, and I've no doubt they're doing their best. But there's so many criminals nowadays, I don't know how they can expect to find any particular one."

"There was a policeman came round to us on Sunday evening, asking Mr Dixon and I if we'd seen anybody go in or out of No. 31 between 3.15 and four. But Mr Dixon was out all Sunday afternoon. He'd gone to see a friend in hospital. And I wasn't noticing anything in the Square because I was that bothered with the outside tap, the one Mr Dixon uses for swilling the area and the steps. Flooding the area it was, and I couldn't stop it. Even with my boots on I got soaked halfway up to the waist trying. The water was coming in beneath the door into the kitchen. I had to put down cloths and newspapers to soak it up. I didn't know what to do. I didn't know what time Mr Dixon would be back, the hospital was out at Harrow. So I rang the Metropolitan Water Board."

"Yes, you can always get them."

"This man came in an hour. It wasn't bad, seeing what sort of a day it was. I know it was exactly an hour because I looked at the clock when I rang, and it was quarter to three. It was just turned the quarter to four when he came."

Mrs Bramley said instantly,

"I suppose he hadn't seen anything? I mean, if he got to you just after quarter to four he'd have been coming along the street the very time they was asking everyone about. He might have seen somebody coming out of No. 31."

"But people go in and out of houses all the time. Who's to notice one more or less?"

"There wouldn't be that many about on an afternoon like last Sunday was."

"I don't think he'd have noticed. He'd been going round since ten o'clock that morning answering calls. His hands was so cold I had to give him a cup of hot tea before he could work on the tap. He wouldn't be thinking of anything much but getting done and getting home."

"No, I suppose not."

"It wasn't the washer; he had to knock the tap up, and now of course we can't use it until we can get the plumber to it. Oh well, we're in February now. Spring will be here before we know where we are. I must be getting along home."

When she had left, Mrs Bramley went upstairs to the first floor to turn some lights on. She thought it was better than leaving the whole house dark so that everyone could see that it was empty.

There was a large parcel in the hall that she had taken in that morning. It was addressed to Miss Mansbridge, but Mrs Bramley knew by the printed label of the manufacturers what it was. It was a new quilted nylon satin coverlet for their bedroom. Miss Mansbridge had been into their room a week or two ago and had said that their coverlet was getting worn out. She'd found some in an advertisement in the paper, and had asked Mrs Bramley what colour she would like, and had sent off for it.

Mrs Bramley stood in the hall holding the parcel and wondering if she ought to put it with the letters that had come for Miss Mansbridge and that Mr Holdsworth had said he was going to fetch. She thought it would be all right to open this; it was for their bed, and lately Mr Bramley had been pulling his dressing gown over the old coverlet. Miss Mansbridge would have liked them to have this one as soon as possible.

Out of the brown paper came the big, puffy, gleaming square in a deep rose red. It's really lovely, Mrs Bramley thought; Miss Mansbridge would have been pleased with it, she liked a bit of bright colour.

She was suddenly shaken by sorrow and regret because Miss Mansbridge could not enjoy anything any more. She thought angrily, I wish they'd get the man that did it, and send him down for life. It seems they ought to be able to find him somehow.

Her mind went back to what Mrs Dixon had said this afternoon about the man from the Water Board. Suppose he had happened to see somebody near No. 31? No harm in asking. The sergeant had said, "If anything, even the smallest thing that might help us comes to your mind…" He wasn't the sort that would snub you if you suggested something that was no good. How, after all, could you know?

Mrs Bramley heaped the coverlet on to the big chair in the hall. She took out of her handbag the slip of paper that Sergeant Newstead had given her with his number on, and the extension. She picked up the receiver and dialled Blent Street.

CHAPTER XXXI

T O ANTHONY THIS SEEMED TO BE THE LONGEST WEEK OF HIS life. Lisa was particularly busy; he himself had nothing what-ever to do and the beginning of February was not an inviting time of year to hang about in.

On Thursday, Lisa, who had been out all the morning, came back to the flat about half past one. It was raining hard; water had taken all the Regency curls out of her uncovered hair and soaked the shoulders of her coat. She kicked off her wet boots.

"Is there anything to eat?"

"I got eggs and butter and cheese. I didn't buy anything else. You said you didn't know whether you'd be in to dinner or not."

"I shan't be. I'll scramble myself some eggs now. You buy anything you want for tonight."

He said assertively,

"I shan't be dining in either."

"Oh, well, that's all right then."

He had as a matter of fact no plans at all. There were friends that he could look up, of course, but he did not want to explain to joint friends that he did not know where Lisa was, and he shrank from being questioned about the murder—he had had enough of that from Corby and the newspapers.

The bell rang. Anthony went to open the door warily, expecting another reporter.

"Good Lord! Marcello."

"May I please come in?"

"Of course."

Marcello put his dripping umbrella behind the door. Although it had kept him fairly dry he looked bedraggled, his shoes soaked, the skirts of his elegant periwinkle coat splashed with mud. He said,

"I have walked about all morning. I do not dare to go in a bus or a tube."

Lisa, turning round from her pan on the stove, offered,

"Would you like some scrambled eggs? I'm just doing some for myself. What's happened? Why can't you go in a bus or a tube?"

"Because I am sure that I am wanted by the police."

"Oh well," Anthony said, "in a sort of way we're all wanted by the police, except Lisa who's out of it. I suppose we all shall be until they find the murderer."

Lisa, stirring the eggs, said to Marcello over her shoulder,

"You didn't actually do it, did you?"

"No, no, no! Why should I? Why should anybody think that I should?"

"I don't suppose they do really. I can't see why you should kill Alberta, you least of all. It was much better for you to have her alive."

"No, I did not kill her, of course. But I have done… other things."

"Don't tell us if you don't want to; in fact I think you'd better not. That detective may turn up here again asking questions."

"But I am desperate. I do not know what to do. I need help."

Anthony said, "What sort of help?" in the same instant as Lisa said "Money?"

"I must get back to Italy. I must get a plane to Milan tonight."

"How much?"

"Of course I shall return the loan to you." With a shadow of his former grandiloquence he added, "Through friends in the Embassy—a little thing like that… in the diplomatic bag—"

Lisa, waving her free hand, dismissed the diplomatic bag.

"How much?"

"£30… for a night flight."

Anthony broke in half-resentfully,

"Why did you come to us?"

Marcello spread out his hands. "Because you are young like me, you can understand how one can make mistakes, and because," he directed his fine eyes at Lisa who was, he knew, the one making good money, "*you* are so kind and so beautiful."

"I'm not going to write you a cheque."

Marcello's face sagged.

"Because they might find out. I don't know what you've done and I don't want to know, but if I write a cheque to you I might get into trouble, and I don't want to help you as much as that."

Anthony wished that she had left out the last sentence; he also wished that she would not leave him out so completely.

Marcello said fervently, "I would never, never tell; I swear."

"Well, I don't know, you might at a pinch. Anyhow, they have ways of finding out all sorts of things. No, I won't give you a cheque. But our bank is just round the corner. Anthony can cash a cheque on our account and give you the money. Lend him your umbrella, we haven't got one. You'd better sit down and have something to eat while he goes."

Anthony, underneath Marcello's umbrella, went to the bank with mixed feelings. He was touched by Lisa's practical kindness; nervous that even without making out a cheque to Marcello she might get into trouble; envious that she could fork out £30 so much more easily than he could.

When he came back with the money, Lisa and Marcello were companionably eating scrambled eggs and drinking coffee. Marcello was smiling and showing his beautiful white teeth and the two, in his opinion, no less beautiful gold ones which had been paid for by a foolish Signora in Rome.

Anthony, seeing them there together, entertained but quickly dismissed a wild suspicion that Lisa had not been as indifferent to Marcello's attempted passes as she had pretended. He really knew that this was nonsense, but she kept him so much on wires nowadays that he saw a rival in every coffee cup.

When Marcello had gone off with the money, Anthony said to Lisa,

"I don't know if you ought to have done that."

She shrugged. "I may be in a jam myself some day. He didn't do the murder. He only told a lot of lies to an old woman who was fool enough to believe him. Is it still raining? Oh blast!"

She hugged herself into her coat and tied a scarf over her head. She paused in the doorway.

"I told them at the office I couldn't do anything tomorrow, with your family coming up for the funeral. We can ask your mother and sisters to dinner here if you like. I'll boil a piece of ham. Ham and sherry, I know that's what people have for funerals."

She suddenly skimmed across the room, and hooked an arm round his neck.

"Don't look so miserable. I'd be a better wife to you if you were a worse husband to me! I suppose it will all work out somehow."

He reached up and pulled her face down to his. They kissed with the passion that just kept their difficult relationship alive.

"Bye! See you later."

The door slammed behind her as it had done every time she or Anthony went out that week, the murder having obliterated all recollection of the Baxters' mild protests.

Anthony was so gratified by her wifely gesture that he at once rang up his mother and invited her and his sisters to dinner on Friday. There was a good deal of "We shouldn't like to give Lisa all that trouble. I think you'd better both come to us at the hotel."

"Oh no, Lisa *insists*," he said proudly.

The empty afternoon stretched before him. He thought that he would go round to the boutique and see how Evelyn was getting on and if he needed any help. It was still raining and the basement flat was dark and felt dank, although it probably wasn't, since they always had their electric fire on and often forgot to turn it off.

As soon as he pushed open the door of Evelyn's, Anthony saw Charlot wearing the brown velvet coat, and prancing to meet a putative customer.

"Oh," he said, checking in his prance, "it's you."

"Where's Evelyn?"

"He's just gone to the post with a parcel."

"I always did that."

"Well you weren't here, were you? I would have gone *of course*, I wanted to go, but I'd had a bit of neuralgia yesterday and Evelyn thought I'd better not go out in the rain. He's such a good employer, isn't he?"

Anthony asked bluntly, "Is he your employer now?"

"Just this week he is. I can't say about anything else for certain. There's no doubt I suit him, we fit into each other's ways perfectly. When are you going to come into your estate in Yorkshire?"

"I told you, there isn't one."

At this moment Evelyn came in, furling a dripping umbrella.

"Hulloa, Anthony." He looked uneasy, almost frightened.

"Evelyn, darling, are you soaked?" Charlot laid a hand on his shoulder.

"No, of course not. It's only just round the corner. How are things going, Anthony? Have they found the murderer?"

"I don't think so. I don't know any more about that. I came round to see if you wanted any help. I've got nothing to do. I thought you might like to go off early."

"That was kind of you. Charlot's helping me out at the moment."

"So I see."

There was a rather uncomfortable pause.

Charlot turned his back, picked up a pair of trousers that were lying on a chair and daintily flicked a piece of fluff off them.

"You don't really want me back, do you, Evelyn?"

"Now don't say that. Of course I was expecting you on Monday."

"But you'd rather have *him*."

"Anthony my lamb…"

"And I'd rather you did. Not that I haven't liked working here with you. But I don't think this is the sort of job I want to go on with permanently. I'm sick of clothes."

"Have you got something else in view?"

"Not at the moment, but I shall have. So I'll say good-bye."

"Wait a minute, wait a minute. You can't just go off like that. You must have this week's pay."

"I haven't done anything for it this week."

"Never mind; it's the right thing. We shan't let you go without it, shall we, Charlot?"

Charlot, who didn't answer, looked as though he wouldn't mind in the least. Evelyn sat down at the beautiful little seventeenth-century escritoire where he made out bills, took a few notes out of a drawer and neatly slipped an elastic band round them.

Anthony thought of making a protest and then stopped himself. You did usually get a week's pay when you left a job, he was very hard up and he knew that Evelyn had meant in a decent, leisurely way to ditch him.

Charlot was still putting on an act of being very busy brushing the dust off dustless clothes. Anthony stuffed the notes into his pocket; he never had a wallet.

"Well, good-bye, Evelyn, and thanks for a pleasant time. I'll be seeing you, I expect. When I'm a successful tycoon I'll come here for my clothes. Meanwhile, good luck."

He nodded to Charlot, grinned at Evelyn who was looking half— but only half—regretful, and went out of the warm, luxurious shop into the rain and near dark of the February afternoon.

"Well," he thought, "that's that. And now I'm unemployed again. They'll all be on at me to go back to Hithamroyd. I must make some sort of plan."

His old idea of consulting Russell Holdsworth recurred to him. If he got a cup of tea somewhere now, so that he could shelter from the rain, he could take a tube after that and reach Holdsworth's house in Putney at six, by which time he should surely be home from work. Holdsworth would then give him a drink and probably some good advice. He was a knowledgeable fellow and he had been kind in a dry way about the overdraft. He knew the whole situation, and would be able to suggest what steps Anthony should take next.

Not really sorry to have finished with the boutique, pleased to have some plan in mind, Anthony turned into an A.B.C. He collected a large, delicious-looking bun and a cup of tea from the counter, bought a new packet of cigarettes from the pay desk, carried his spoils to an empty table in a far corner and sat down to pass the time in peace.

CHAPTER XXXII

CORBY SAT AT ONE END OF THE TABLE IN HIS ROOM AT BLENT Street. Iris Shadburn sat opposite to him. Newstead, his notebook open on the table in front of him, was on her right. Margaret Poley, a young C.I.D. officer, sat patiently on a chair just inside the door.

Iris Shadburn looked strained and exhausted, but she was still holding out on them as much as she could. She had decided that she did not want her solicitor, probably, Corby thought, because whatever solicitor she had had at the time of the divorce was unaware of her recent activities.

She repeated for the tenth time,

"There was nothing wrong in it. Anybody can open an account at a bank. We meant to get this business started and then I haven't been strong since my breakdown, and like I said it takes time to form a connection. Russell, Mr Holdsworth, said that of course I should need capital to start on so he paid some money into my account, and of course he would have got it back later when the business was a going concern."

"We've seen the Shadburn's Supplies and Services account. You were not building up capital for a business at all. You were living on the money."

"Well I had to keep going, didn't I, till I could live on the returns from the business? Me being so delicate, that was what upset the time-schedule. My ex-husband didn't always pay my alimony. I could have taken him to court of course, but well, when you've been married to a man for some years you don't always like to, do you? It's too sordid."

"More sordid than embezzlement? You paid this money into the bank, you endorsed the cheques. You saw where they came from, the Albert Mansbridge Memorial Fund, and from one or two other trusts of which Holdsworth has been the treasurer. Didn't you realize that he was stealing the money?"

"I didn't know what arrangements he had with those companies. He told me it was all right. I expect he balanced it up in some other way. I don't understand finance."

"When we first saw you yesterday, you told us that your Supplies and Services had been engaging staff for the Orphanage and buying bulk foods and blankets and so on for them. That was a complete lie. You never spent a penny on them."

She ran her tongue along her lips; she had done it so often that only a thin crust of lipstick remained.

"I'd ordered things for them. The bills hadn't come in yet. I was going to pay for them."

"Where were the copies of the orders? You had no files. We've searched your place. You said that the books were at the auditor's, but there are no books. You've been living on stolen money. You must have known it. You must know now that Holdsworth was fiddling the accounts of several trust funds."

"I don't understand about all that. He probably has some explanation."

"He'd better have. Did you know that there had been complaints from the Orphanage about shortage of everything there at a time when Miss Mansbridge was paying extra money into the Orphanage account to help them? Did you know that she had found out that the extra help was not reaching the Orphanage? Did you know that she had lately been up to the Orphanage herself to find out what was happening?"

Iris Shadburn said sulkily,

"I didn't know anything about her. Russell never talked about her. Why don't you ask him to explain what he was doing?"

"We shall. When did you last see him?"

"Thursday evening last week. We went out to dinner together."

"Did he tell you that he was going to tea with Miss Mansbridge on Sunday?"

"No. I never asked about his weekends. I knew he had to spend them with his family. I never expected to see him on Sundays. I never had any wish to break up his family life." She assumed a look of virtue. "I've had that done to me and I wouldn't do it to anyone else. Russell and I both knew that his wife and the two kids are his duty. I am his pleasure."

It was probably true. In spite of her situation she said this with an air of happy confidence and her smile was almost girlish.

Corby asked suddenly,

"Does Holdsworth often ring you up?"

"Yes, every day."

"From his office?"

"Yes, or from a call box if he happens to be out of the office."

"He has already rung your flat four times this morning."

"He won't understand my not answering. He always rings before eleven. I don't go out to do my shopping till I've heard from him."

"Has he telephoned to you as usual this week?"

"Yes, except yesterday; he went off to drive his wife and daughter into the country to spend a week with her mother. The boy is away at boarding school."

"Did he say anything about the murder of Miss Mansbridge?"

"No. Why should he? What he said on Tuesday was that with his family going away he would be able to spend all the weekend with me; he'd come here early on Saturday and we'd go out somewhere for lunch and then he'd be able to stay the night."

"Did he sound to you the same as he always was?"

"Yes, well, he was, more eager, you know, because they were going to be out of the way I suppose. More... more lover-like. He kept on saying, 'We'll have one weekend anyhow, whatever happens'."

"What did you think he meant by that?"

"Well, we don't get many chances of that kind. When he goes on holiday or away for a weekend it's usually with her and the kids."

"You didn't get the impression that he was worried about anything? What did he mean by 'whatever happens'?"

Corby saw her hesitate for a fraction of a second, thought he saw a flicker of fear in her eyes. She replied calmly,

"I don't know, unless he was afraid of his wife finding out about us, or unless she had. I daresay that would send her running to her mother. I was a bit surprised at her taking Gillian, that's the daughter, away for a week in term-time."

There was a pause. Iris Shadburn said with an air of bravado, "Are you going to let me go now?"

"No. I'm going to take you down to the charge room, and charge you with receiving money which you knew was unlawfully obtained."

"I want my solicitor here."

"You can have him now. Give the number to Sergeant Newstead." She hesitated.

"It's so long since I've had any dealings with him, I don't know if it would be much use. May I have a call put through to Russell Holdsworth?"

"No."

She had, of course, expected this answer. She shrugged and let Margaret Poley take her down to the charge room, Corby following.

CHAPTER XXXIII

WHEN CORBY CAME BACK, NEWSTEAD WAS SPEAKING ON THE telephone. He turned round with the nearest approach to excitement that Corby had yet seen in him.

"We may have got a useful witness. That was Mrs Bramley on the telephone. It seems she was talking to a friend of hers who lives further down that side of the Square and who was expecting a man from the Metropolitan Water Board on Sunday afternoon. She knew he came just after a quarter to four because she was in a fluster about how long he was going to be, and was watching the clock. Mrs Bramley says he must have walked along that side of the Square, and he must have been looking at the numbers of the houses to find the one he was called to. I'll get on to the Water Board now, and ask them to find which of their men answered the Porlock Square call on Sunday afternoon and send him round here at once."

"Get someone else to do it. Let's have a look at the file again before I type out my report."

Corby, who secretly hated having to make any report on a case until he had come to the end of it, was always glad to postpone this duty. Those parts of C.I.D. work bored him, though he had trained himself to do them thoroughly.

"Nothing more on Slater?"

"No."

"What's the report on the doctor?"

"Hewitt who was watching the house last night said the light in the front room was on very late, then it was all quiet till morning.

Thompson relieved Hewitt at seven. The doctor came out just after 8.30 with a small bag, got his car out of the garage and drove to the hospital. He parked his car in the inner courtyard, and he's been inside the hospital ever since. Thompson says it's difficult to keep a tally on him there because there's several entrances, but he's got his eye all the time on the car."

"That's not good enough. If the doctor wanted to make a get-away he could easily walk out by another entrance and pick up a taxi or slip into the tube. He'll be near the end of his hospital morning now, but if we're still tailing him tomorrow morning we'd better have two of them on it. Who is on Holdsworth now?"

"Daly has just relieved Cunliffe. He reported ten minutes ago that Holdsworth is still in his office. The telephone exchange says he's tried to ring Shadburn seven times this morning."

"He'll go round there before long. Warn Daly to keep a close eye on him, especially after he finds out that she's not there. We could pull him in now, for embezzlement, but we'd be no further on about the murder. I want to leave them both free as long as we can."

Newstead went up to lunch in the canteen, but Corby pushed out into the rain and walked to a pub some little way off where he was not likely to find any of his colleagues. At this stage in an investigation when everything seemed to be moving towards a still uncertain point, he needed to be alone to think. He was fairly sure of his quarry, but with a murder so ably planned, proof was hard to come by.

Reports came in from Hewitt and Daly during the afternoon. The doctor appeared to be following his normal day. Holdsworth had left his office just before one, had gone into a nearby pub, drunk two double Scotches, and ordered a sandwich. He had then got his car from the side-street where it was parked and driven to Shovel Road. Daley had seen him go up to No. 18 and ring the top bell twice. After that he had rung the bottom bell and a young woman had answered it; Holdsworth had followed her in, and Daly could see him in the downstairs front room talking to her and to a child.

He came out again and drove back at top speed to his office. He went in for a few minutes leaving his car just round the corner. Then he came out and went on foot to a bank at the other end of the street. Daly saw him push a cheque across the counter and scoop up a handful of notes. He got near enough to see that there was a hundred pound note on top of the pile.

Holdsworth packed the money into his wallet and went out. Daly said that he looked very white and staggered a bit as he came out of the bank. He stood for a minute on the pavement as if recovering himself, then he walked along and turned in at the doorway of a travel agency.

There was a small queue at the counter. Daly picked up a handful of brochures and moved into the queue behind Holdsworth. He stood there leafing through the brochures and heard Holdsworth try to book a flight to Montevideo for that night. There was no plane leaving until the next afternoon and he was told that he would have to book a flight to Lisbon. After waiting while the clerk telephoned the airport he got his ticket and went round to the office again. He was still there.

"You're doing fine, Daly," Corby said. "Stick to him. Did you manage to hear what time his plane was going to leave?"

"Nine o'clock, sir."

"I expect he'll go home first. Keep in touch."

"He knows now we've got Iris Shadburn," Corby said. "I expect the kid playing in the garden had seen two men take her away in a car. I'll get an open warrant, though I don't want to pick him up for embezzlement until the last minute."

At four o'clock Daly reported that Holdsworth had come out of his office and was getting into his car.

"Follow him, and let us know."

Newstead ventured, "Are we cutting it a bit fine, sir?"

"He won't be going to the airport yet, and we've got them alerted anyhow. My guess is he's going home to pick up some clothes, and his passport."

The Inspector began all the same to walk up and down the room.

"Taking their time, that bloody Water Board. They know outside that we want that man in here at once, don't they?"

"Yes, sir, but I'll go and make sure."

Before Newstead reached the door it opened, and the Station sergeant ushered in a young man wearing a dark blue uniform which he had enlivened by a peacock blue shirt and a flowing tie of the same colour.

"Mr O'Gorman from the Water Board."

The young man, who seemed unimpressed by his surroundings, grinned cheerfully.

"Sit down, Mr O'Gorman. I am Inspector Corby of the C.I.D. here and this is Sergeant Newstead. We are wondering if you can help us?"

"Helping the police with their inquiries?"

"Yes, exactly, and that doesn't always mean what people think it means. Were you on duty last Sunday afternoon?"

"I was. I should by rights have gone off at two o'clock but we had three men away sick and more calls than we could get round before dark so I worked overtime."

"Did you go to a house in Porlock Square between three and four o'clock?"

"I did so; there was one with a broken tap that was flooding all the area and coming into the kitchen. The old biddy gave me a cup of tea and a slice of buttered toast."

"Do you remember the number of the house you called at?"

"It was No. 49. I know it took me a bit of time to find it because the snow was blowing up against the fronts of the houses, and a lot of the numbers was covered. There's some of the houses in that Square have the numbers on the pillars and I couldn't see them, only the ones that have the numbers on the glass over the front doors."

"When you were walking along that side of the Square towards No. 49, did anybody come out of the houses you passed?"

O'Gorman considered.

"Yes. I seen a fellow come out of No. 31."

Corby leaned forward, every nerve tingling.

"How did you know it was No. 31?"

"Because it was the first house on that side that had the number up on the glass fanlight over the door."

"Were you able to see this man who came out?"

"I noticed him because he came out very quickly and the door shut behind him with a bang. He seemed as if he'd been running. He stood on top of the steps and looked up and down the street as if he expected to see someone coming."

"You are an excellent observer, Mr O'Gorman. Can you tell me what this man looked like?"

O'Gorman hesitated, as if nonplussed.

"Was he tall or short? Young or old?"

"He wasn't tall nor yet he wasn't young. There wasn't anything to say about him really... except he was wearing spectacles."

"What kind of spectacles?"

"The kind with thin gold rims."

Corby sat back. "Do you think you would recognize this man if you saw him again?"

O'Gorman said doubtfully,

"I couldn't swear to it, him being so much like a lot of other people. But I think I would. I took notice because of there being so few people about and because he came out of the house as if he'd been shot out. But I only saw him for a minute. He put up his umbrella and walked away."

"Thank you very much, Mr O'Gorman, you've been most helpful. We may have to ask you to come here again to see if you can identify this man. We would, of course, get in touch with your employers."

"Oh, that will be all right," O'Gorman said cheerfully.

When he had gone out Corby and Newstead looked at one another.

"Holdsworth was the only one wearing spectacles. Would O'Gorman be able to pick him out at an identity parade? But even so it's not enough. That a man came out of a house at about the time of a murder is a strong argument in favour of his having done it, but it isn't proof. We need something more, but I'm damned if I see where we're going to get it. We can't leave him much longer. We shall have to pull him in for embezzlement, and try and break him down with what we've got."

"Shall we go after him now?"

"Let's see what Daly has to say."

Corby picked up the personal radio on the table in front of him.

"Daly? Corby speaking."

"Daly here, sir, outside Holdsworth's house. He went in there twenty minutes ago. His car's outside the front door. He's got a lot of lights on inside, upstairs and down."

"What kind of house is it?"

"A fairly big villa with a bit of garden in front going round the side of the house, and more behind. I've had a look round behind the house. There's no exit there, except he might climb a fence into the next garden. The garage is at the side of the house. I'm drawn up at the side of the road, a little back from the entrance. There's quite a lot of cars parked along this road. I'm not noticeable."

"We'll ring Putney Station and ask them to let you have a man to watch the back of the house, just in case. We're coming now to pick Holdsworth up. If he leaves before we get there, go after him, of course; we'll follow."

"Right. Oh, one minute, sir. There's somebody going up to the house. He just got off the bus, the stop's near the gate. It's a tall young man wearing a dufflecoat. I saw him under the street lamp, he's got very fair hair. He's ringing the front door bell."

"Good God! Keep an eye on him too, Daly. We're coming."

As they settled into the car and Newstead let in the clutch, Corby said,

"Daly reports a tall young man with very fair hair going to the house. That could be young Seldon. Now what the hell is he doing there? Have I been diddled by him? Is he in it too?"

Their car, sirens sounding, shot through the London streets followed by a car containing two uniformed policemen. They streaked through the evening traffic that reluctantly let them pass. They had a glimpse of dark water below, slashed with light, as they raced over Putney Bridge and turned left of the Heath.

CHAPTER XXXIV

IT DID NOT OCCUR TO ANTHONY TO TELEPHONE HOLDSWORTH to ask if it would be convenient to see him. The young Seldons ran their social life by dropping in. If, for some unexpected reason, such as acute illness or absence, the dropped-in-on could not do with them, they passed by and dropped in somewhere else.

When Anthony turned in at the gateway of Twin Gables he saw that the front door was open, letting out a slanting oblong of light in which the car stood with the lid of the boot raised. As he was lifting his hand to the bell, Holdsworth came out carrying a suitcase. He jerked to a stop and peered at Anthony.

"Who's that? Who's that?"

"It's me, Anthony Seldon."

"You! What are you doing here? Who sent you?"

"Nobody sent me. I just wanted to have a word with you. I wanted to ask you for some advice."

"Advice? What do you mean?"

Anthony began to realize that he had not come at the most favourable moment.

"But you don't... you're just going out, aren't you?"

"I can't see you now."

"All right, of course. I'll come again some other time."

"No, wait a minute." Holdsworth peered beyond Anthony into the dark. "Are you alone? You're not alone, are you?"

"Yes, I am." Holdsworth's manner was so strange that Anthony wondered vaguely if something had happened to Mrs Holdsworth or to one of the children.

"I won't bother you now. Another time will do."

He turned to go.

"Stop! Did anyone send you here?"

"No. I just wanted to consult you about a job, that's all."

There was a pause, then Holdsworth said, "You'd better come in."

"No, if…"

"Come in."

Holdsworth lifted the suitcase into the boot, crashed down the lid, and led the way into the house. Anthony followed him doubtfully. He felt that there was something peculiar about Holdsworth, but then older people were so often peculiar; they got into fusses about nothing, you never knew.

Inside the hall there were further signs of departure. A cupboard was open, a rug was lying across a chair. On a table were a bundle of papers that looked as if they had been hastily crushed together.

"I hope there's nothing wrong," Anthony said.

"Why? What do you mean?"

"With Mrs Holdsworth or the children."

"They're away. You'd better come in and have a drink."

"Thanks." Anthony, brightening, followed Holdsworth into the sitting-room.

It was a pretty room, like dozens of other pretty suburban rooms, full of chintz and pink lampshades and crystal flower vases. A coat, a warm scarf and a briefcase lay on the chair. There was a drinks tray on the side-table. Holdsworth crossed to it, poured some whisky into a glass and drank it at a gulp.

"What do *you* want? Scotch?"

"Fine, thanks."

Anthony spoke with unnatural heartiness. He felt disconcerted: something was up, surely. He heard bottles and glasses clinking together, but he could only see Holdsworth's narrow back in his dark city suit; he could not see the movements of his hands.

Holdsworth turned round and held out a full glass in a hand that shook. Been drinking a lot already, thought Anthony, suddenly seeing daylight.

"Sit down. Tell me why you came here. Be quick."

Anthony encouraged himself with a good swig of whisky.

"Well it's like this. You know I had a job in that boutique?"

"What? What job?"

Fancy him not remembering!

"In a boutique for men's clothes. I've left it."

Holdsworth appeared to be listening, but not to Anthony.

"What was that?"

"A boutique," Anthony repeated, "for men's clothes."

"No, outside the door. I heard somebody."

He'd be seeing pink elephants next.

"I didn't hear anything. It's the wind. It's making the branches creak."

"You didn't come here alone, did you?"

"Yes, of course I did." And I'll go as soon as I've swallowed this. No use talking to him when he's half stoned.

Holdsworth, who had poured another drink for himself, sat down with it in his hand. He seemed to collect himself. He said in something more like his usual manner,

"Well, what is it you want?"

"I want another job. Something worth doing with some prospects."

"A good many people want that."

"Yes, I know. That's why I came to ask if you could advise me how to get one."

"No, I can't."

"Oh well then, that's that." Anthony began to drink his whisky quickly. He'd drawn a blank, and he'd better get out of here as soon as he could; he wanted to get out. By way of making a bit of polite conversation he asked,

"Have you heard anything more about the murder? Have you seen Corby lately?"

"No. But you have, haven't you?"

"I saw him." Anthony paused to remember; the days of this interminable week seemed to have got mixed. "Monday, I think it was."

"What did he say?"

"He asked me a lot of questions."

"What about?"

"Oh, about Marcello—he's off, by the way, he's bolted—and about whether I could think of anything that might help."

"What did he ask you about me?"

"Nothing about you."

"Well he will now when—if—you leave here."

Anthony decided to abandon half a glass of good whisky and get out. Holdsworth was having a nervous breakdown or something. Anyhow this visit was a dead loss. He put his glass down and got up.

"Well, thanks for the drink. I won't take up any more of your time."

"Sit down again. I can give you the address of somebody who might be able to help you."

"Thanks a lot."

"If I can remember it." Holdsworth stooped forward in his chair and covered his face with his hands.

"Please don't bother now. You could send it to me, or give it to me next time you see me."

"No, I've got it. Write it down."

Anthony felt in his pocket and pulled out a biro and a packet of cigarettes. He looked expectantly at Holdsworth.

"No, no, you can't write it on that. You'll lose it. Sit down at my desk and write it properly."

This, the sort of thing that people had been saying to Anthony all his life, sounded familiar and reassuring.

He crossed to the desk and sat down. The flap was open, there was a clean note-pad on it.

"Yes?" Anthony said. "Fire away. I'm ready."

Holdsworth said nothing. Anthony was surprised by a bead of sweat which ran down his own face into his eye and made it smart.

"Yes?" he said again and was turning when something thick was round his neck, jerking his head back, pulling tight so that his breathing was half stopped and his heart began to beat like a piston.

He had a second, two seconds, of shock and surprise, in which he afterwards realized that he had heard a whistle somewhere near. Then he tore with both hands at the scarf round his neck. He managed to screw himself round and lunged upwards at the face near him. It was an awkward, glancing blow but it caught Holdsworth's spectacles and sent them flying. There was a rush of feet, the stifling grip relaxed, there was a scuffle going on—Holdsworth, a man in a mackintosh and a uniformed policeman. Anthony staggered back against the table feeling his neck; the tray of bottles and glasses crashed to the floor. More men were running into the room, the two already there jerked Holdsworth to his feet. Something clinked. Anthony saw Holdsworth's hands fastened together by handcuffs. Corby and the sergeant were there now; the sergeant asked Anthony if he was all right. He nodded, surprised and relieved to find that he was. He had a glimpse of Holdsworth's face, squinting and distorted. He heard Corby say,

"Russell Holdsworth, I have a warrant for your arrest. I charge you with the murder of Alberta Mansbridge and I have to warn you that anything you say will be taken down as evidence and may be used against you…"

CHAPTER XXXV

"I SUPPOSE HE MIGHT HAVE BEEN A RESPECTABLE ACCOUNTANT all his life," Corby observed, "if he hadn't met Iris Shadburn. Or would it have been somebody else that brought the crazy bit of him up from the bottom?"

This was not the kind of speculation that interested Newstead.

"Do you think we would have had enough evidence to convince a jury, sir, if he hadn't confessed?"

"I think so, with the second lunatic attempt on Seldon, and evidence of the man from the Water Board. It was enough to break him down anyhow. He held out a long time, didn't he? Seemed to go out of his mind and then come back into it. I expect his counsel will try for diminished responsibility, but I don't think he'll get it. Well, let's see where we are on those small jobs and then go home early. I'm expecting the doctor at four; it's just on that now."

The doctor, Corby saw, looked as if a weight had been lifted off his head. He began at once.

"I've told my wife. She was… all that I didn't deserve. And I've been to see my solicitors. It seems I don't come into your province. It's over seven years since Brenda disappeared, and apparently a bigamy charge doesn't lie after seven years. Under the new Act there will be no difficulty about getting a divorce. But of course that's only the legal part of it. I've written to friends in Australia to find Brenda and see that she's looked after, until I can go out there. Elaine is as anxious as I am that everything that can be done for Brenda should be done. I don't know whether she'll decide to go on living in Australia or want to come home. But I shall see that she is comfortable some-where—wherever she wants."

And she'll be a problem to you and your Elaine as long as she lives, Corby thought.

"You will see in the evening paper that Holdsworth appeared before the magistrate this morning and was remanded without bail to the Assizes. Oh, and by the way there's been news of another of the tea party. Young Slater, who had been around again with his old confederates, was caught last night breaking into a transistor factory near Slough."

"Sad, after all Alberta tried to do for him! I'm glad she didn't know it."

"Do you think she would have been surprised?"

"No, I think she guessed. I am afraid she found out several unpleasant things at the end of her life. Well, I won't take up any more of your time."

When the doctor had gone out, Corby tried to concentrate on some of the paperwork that he had been obliged to postpone, but he was sleepy after half the night spent in extracting Holdsworth's confession. Strange how you lived with a group of people for a few days, your mind on the stretch to pick up every crumb of information about them, to understand them, almost to live in their lives. And then it was over like a book you had taken back to the library. He was glad anyhow that he would be at home for Tilly's birthday party.

Newstead came back into the room.

"Young Seldon is here, sir, asking if you could spare him a few minutes."

"Probably remembered something else he thinks ought to go into his statement. Let's have him in."

Anthony, wearing a dark suit and a sober tie that his mother had insisted on buying him for the funeral, looked unnaturally respect-able and almost portentous.

"I do hope I'm not wasting your time," he began.

Corby grinned at him. "We'll soon let you know if you are. What can we do for you?"

"It's really that I just wanted to ask you for some advice. You see it's like this—I haven't got a job at the moment. And I'm rather sick of the kind of jobs I have been doing. I want to do something... more—more responsible. I can't go into the family firm; I don't want to anyhow, but there's probably going to be a take-over and they wouldn't want me without any experience. So I wondered... whether there would be a chance that I could join you? Naturally I mean starting at the bottom and working up. But it's something I feel I could do, if you think it's a good idea. Would you advise me to be a policeman?"

ALSO AVAILABLE

"You have to reach for the greatest of the Great Names
(Agatha Christie, John Dickson Carr, Ellery Queen) to find
Christianna Brand's rivals in the subtleties of the trade."

Anthony Boucher in the *New York Times*

Night falls in the capital, and a "London particular" pea-souper fog
envelops the city. In Maida Vale, Rose and her family doctor Tedwards
struggle through the dark after a man has telephoned from Rose's
house, claiming to have been attacked. By the time they arrive the
victim, Raoul Vernet, is dead. The news he brought from Switzerland
for Rose's mother has died with him.

Arriving to the scene, Inspector Cockrill faces a fiendish case with
seven suspects who could have murdered their guest – family members
and friends with alibis muddled by the suffocating fog and motives
wrapped in mystery. Now, the race is on to find the truth before the
killer strikes again.

First published in 1952, *London Particular* was Brand's favourite among
her own books, and it remains a fast-paced and witty masterpiece of
the genre, showing off the author's signature flair for the ruthless twist.

ALSO AVAILABLE

"It is past the half-hour.
My time is coming nearer with every tick of the clock."

Horace Manning, scientist, recluse and 'closed book' even to his friends is found dead in his study at 4am, following a dinner in honour of his daughter's engagement. An ivory-handled carving knife rests between his shoulder blades as the houseguests gather round to witness the awful crime. The telephone line has been sabotaged – a calculated murder has been committed.

Rewinding twelve hours, the events of the afternoon and evening unfold, revealing a multitude of clues and motives from a closed cast of suspects until the narrative reaches 4am again – then races on to its riveting conclusion at 4pm as the reader is led twice round the clock.

First published in 1935, the sole novel from the actor and dancer Billie Houston is a lively country house mystery and a true lost gem of the Golden Age of crime writing.

ALSO AVAILABLE
IN THE BRITISH LIBRARY
CRIME CLASSICS SERIES

Many of our titles are also available
in eBook, large print and audio editions